W9-BHU-204

Secrets of Willow House

BOOKS BY SUSANNE O'LEARY

The Road Trip

A Holiday to Remember

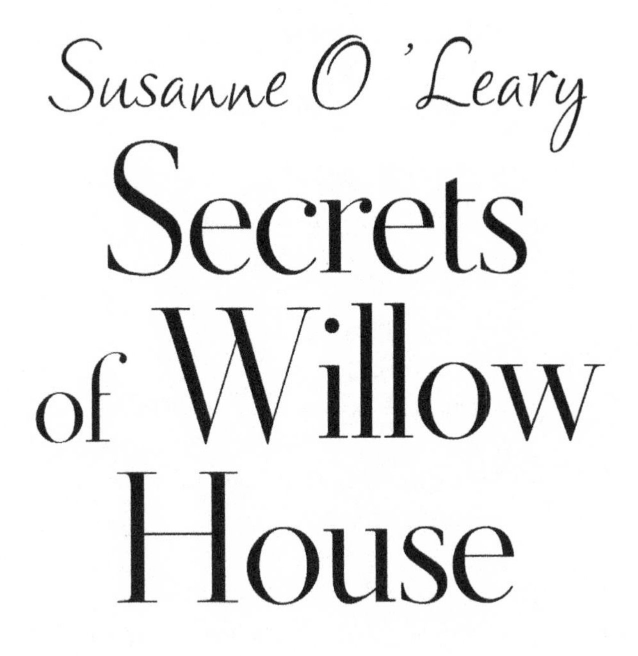

Bookouture

Published by Bookouture in 2019

An imprint of StoryFire Ltd.

Carmelite House
50 Victoria Embankment
London EC4Y 0DZ

www.bookouture.com

Copyright © Susanne O'Leary, 2019

Susanne O'Leary has asserted her right to be identified
as the author of this work.

All rights reserved. No part of this publication may be reproduced, stored in any retrieval system, or transmitted, in any form or by any means, electronic, mechanical, photocopying, recording or otherwise, without the prior written permission of the publishers.

ISBN: 978-1-78681-853-9
eBook ISBN: 978-1-78681-852-2

This book is a work of fiction. Names, characters, businesses, organizations, places and events other than those clearly in the public domain, are either the product of the author's imagination or are used fictitiously. Any resemblance to actual persons, living or dead, events or locales is entirely coincidental.

To Margaret, Katie and Mairead, my favourite Kerry girls.

Chapter One

When Maeve was still in the office at eleven thirty on Saturday night, searching online for a loo seat with a floral design, she had a feeling something had to be wrong with her life. And when a client phoned her at six the next morning, screeching that the curtains in her bedroom were the wrong shade of purple, she knew things had to change. But it wasn't until she was at the surgery of her local GP a week later and heard the words 'exhaustion' and 'panic attacks that could turn into heart arrhythmia' that she was forced to make a decision.

'You need to take some time off,' her doctor said as she lay like a dead fish on the examination table.

'Not possible,' she mumbled. She struggled to sit and buttoned up her shirt. 'We have taken on a huge amount of work at the office and I'm one of the top—'

He looked at her sceptically. 'Top what? Rocket scientists?'

'No. Interior designers.'

'And that's so stressful you end up in casualty twice with panic attacks and a pulse of over a hundred?'

'You haven't met our clients.'

'I don't think I'd like to.' He put his stethoscope back around his neck and pushed his glasses up his nose as he sat down behind his desk. 'I'm going to give you a prescription for some beta blockers. But that doesn't mean you can pop them like Smarties and carry on.' He looked at her sternly. 'I've seen so many young women like you ending up with serious health problems because they're so bloody driven. Please don't be one of them. Take some time off, relax, get some exercise and then see if you can't manage your time a bit better.'

'I'll try,' she promised, knowing it would be next to impossible. Her mobile rang as she put on her shoes.

'Ignore that,' the doctor ordered as she reached for it. 'Learn to turn off your phone and not be available all the time.'

'Is that what you do?' she asked cheekily. The doctor looked quite tired himself.

He looked startled. 'Er, okay,' he said with a wry smile. 'Maybe not as much as I should. But my job is a tad more important to humanity than yours, I would imagine.'

Maeve had to giggle. 'Yeah, I know. The wallpaper clashing with the upholstery is not exactly life-threatening, of course.' She paused and looked at him. 'Your waiting room needs a little update, now that we're on the subject.'

'I know,' he said with a sigh. 'The magazines are out of date.'

'Yeah, well, that too. And they were all messed up, so I straightened them and organised them in chronological order.' Maeve felt a dart of pride. He was sure to be grateful for that little favour.

'You do need a break, my dear,' the doctor said, with a hint of exasperation. 'Could you try to turn your mind away from such things for a while? Maybe go out with your boyfriend to a movie or dinner?'

'I would if I had one,' Maeve said wistfully. 'But going out alone isn't much fun.'

'Oh. Sorry. I had no idea. But do try to take time off in any case.'

'I will,' Maeve promised. 'I just want to tell you about the waiting room. It's very depressing, you know. That green paint on the walls and the burgundy fabric on the chairs clash horrendously.'

The doctor lifted one eyebrow. 'That's hardly any concern of yours.'

'It is if I have to sit there waiting for half an hour,' Maeve argued. 'It would give anyone a headache. But you know what? It's easy to fix. Dulux does this lovely white paint with a pink undertone. And IKEA has some great chairs right now. I got a few for a client recently. Very cheery colours and really comfortable.'

'Lovely,' he said and handed her a prescription. 'Take these beta blockers and a couple of weeks off and you'll be fine. I want to see you back for a check-up in a month with a tan, a smile on your face and a little more flesh on your bones. Stop even thinking about design or other people's houses. Go out there and have fun, drink wine – and why not even fall in love, if that's possible.'

'I'll do my best,' she said, knowing the falling in love bit was the greatest challenge. Fat chance of finding some man out there in the dating jungle. Been there, done that, got dumped and picked herself up. Bitter? No, but still in pain – even after three years – and determined not to get fooled again. She didn't have the mental energy to go out there and be fascinating enough to catch whoever might take her fancy.

Maeve took the prescription, wishing it included some kind of medicine for broken hearts.

'He said I have to slow down,' Maeve told her boss later that day. 'Or I will have a heart attack... or something,' she ended lamely.

She looked at Ava across the desk, which was littered with bits of fabric and books of wallpaper samples. 'I'm run down. Burnt out. I need a break. Right now. Doctor's orders.'

Ava fixed her with a steely look. 'A break? Right now? You mean you won't finish the townhouse in Knightsbridge? Or the flat in South Kensington?'

'I can do the Knightsbridge one,' Maeve sighed. 'But not the South Ken one. That woman is driving me nuts.'

Ava rolled her eyes. 'Don't they all?' Her mobile rang. She looked at the caller ID and turned it off. 'The rich bitch in Battersea. For the fifth time today. You were saying?'

'I need some time off,' Maeve stated. 'My doctor is worried.'

Ava lifted a perfectly arched eyebrow. 'Worried? About a young woman like you? You're only in your thirties. What could possibly be wrong with you? Wait till you're my age, then we can talk about health problems.'

Maeve sat up straighter. 'Look, Ava, I'm about to turn forty. Not that I'll be shouting it from the rooftops, but that's the fact. My workload has been impossible lately. You have given me all the new clients we've been flooded with since that house was featured in *Vogue*. It's nearly impossible to keep up.'

Ava fixed Maeve with a steely look in her pale blue eyes. 'We *can* keep up. We have to, and we will. End of story. I'm doing two houses, a flat and a boutique hotel at the moment. If I can cope, so can you.'

Maeve met Ava's gaze with a stern look of her own. 'You've given me six new clients in the past two weeks. That's more than I can cope with. My dreams are full of wallpaper designs and sofa cushions, and clients call me at six in the morning. On a fecking Sunday!' She paused and lowered her voice. 'I'm taking two weeks off. Doctor's orders. My summer holidays are overdue anyway. I was supposed to have my break three weeks ago, remember? I delayed it because of all the new jobs.' Maeve sighed, feeling a knot of tension in her chest. She took a deep breath and tried to relax her shoulders. 'Please?' she asked. 'Just two weeks. My doctor told me to take a break or I'll have to go on sick leave. Can't you get Rufus to take over? He's been chomping at the bit since he started last spring. And then there's that nice trainee we took on – she seems terrific.'

'I gave Rufus all the house doctor jobs so you could have more time for the new clients. And the new girl has to be broken in slowly.'

'I know. But you can free up Rufus by giving the trainee the house doctor jobs, can't you? Those are quite easy and the most fun. I loved making houses and flats look enticing for the property market when I first started.'

'We're not here to have fun.' Ava sighed and flicked her sleek blonde mane behind her shoulders. 'Okay, then. It's against my better judgement to let you take leave now, but I have to say you do look bloody awful. Not a sight we want our posh clients to be confronted with. But I want you back in time to prepare for the interior design fair in October. We'll have a stand there and I'll need you with me.'

'I'll be back in plenty of time, I swear,' Maeve said in a near whisper, knowing she'd promise anything so she could have some time off. She knew without glancing in the mirror that she looked more than a little under the weather. Her usually rosy cheeks were a sickly white, there were bags under her normally sparkly green eyes, and her thick auburn hair hung lankly down her back. She had lost at least five pounds in the last few months, not because of dieting, but because she hadn't had time to eat properly.

'Where are you going?' Ava asked.

'Home,' Maeve said. 'To Ireland.'

She met Ava's eyes and noticed a flicker of concern. Her boss wasn't without empathy, she was just a very driven woman who fought hard to make her business run smoothly and to keep earning enough money to support her family. Two teenage girls, a flat in Chelsea and an actor husband constantly 'resting', as actors say when they're out of work, didn't come cheap.

Maeve had joined Ava's firm three years earlier, having left everything behind in Ireland following a painful breakup with her boyfriend. The breakup had struck her like a thunderbolt, shattering her well-ordered life, which had included a job at an interior design firm in fashionable Ballsbridge, a good enough income and a wide circle of friends, all fun-loving young professionals with money to spend. Marriage and a family had never been part of her plan. She just wasn't the motherly type – or so she'd been told by her stockbroker boyfriend of the time, who had declared he was not into that scene at all either. Until he'd fallen in love with someone else, and had marched his blushing and heavily pregnant bride down the aisle in double-quick time following his and Maeve's breakup. Maeve had read the announcement of their wedding in the *Irish Times*, swiftly followed by the news of the bouncing baby boy born shortly afterwards. It had been like a stab right into her heart. Breaking up was bad enough, but finding out by the timing of the pregnancy that he had cheated on her had been a huge betrayal. He had been carrying on with this other woman for months before he and Maeve had broken up, lying and going behind Maeve's back. She couldn't begin to understand why. If he'd wanted children, why hadn't he said so? Or was it that he hadn't wanted to have children with *her*? Was there something wrong with her? These sort of thoughts went on and on, and still popped up now, when she was feeling low. She now felt herself bristle whenever a man tried to get close. Would those wounds never heal?

'Where in Ireland?' Ava asked, pulling Maeve out of her thoughts.

Maeve shrugged. 'Haven't decided yet.'

'You have family in Dublin?'

'My parents retired to Spain a few years ago but I might stay with my sister in Dublin for a bit. Then maybe a week in the west. I'll think of something. Ireland is lovely in September.'

'Oh?' Ava looked surprised. 'I thought it'd be overrun by tourists.'

'Some parts, yes. But if you stay out of the tourist hot-spots, it's pretty quiet.' Maeve suddenly had an idea. She felt a spark of something akin to excitement. Why hadn't she thought of it before? 'I have an aunt who lives in a very remote part of Kerry. I might see if I can go and stay with her. Old wreck of a house, but it's very pretty.' She hadn't thought of her aunt or the old house in Kerry for a long time. But now, the more she thought about it, the better an idea it seemed.

'Sounds nice,' Ava said, picking up a brochure. 'Okay, then, darling. You can go on your break on Monday. Make sure you have everything tied up in the Knightsbridge place, and I'll take over that cow in South Ken. Get Rufus to help you. It's time he started earning the rather generous salary I pay him. And if you could be available by email so we can discuss all the other pending jobs, that'd be terrific.'

'Of course,' Maeve promised, knowing that would mean several emails a day, but this was better than being up close and personal with demanding clients. 'I can do lots of stuff online, no problem.'

'Super,' Ava said and picked up her phone.

Maeve slowly got to her feet and tried not to stagger as she went to her cubby hole of an office to tie things up and see what could be left for Rufus to do. Waves of fatigue hit her as she slumped in her chair. *Two weeks*, she thought. It seemed like a mirage. Two weeks of doing nothing. She would go down to Kerry, to her aunt, after a short stint with her sister in Dublin. Sandy Cove… A little village on the edge of the Ring of Kerry, an enchanting place in the summer. And Willow House, where she had spent so many childhood summers, right on the wild beach against a backdrop of the constantly changing lights of the ocean and sky. Not a wildly fashionable place, but Maeve had had enough of that sort of thing after her busy London life.

Who would have thought interior design would be so stressful? Ava's was one of the most sought-after firms, which had been fun and glamorous to work in at first. That was before Maeve had seen the ugly side of spoilt rich people snapping their fingers at anyone they hired. Suddenly, they thought they owned you and had the right to order you around, even on Sunday mornings. There was absolutely no creative freedom in simply doing what the clients wanted, in having to agree with everything – even if they wanted a horrific stuffed polar bear in the middle of their living room.

Maeve closed her eyes for a moment and took a deep breath. *I just have to get through this week and I'll be there*, she thought, and jumped as her phone rang. She was about to answer, but someone standing behind her reached over and grabbed the receiver.

'Ava McDonald Interiors,' Rufus' silky voice answered. 'How can we help you?' He listened for a while. 'She's just stepped out of the office for a moment, but I think I can help you with that. The Italian silk curtains, you said? I know the fabric was being woven in Milan to your specifications, but I'll have to check and see if it's ready. Can I call you back in few minutes?' Rufus said goodbye, hung up and directed his velvet brown eyes at Maeve. 'That was the old thing in Chelsea. The one who can't decide what to have for breakfast, never mind fabrics and stuff. I have a feeling she wants to change the design of the drawing room curtains. Again. Do you want me to handle that?'

'Oh, Rufus, would you? That woman is a total nightmare. I'm so tired and I've been ordered to take some time off by my doctor. I just managed to convince Ava to give me two weeks' holiday.'

'In that case I'll deal with the old bat. Anything for you, my darling.' Rufus picked up the receiver and dialled a number. 'Hello there. It's Rufus at Ava McDonald again. I'll check that order for you straight away, but I just wanted to know if you're positive you want that particular—' He paused while he listened to the high-pitched chatter at the other end. 'Yes, that's what I thought. I could hear by your voice that you were a little unsure… Of course. I can call around with some samples for you this evening. Maeve is going away for a break, but I will be available for you whenever you need me.' More excited chatter. 'Fabulous. See you at six, then, Mrs Hetherington.' He hung up, turned to Maeve and winked. 'There. I just poached that client from you.'

'You can have them all,' Maeve sighed. 'Except the client in Holland Street. I like him and we get on. His fiancée never comes to the meetings any more, so he does it all now. So refreshing to work with someone who's courteous even if he doesn't follow all my advice.'

'I know what you mean.' Rufus smiled, showing nearly every one of his perfect, dazzling white teeth. 'But I like them. I wish Ava would give me a bit more responsibility. House doctoring is fun, but I could do it in my sleep. I need something real to dig my teeth into.'

Fascinated, Maeve looked at him. 'You have gorgeous teeth. How do you get them so white?'

'Regular bleaching.' He shook his head and laughed. 'But we were talking about challenges, not teeth.' He touched her shoulder. 'You do need that time off. And a haircut.'

Maeve tucked her hair behind her ears. 'I know.'

'My partner is a hairdresser at Gielly Green. I could get you a special deal.'

'Gosh, aren't they incredibly busy? But…' She hesitated. It would be nice to be pampered before she set off to Ireland. She hadn't treated herself to a good haircut in months. 'Maybe you could call him and see if he can fit me in?'

'*She*,' Rufus corrected. 'Bloody hell,' he groaned. 'Why does everyone think I'm gay? Is it because I'm an interior designer?'

'No,' Maeve laughed, trying to cover her embarrassment. 'It's because you're so handsome, so impeccably dressed and so… well, fecking *nice*. And hey,' she added. 'Don't tell me you don't play that card with clients.'

Rufus smiled cheekily and adjusted the handkerchief in the top pocket of his Armani blazer. 'Yeah, okay. I go over the top a bit. But that's what they expect. And they feel safe with me.'

Maeve giggled. 'You're a hoot, Rufus.'

He grinned and winked at her. 'I'll miss you.'

'Yeah, right. I'll come back and find myself with no clients. But that's okay. Except for the nice guy in Holland Street. He's mine.'

'I won't go near him,' Rufus promised. 'Where are you going for your break?'

'First to see my sister. And then to Willow House,' Maeve replied, feeling a strange calm as she said it. 'An old house on the very edge of the Irish Atlantic coast.'

'Sounds magical.'

'It is,' Maeve said dreamily. 'The house is lovely. Built by my great-great-grandfather in 1912. And the coast there is amazing. Wild, windswept, beautiful and remote.'

'But…? I hear a "but" in your voice.'

Maeve shrugged. 'I haven't been there for ages. And I haven't kept in touch with my aunt. My uncle died a year ago and I couldn't go to the funeral because I was stuck with a client in the Cotswolds, but I wrote her a letter. She sent me a thank you note, but I haven't heard from her since then. Or her from me. I haven't had time to keep up with my family lately.' She sighed, suddenly overcome with guilt. 'I haven't even had time for me.'

Rufus put his hands on her shoulders and looked into her eyes. 'But now you do. Go, Maeve. Go to Willow House and find yourself again.'

Chapter Two

Although preparing to go to Willow House to 'find herself' was going to take a little time, getting her remaining clients to work with Rufus wasn't as difficult as Maeve had imagined. They were all delighted to have him. With his flashy good looks and impeccable manners, even Ava had to admit he was a welcome addition to the firm. Maeve found herself beginning to wonder whether he'd take over while she was away. But by this stage she was so tired, she didn't care.

It was a relief to take a little time to herself, to get her tiny flat tidied up and her clothes sorted. Rufus's partner managed to squeeze her in the next day at the fashionable salon where she worked, and this was one of the high points of Maeve's week. The curvy blonde – aptly named Barbie – cut Maeve's hair into a lovely shoulder-length bob and gave her a fancy conditioning treatment. Maeve gazed at her reflection in the mirror and smiled. Her shiny auburn hair now softened her square jaw and gave her green eyes a sparkle she hadn't seen for a long time.

The new hairdo did wonders for Maeve's mood and gave her a new pep in her step. It also made her favourite Holland Street client, a tall, silver-haired man, smile at her with a twinkle in his eyes.

'You're looking very fetching, if I may be so bold,' he said, as she stepped into the still-unfurnished hall.

She smiled back at him. 'Thank you, Mr Taylor. I had my hair cut.'

'Very nice.' He led the way into the living room, which had been painted the green called 'Arsenic' in the fancy Farrow & Ball range. The few pieces of antique furniture were swathed in dust covers and the paintings were stacked against the far wall. The bare sash windows overlooked a tiny but well-tended garden, and the traffic of the city was only a distant murmur. 'As you can see, they've finished painting. But I'm afraid we'll have to cover it up with wallpaper. My fiancée has changed her mind. So if you've brought some samples, we could take a look and see if you have what she wants…'

Maeve had only met Belinda once, but knew that it was typical of her to constantly change her mind. She'd get an idea from a celebrity home she had spotted in *Hello!* magazine and then want the same thing, until she saw something else. Then she would phone Maeve and announce in her affected baby voice that this was the 'in' look and she wanted it, like, yesterday. She was at least thirty years younger than her future husband and very determined to get her hands on his money once they were married. What a relief that she was so busy with her wedding plans and had let her charming fiancé take over.

Maeve smiled at him and placed the big canvas bag on a small table by the window. 'I did bring some wallpaper books and fabric samples, just in case.'

'Ah, good. My son's coming a little later to help out. I have a feeling he wanted to stick with the green, though. But Belinda…'

'Maybe I should talk to her directly?' Maeve suggested.

Mr Taylor smiled and shrugged. 'Not possible, I'm afraid. She's at a yoga retreat in India and will be back tomorrow. But then she'll need at least a week to rest, or so she told me when I spoke to her yesterday.'

Maeve sighed theatrically. 'I know. Yoga can be so draining, with all that stretching and chanting and breathing through your nose. I tried it once. The corpse pose was my favourite.'

Mr Taylor laughed. 'Not my kind of thing, I have to confess. But she says it makes her chakra stronger.'

'Oh, the chakra.' Maeve nodded, even though she hadn't a clue what it was. 'It's good she gets that one looked after. But maybe you should put things on hold until she comes back and is ready to tackle things again?'

'Not a good idea, as we have booked the workmen and they have a tight schedule. And Belinda wants to get it all started and on the way. We're getting married in two months, so…' He brightened as there was a sound from the hall. 'Ah, that must be Stephen now.'

The parquet floor creaked as a man walked into the room. Momentarily dazzled by a shaft of sunlight, Maeve couldn't see him clearly at first. Then he stepped a little further towards her, out of the light. As tall as his father, with the same bright blue eyes, he had gleaming blond hair and a smile so dazzling Maeve couldn't help smiling back. Dressed in a grey suit that shouted Savile Row and a light blue button-down shirt, he exuded confidence and wealth.

He held out his hand. 'Hello. I'm Stephen Taylor. And you're the lovely Mary, I take it?'

'Well… No, my name's Maeve,' she mumbled, slightly flustered by his deep voice and broad smile. She pulled herself together and shook his hand. 'Hello. Nice to meet you.'

'It certainly is,' Stephen said, holding her hand a little longer than absolutely necessary. 'Sorry about the name. Maeve, of course.' He looked around the room. 'So where were you when I came in?'

'We're debating about wallpaper,' his father said.

Stephen looked at the walls. 'What's to debate? This is the right colour and wallpaper would be wrong. In any case, the place will be plastered with paintings, so whatever is underneath is of little importance.'

Mr Taylor Senior winked at Maeve. 'What did I tell you?' He looked at Stephen. 'I'm afraid Belinda has changed her mind. She wants wallpaper. The William Morris one called—' he thought for a while '—Strawberry Thief? In blue. With matching curtains.'

'Oh, yes.' Maeve rummaged in her bag and brought out a folder. 'I have it here. Quite right for the period, but perhaps a little busy with matching curtains and all those paintings you're going to hang…'

Stephen Taylor glanced at the pattern in the book Maeve had opened. 'Nice. But too much. This room will be a total nightmare with all the patterns.' He shrugged. 'But Belinda rules, right, Father?'

'I'm afraid so,' Mr Taylor Senior said ruefully.

Stephen consulted his watch. 'What's next? I'm meeting Zoe in Sloane Square in half an hour. Not sure what I'm doing here at all, to be honest, as good old Belinda seems to decide everything all the way from India.'

'Just the rest of downstairs to do for now. The kitchen and what will be the dining room,' Maeve replied. 'That's as far as we've got.

The study and bedrooms upstairs are fine for the moment, your father said.'

'Yes,' Mr Taylor Senior agreed. 'That can wait until she comes back and then we'll have another blast.' He laughed. 'I haven't really a clue about bedrooms and bathrooms and such. She's putting in a four poster and we're looking at Jacuzzis. And we're knocking out a wall to make an en-suite and a walk-in closet, that's all I know.'

'Sounds enchanting,' Stephen said in voice that was dripping with sarcasm. 'Let's have a look at the rest, then.'

They continued down the corridor to the bright, sunny kitchen, where the original cupboards and marble counter tops would soon be replaced by new units. Maeve looked around with a feeling of regret. Such a pity to rip out the solid oak cupboards when they could have been painted and lovingly restored instead of being replaced by something soulless and modern.

'Vandalism,' Stephen exclaimed, as he looked at the plans. 'And she wants a bloody island? Whatever for? She can't cook, for God's sake!' He shot a puzzled look at Maeve. 'You agreed to all of this? Turning an architectural gem into something from a trashy magazine?'

Maeve sighed. 'You're right. It's a great pity. I said so to your father a few weeks ago. But the clients have the last say.' She glanced at the older man. 'I'm afraid I agree with your son, Mr Taylor. But in the end, I'll do what you want, of course.'

Taylor sighed and shrugged. 'Belinda is going to cordon bleu cooking classes. Then we'll have dinner parties here, in what will be the kitchen-diner when the walls are knocked out. She thinks it'll be great fun.' He paused as he looked at his son. 'I'm looking forward to that. Dinner parties with Belinda cooking – and maybe even burning – the dinner! It'll be a laugh. She's a real tonic and has truly brightened up my life.'

'And she has been spending your money like water.'

Mr Taylor Senior shrugged again. 'So what? It's only money. Belinda loves being pampered and I love making her happy. So there might not be much left by the time I pop off, but in the meantime, I'm having a ball, as the kids say. If Belinda wants to turn this house into an amusement park, I'm going to let her. So you can wipe that sour look off your face, Stephen.'

'She'll be the death of you, Dad.'

Mr Taylor winked. 'Then I'll die happy. Please stop worrying. I'm having more fun than you are. Maybe that's your problem?'

Maeve stepped away, pretending to check her messages on her phone. The conversation between father and son was turning a little too personal for her taste.

'Oh, whatever,' Stephen muttered. 'It's your life. I have to go. Thanks for coming, Maeve.' He touched his father's shoulder. 'Sorry about the sour face. Things are a little tricky right now with the divorce and custody problems. We'll have dinner before Belinda comes back, okay?'

Mr Taylor nodded. 'Okay, Stephen. Say hello to Zoe.'

He looked at Maeve with a touch of embarrassment when his son had left. 'Sorry about that. Stephen has a bit of a temper, I'm afraid.'

'He doesn't get on with Belinda?' Maeve asked.

'That's putting it mildly.'

'Must be hard.'

'Not really. I ignore his bad temper and do my own thing. He has a lot of problems at the moment.'

'Oh? That's a pity.' Maeve took out her phone. 'So, let's just go through this, shall we?'

When they had worked out the details of the kitchen, Maeve picked up her bag from the living room, said goodbye to Mr Taylor and walked down the garden path, her thoughts on her trip to Ireland. Only two days away. The big canvas bag dragged on her shoulder, and she was just contemplating taking a taxi, when a voice from a car startled her.

'That looks heavy. Would you like a lift?'

Maeve peered at the silver Audi and discovered Stephen Taylor at the wheel. 'Oh,' she said. 'I thought you were meeting someone in Sloane Square?'

'My daughter. She just cancelled. Had something better to do. Teenagers, huh?'

'I wouldn't know. I haven't got any children. Just three wild nephews in Ireland. But I haven't seen them for—' She stopped, knowing she was babbling. She hitched the bag higher on her shoulder. It weighed a ton. It had been a struggle to get it here on the Tube and she wasn't looking forward to repeating the journey back. 'A lift would be nice,' she said. 'But I don't want to put you to any trouble. The office is in Fulham.'

'No problem,' he said, and got out to help her with the bag. 'I had freed up this afternoon for Zoe, so now I have all the time in the world. It's only three o'clock, so the traffic won't be too bad. I'll have you back in the office in half an hour or so. Quicker on the Tube, I suspect, but a lot less comfortable.'

'That's for sure,' Maeve said, settling into the passenger seat, admiring the plush interior. The cream leather felt butter-soft and the mahogany panelling on the dashboard added to the luxurious feel. The car even smelled expensive.

Stephen's phone rang as he started the engine. He glanced at the caller ID. 'Client,' he grunted. 'I'll take that later.'

'What do you do?' Maeve couldn't help asking.

He glanced at her as they drew up at a red light. 'What would you guess?'

'Hmm.' Maeve thought for a while. 'You said client… And they call you on your mobile… You're not a stockbroker, are you?'

'I hear a note of panic,' he said, laughing. 'What's wrong with being a stockbroker?'

'Everything,' Maeve muttered. 'But that's a private matter.'

'Oh?' The lights changed. Stephen put the car in first gear and it rolled into the traffic. 'No, I'm not a stockbroker. I'm a literary agent. You might have heard of me. The Taylor Agency. One of the biggest agencies in London right now.'

'Eh, no. Not really in touch with publishing and literature. I'm sure it's very interesting work, though.'

'It's fabulous. We sailed through the bad times in publishing by making a few sacrifices, and it paid off.'

'What kind of sacrifices?'

'Oh,' he said airily. 'We took on some of the more popular authors in the romance genre. It took a bit of soul searching, but we had to do it to save the agency. Proved to be a good move, even if it was a little painful.'

'How very brave of you,' she replied with a teasing smile.

He shot her a glance but seemed to take her remark as praise rather than sarcasm. 'Yes. But sometimes you have to go with what makes the money to stay afloat.'

'I know. That's why I have to wreck architectural gems sometimes. All for the sake of staying afloat.'

He laughed. 'Touché.' He looked at her as they pulled up at a set of traffic lights. 'Are all Irish girls this witty?'

'I don't know,' she replied, returning his smile. 'I wouldn't call myself witty, either. Maybe just good at the old repartee.'

'I would agree with that.' His smile widened. 'I like someone who can bounce the ball back.'

'As long as it doesn't hit you where it hurts, I bet.'

'Absolutely.' Their eyes met for a second before the lights changed, and Maeve felt a spark between them, something she hadn't experienced for a long time.

As the traffic grew heavy, they didn't speak while Stephen expertly weaved in and out of lanes, dodging taxis, trucks and buses, and taking shortcuts through narrow streets. He finally pulled up outside the Victorian building where Maeve's office was situated. 'This is it?'

'Yes.'

He glanced up at the façade. 'Nice house.'

'On the outside, yes. Our office is in the basement, down the steps. A bit dark, but I don't spend that much time there.'

'I see.' He looked at her for a moment. 'I know this is short notice, but would you like to go out for a bite later?'

'A bite? You mean dinner?' she asked, confused. 'But… your… or whatever, uh, I mean…'

'No wife, as you might have heard. No significant other either at the moment. You?'

'Not at the moment, no,' she replied. She'd been single for over three years – the whole time she'd been in London. Not that she'd admit that to him right now.

He smiled and held out his hand. 'Let me introduce myself properly. Stephen Taylor. Soon to be divorced. Father of the dreadful but very loveable Zoe. Literary agent at the Taylor Literary Agency.'

Maeve returned his smile and shook his hand. 'Nice to meet you, Stephen. I'm Maeve McKenna from Dublin. Single, but still hopeful. Haven't found that significant other. But maybe I'm getting too old and picky.'

'You don't look old to me.'

'Right now I feel about sixty. Work, work, work, you know?' She grimaced as her phone rang, and checked the caller ID. 'Got to take this, sorry. Bathroom tiles gone wrong.'

'How about that bite to eat later? I hate eating alone. I'll come back around seven, if you're free then?'

'Yes, I should have finished then.' Maeve smiled and nodded, getting out of the car, answering her phone at the same time. Stephen lifted her bag out, placed it on the ground beside her and drove off. In deep discussion about bathroom tiles, Maeve took her bag, walked down the area steps and entered the office. Once she had promised the client that she would call the supplier and the decorating firm and had hung up, she sat down at her desk and tried to remember what she had said to Stephen before that phone call. Had she really agreed to go out to dinner? Well, why not? She could do with some food and a bit of a laugh. He seemed capable of delivering both. He just wanted company, anyway. She looked at the calendar hanging on the wall. Wednesday. Two days and she'd be off to Ireland. Which reminded her that she hadn't yet got around to call either her sister or her aunt to say she was coming. All she had managed to do was book her flight to Dublin. Great planning.

Her phone rang again and she answered, her mind still on bathroom tiles and curtain fabrics. 'Ava McDonald Interiors, Maeve McKenna speaking.'

'Maeve!' the voice exclaimed. 'The very woman.'

'Yes?' Maeve said, puzzled. The Irish voice, laced with a Kerry accent, was so familiar. 'Who…?'

'It's Phil, me darlin'. Your auld auntie in Kerry.'

'Aunt Philomena?'

'Bingo! Gee, you're gettin' slow in your old age. Forty, is it?'

'Not yet.' Maeve burst out laughing. 'You sure haven't changed. How are you?'

'Ah sure, I'm grand,' Aunt Philomena replied. 'A bit lonely and sad of course. But that's life, isn't it?'

'I'm so sorry, Auntie Phil,' Maeve exclaimed. 'It must be so hard for you.'

'Yes, but I have to go on living… Anyway,' Aunt Philomena breezed on. 'I was wondering if you could help me out with something that has popped up. It's a bit… puzzling. I'm after discovering something alarming in Joe's computer.'

'Oh? Like what?'

'I'm not sure. It's about the Internet and such. And… things.' Philomena sighed loudly. 'I need help to sort it all out. There's no one else I could ask. I remembered how good you were with computers and things on the Internet, so I decided to call you and…' Aunt Philomena paused. 'I know you're very busy, but I've missed you so much. So I was wondering if maybe you might come over for a weekend or something soon?'

'Well, yes. Funny you should call right now. I am actually planning to take a break,' Maeve replied, her eyes suddenly welling up. Poor Auntie Phil. She must be so lost and lonely. 'I was actually about to contact you and ask if I could come and stay for a week or two.'

'Lovely!' Auntie Phil said, laughing. 'Must be telepathy. Please come as soon as you can, darlin'. I'd love to see you, and Sandy Cove is so beautiful right now.'

An image of the village popped into Maeve's mind, with Willow House perched on the edge of the cliff and the sea crashing below. The blue ocean, the seagulls, the beach. Swimming in the water warmed by the Gulf Stream. The glittering stars at night and the fresh air…

'I can't wait,' she heard herself say. 'I'll spend the weekend at Roisin's and then rent a car and drive down. I could be there on Monday night. Would that be okay?'

'It would be heaven, my sweet,' Philomena said with a sigh. 'I'll air your bedroom and make the bed. See you at around teatime on Monday, then?'

'I'll be there,' Maeve promised, feeling her spirits rise. She hung up, wondering why Philomena needed her so badly. It had to be more than just for the company. Something a bit alarming to do with her late husband, she said… Maybe she had found emails Uncle Joe had sent to someone? Or… Maeve shook her head and told herself to stop making things up. She'd find out soon enough. The phone rang again and she took the call, this time from workmen asking about paints and plumbing in a house in north London.

The rest of the busy afternoon whizzed past, and when Maeve emerged from the office a little after seven, she was startled to see Stephen Taylor leaning against his car, smiling when he spotted her. She had been so wrapped up in everything at the office and Auntie Phil's phone call, she had forgotten all about their arrangement.

'Hello, there. All finished?' he asked.

Maeve smiled at him. 'Yes,' she said, blowing a lock of hair out of her eyes, 'Finally, phew.' She looked down at her creased skirt that looked more like an accordion than a pencil. 'But I'm not fit to go into a restaurant.'

'How about a pub, then? There's a nice one only five minutes away. Fish and chips, a glass of Pinot Grigio, what do you say?'

Maeve was suddenly starving. 'Sounds perfect.'

He locked his car and walked to her side. 'It's just around the corner. Do you want me to carry anything?'

'No, thank you, I left the samples in the office. I just have my handbag.'

He glanced at her large leather tote. 'Looks pretty hefty to me. What do women have in those big bags anyway? Tea for five and a spare motorbike?'

Maeve laughed. 'Nearly. I have my gym clothes and a change of shoes. Keys, phone, wallet, some make-up and my Filofax.'

'Bloody hell.'

'Yeah, well I spend all day away and often don't get home until very late. So I need all that stuff.'

'I see. We're nearly there. Just around this corner,' he said, leading the way down a narrow street until they came to a stop outside a pub with the name 'J.K. Walsh' on a painted sign above the entrance. They walked into a small, cosy bar with tables and chairs near the window and barstools at the counter. The pub was nearly empty, except for a couple at one of the tables and a man at the bar counter enjoying a pint of beer. The smell of freshly cooked fish and chips made Maeve's stomach rumble.

Stephen walked ahead to the bar and waved at the bartender. 'Fish and chips for two, please, old sport. And a glass of Pinot each.' He glanced at Maeve. 'Is that okay with you?'

'Perfect.'

'Good. We'll be at the table over there by the window.'

'You've been here before,' Maeve said as he pulled out her chair.

'Oh, yes. I often come here after a rugby match at Twickers. Great food and quick service. And it's never so packed you can't get a table. And I like the décor.'

Maeve scanned the room. 'It's nice, except for those curtains. I'd have gone for a more rustic look rather than the paisley design. A bit too girly for a pub. And if they painted the wainscoting white, it would a be lot brighter.'

He laughed. 'I'd never noticed. But then I'm not a designer like you.'

'I'm afraid it's in my blood by now. But the view is nice,' Maeve remarked, looking out the window at the leafy street lined with Victorian houses.

'Very nice,' Stephen agreed, looking at her so intently it made her blush.

'Do you live around here?' Maeve asked, trying to regain her composure.

'No, I live in Maida Vale.'

'Oh. Very posh.'

'Nice area,' he said, a little stiffly. 'And where do you live?'

'Tiny flat in Stockwell.'

'Exquisitely decorated, no doubt.'

Maeve laughed. 'Oh yeah. It's gorgeous. That boho-not-so-chic look with flaking paint, brown lino and leaking taps. I rent it and the landlord would start charging more if I did anything to improve it. Even if I paid for the improvements myself.'

'Ouch. Must be painful.'

Maeve sighed. 'It's very depressing. I'm dying to redecorate it. I've done what I can with curtains and sofa cushions, but it's still depressing. But I have my eye on a nice flat in this area, so I'll be looking into that when I get back from my holiday.'

'You're going away?'

'Just for a break. Doctor's orders. I have a few health problems. Stress-related, apparently.'

His eyebrows shot up. 'Stress-related?'

'I know. Sounds pathetic, doesn't it? What can be stressful about picking out the perfect wallpaper to go with the perfect couch?' She stopped, feeling stupid. 'It's not about the actual work though, it's about the clients. They want everything done at the click of their fingers. And then there's my quest for perfection, too.'

'Oh.' He looked at her appraisingly. 'We're a bit of a perfectionist, are we?'

'What makes you say that?'

'The way you rearranged the salt and pepper on the table as soon as we sat down. And put the mustard pot behind them.'

'Oh. Yes, well…' She bristled slightly at his teasing tone. 'I like straight lines.'

'And hospital corners?'

She had to laugh. 'That too.'

'I suspect it's your personality that landed you in the doctor's office more than the actual job.'

Maeve shrugged. 'A bit of both, I think. But I do have a huge amount of work on right now, so that doesn't help. Then the doctor told me to go off and have fun, fall in love, drink wine and get a tan, if you could believe that.'

Stephen smiled. 'Alcohol, sex and tanning? Sounds like a great doctor. So where are you going to find all that?'

'A little village in the west of Ireland,' Maeve laughed, suddenly relaxing at the thought of her holiday.

'Ireland?' he said, in an incredulous voice that annoyed her.

'Yes. Why not?'

'Oh, I don't know. Never been there. Seems a little provincial and old-fashioned.'

'It's a lot more than that. But I suppose it's nowhere near fashionable enough for someone who lives in Maida Vale and played rugby for Oxford.' The sentence was out of her mouth before she had the common sense to hold it in.

'How did you know? About the rugby and Oxford?'

'Just a wild guess.'

'Or maybe you're psychic?' He glanced at her. 'I didn't mean to sound snobbish.'

She sighed. 'Sorry. I'm very tired and that makes me touchy. Just ignore me.'

'Stress can make a person edgy.'

Her shoulders slumped. 'It sure can. Everything seems like such hard work right now. I don't have much of a personal life. Not many friends in London, no significant other, just my job and my crappy flat. Love my job though, so at least that's something.'

'Including the clients?'

'Most of them. But there are some difficult ones, of course.'

'Like my future stepmother,' he said, rolling his eyes.

'But your dad's lovely.'

'Yes. He didn't deserve to be trapped by that little gold-digger. He had the bad idea to go on a dating site after my mother died, and Belinda was there, winking at him with her big boobs and long legs.'

'She winked with her boobs? Must be very talented.'

Stephen laughed. 'Ha, yes. Very talented.'

They were interrupted by a waiter bringing their order. A big plate of crispy fish in batter and a pile of hot chips was placed in front of Maeve. She inhaled the delicious smell, feeling ravenous. 'This looks wonderful,' she said, helping herself to tartare sauce as the waiter laid down two glasses of white wine and a carafe of iced water.

They ate in silence for a while, smiling at each other and taking sips of the crisp, cold wine. 'Let me know if you want more wine,' Stephen said. 'I have to be careful as I'm driving.'

'Thanks, this is grand,' Maeve mumbled through a mouthful of succulent fish. Her phone rang in her handbag, but she reached inside and turned it off.

'You're not going to answer that?' Stephen asked.

'Nope. Doctor's orders.' However, she pulled out the phone and checked the caller ID. 'Oops. That was my sister. I'll call her back later. In any case, she'll be free to talk then. Right now she must be in the middle of homework and dinner. She has teenagers.'

'That would keep her busy,' Stephen remarked. 'I only have one of those and when she's around, it's all hands on deck. Homework, making dinner, keeping her off her phone and listening to her moaning.'

Maeve laughed. 'Sounds familiar. Multiplied by three for my sister. Except her husband helps out too, of course. They run a consultancy business together, so life's hectic.'

'Must be. Three of them, eh? That would be hard work.' He sat back. 'But don't get me wrong, Zoe is very important to me. I just wish I could see her more often. We're going through a custody case right now, which is quite harrowing.'

'Oh,' Maeve exclaimed, noticing the touch of sadness in his eyes. 'That must be nerve-racking.'

'Yes, it is. One can only hope for the best. But what about you?' Stephen asked. 'Not to be nosey, but…'

'But at my age I should at least be married with a child or two?' Maeve filled in. 'I never had that urge, to be honest,' she breezed on, before he had a chance to reply. 'I had a boyfriend for five years but we were both very much free spirits. Neither of us felt the need to get married or have a family. Or so I thought. Then he had an affair behind my back and when we split up, he rushed into marriage before I could blink. And now he's playing happy families with a wife and child.' She tried to keep the bitterness out of her voice.

'The stockbroker?'

'Yes.' Maeve avoided his eyes while she picked up a chip and dipped it into the sauce before popping it into her mouth, enjoying the tangy flavour.

'Must have been tough.'

'It stung. Still does a bit. But then I decided I needed a change and came to London. I was lucky to be hired by Ava, my boss. I got so busy I didn't have time to think, which was a good thing. But maybe not so good for my social life.' She drew breath. 'Boring, huh?'

He looked confused. 'What's boring?'

'The story of my life.'

He pushed his plate away and leaned forward. 'Not boring at all, just a bit sad. But aren't we all? I'm going through a divorce and here I am, at forty-two, suddenly single, a little lonely and wondering what to do with the rest of my life.'

'Oh, but…' Maeve stopped. 'You seem to be quite eligible,' she continued. What was he going on about? With his good looks and interesting job, he would be quite a catch.

Stephen laughed and shrugged. 'Eligible? I take that as a compliment. But I rushed into marriage with the wrong woman and now I find myself all alone.'

'Maybe you should be more careful next time?' Maeve suggested.

'I should be more picky like you.'

'Oh,' she said airily. 'I'm not that bad. But I have certain standards all the same. I take things as they come these days, not trying too hard, hoping it will happen one day. Looking for Mr Right is so bloody tiring.'

'And now you're taking off to Ireland.'

Maeve nodded and finished her chips. 'Can't wait. Two weeks at Sandy Cove will be heaven.'

'That sounds poetic. Is it a real place?'

'It's a village in the west of Ireland. The house is called Willow House. A gorgeous pink Edwardian building. My aunt lives there. I spent many childhood summers in that house with her and my uncle. But he died last year, so now she's on her own.'

'I'm sure she'll love your company.'

'I hope so. We were quite close when I grew up. The kind of fun auntie every teenager should have,' Maeve said, smiling as she remembered Auntie Phil and her unconventional ways. 'My mother thought she was irresponsible. I think it was because she had no children of her own, so she liked to spoil us.'

'And your uncle?'

'He was quite serious and very correct. He had a long, distinguished career as an international lawyer. They only used Willow House in the summertime when they were on holiday. Auntie Phil used to love putting on jeans and a T-shirt, such a relief from all the gala clothes, she said. But she was so elegant, even in the jeans. Still is, I think. Even at seventy-two.'

'Same age as my father.'

'Great generation. I think they had the best time back in the sixties. Seems to me to have been such an idyllic world. No worries, just a lot of fun.'

Stephen drained his glass of wine. 'Oh, we always think that when we look back at the past, don't we? I'm sure there were plenty of troubles. The cold war, the threat of nuclear attacks, women's rights, unemployment...'

Maeve laughed. 'I suppose so. I just thought: swinging London, the Beatles, Carnaby Street, miniskirts, great fashion and all that fun stuff.'

Stephen smiled. 'You look at the bright side; I'm more gloomy. But you're right. It was probably a great time to be young.'

'Until they had to face adulthood, of course.'

'Some never did.'

'Like my auntie. She's forever the teenager.'

'Sounds like a marvellous woman.' He looked at their empty plates. 'Would you like dessert? Or more wine?'

'No, thanks.' Maeve checked her watch. 'I think I'll get going. It's getting late and I have an early start tomorrow. A client in Ascot. She wants me to call in before she flies off to New York, so I agreed to be there at seven.'

'You do work hard. Don't you ever say no?'

'Do you?'

He laughed. 'All the time. I can write rejection letters in my sleep. "Dear so and so,"' he drawled, '"many thanks for letting us read your work. We enjoyed it but I'm afraid it's not the right fit for us. Wishing you the best of luck with your future career, blah, blah."'

'Must be difficult. Shattering people's dreams like that.'

'Not in the slightest. It's business.' Stephen waved at the waiter for the bill.

Maeve took out her wallet. 'Let's split this.'

'No, this is on me,' Stephen insisted. 'I invited you, remember?'

'Thanks, but…'

'Please. I want to thank you for putting up with the dreadful Belinda. Paying for dinner is the least I can do.'

Too tired to argue, Maeve put her wallet back in her bag. 'That's very kind. Thank you.'

'You're welcome.' When he had paid, he got up and pulled out Maeve's chair. 'Let me drive you home.'

Maeve picked up her bag. 'No thanks, it's really out of your way. And I want to walk for a bit before I get on the Tube. Clears the head.'

'It's a nice evening.' He held the door open for her and they headed out into the warm evening, the traffic a distant roar and the sky darkening. 'Thanks for the company,' he said as they reached his car.

He leaned forward as if to kiss her cheek, but something made her step back a fraction and hold out her hand. 'You're welcome,' she said, a little stiffly. 'It was fun.'

He shook her hand. 'Maybe another time?' He took a card from his breast pocket and handed it to her. 'Here's my card, in case you want to get in touch.'

'Thanks.' She stuffed the card into her bag. 'Who knows? Some evening when we're both at a loose end.' She knew she sounded cold, but she was determined not to be pulled in by a man before she knew she could trust him. Never again, she had promised herself.

'Have a great holiday there, in the wild west.'

'Thank you, I will. Bye, Stephen. And thanks for dinner.' She walked away, knowing he was still standing there, looking at her. This made her toss her hair and wiggle her hips while she walked. She had found herself very attracted to his posh accent and polished good looks, which made her a little nervous. Had she been a little too stiff with him? she wondered. But she was probably being paranoid after what Lorcan had done to her, she told herself. Stephen had been perfectly nice and had looked at her with more than an appreciative glance. Why not give him a chance?

But right now, her holiday beckoned. She forgot all about him as she walked away, her mind on her trip to that magic place she always thought of as home.

Chapter Three

The planned weekend at her sister's house in Dublin wasn't quite what Maeve had hoped. School was starting the following Monday and when Maeve arrived on Friday evening, the house was a mess of uniforms, stacks of new books and sports equipment. Her sister, Roisin, and her brother-in-law, Cian, were about to depart for a wedding in County Wicklow at the weekend, with Cian's mother in charge of the house and the boys while they were away. Amidst all the chaos, Maeve managed a quick cup of tea in the kitchen while Roisin yelled at the boys to get their stuff together for their various sport activities the next day and sort out their books and bags, argued with her husband about who should take the dog for a walk and wrote a long list for her mother-in law.

'You need a holiday more than I do,' Maeve remarked, looking at Roisin's tired face, her fair hair tied up in a messy bun and her wrinkly T-shirt. But Roisin had never worried too much about looking smart. Life was all about her husband and her children. Did she ever have any me-time? Maeve wondered.

'Tell me about it,' Roisin muttered. 'The start of term is always stressful. And then we have to go to this wedding so I want to have everything organised for Monday morning.' She pulled at a strand of hair falling down from the top of her head. 'And I know you think I should smarten myself up. But I've booked into the hairdresser's at the hotel, so don't worry.'

'That's a good idea. Get a massage and facial while you're at it.'

'I think I might while Cian is checking emails and stuff. We have a lot of work piled up at the moment.'

'I don't know how you cope,' Maeve said, thinking how different they were in looks, yet so similar in character. Roisin had their mother's golden blonde hair, blue eyes and a curvy figure, while Maeve, with her auburn hair, green eyes and slim, athletic frame was the spitting image of their father. But they had both inherited their mother's drive and ambition.

Roisin shrugged. 'You know how it goes. You just manage to squeeze as much as you can into the day and then you collapse into bed. Rinse, repeat, and so on.'

'I know. And that's what landed me in the doctor's office. So I will have to break that cycle.'

'If you succeed, let me have the recipe.'

'I'll let you know how I get on. Thanks for letting me have your car.'

'No problem. I can use Cian's car for the two weeks.' Roisin glanced over Maeve's shoulder at the shelf over the sink. 'You did it again, didn't you?'

'What?'

'You rearranged all the mugs on that shelf.'

'They looked a little untidy. But now the colours match.'

'How wonderful.' Roisin got up and opened a cupboard door. 'And you even managed to change everything in the food cupboard while I was taking in the washing.'

'I did.' Maeve smiled proudly. 'Much easier to find things now.'

'Gee, Maeve, was that really necessary? Can't you stop redecorating for one second?'

'I thought you'd like it,' Maeve sighed. 'I know what you're thinking. But it disturbs my sense of design when I see things that don't go together. I suppose the food cupboard was a little over the top.'

'To put it mildly.'

'Okay.' Maeve held up her hands. 'I'll stop. I won't even tell you that you should get new curtains for the kitchen, or that…' She paused as Roisin shook her head. 'Okay, okay, you're right. I'm getting a little obsessed.'

'More than a little. I don't mind lending you my car. Keep it as long as you need it. And enjoy the trip down to Sandy Cove.' Roisin smiled fondly at Maeve. 'I'm sorry I can't just send the boys away and come with you instead. Wouldn't that be a blast?'

'It would be fabulous. Like the old days when we stayed with Auntie Phil and Uncle Joe.'

'Them were the days,' Roisin said, sighing. 'But I couldn't land Cian's mum with the boys for longer than a weekend. They're hard work at the moment. Teenagers, huh? I wish they could stay at the cute ages. Like ten or something. That's such a lovely age.'

'I think they're lovely at any age. Even now,' Maeve said, smiling at her tall, lanky nephew who had just walked into the kitchen. 'Hi, Darragh.'

'Yo, Auntie M.' Darragh gave her a glimmer of a smile before he opened the fridge and started to rummage around. 'Where's the salami that was here this morning?'

'One of your brothers ate it,' Roisin replied with an exasperated sigh. 'Jesus, you boys never stop eating. Go and get your school stuff organised, will you? I told you I want everything ready for Monday if we come back late on Sunday night. And tell Dad to take in the bin when he comes back from the walk. We're leaving in an hour.'

'Okay,' Darragh muttered before he shuffled out of the kitchen. 'Take care, Auntie M. Have a nice one.'

'A nice what?' Maeve asked.

'Holiday, I suppose,' Roisin replied. 'They seem to find it too exhausting to utter more than a couple of syllables at this age. Don't open their mouths much, except for putting food into them.'

Maeve laughed. 'Ah, but they're sweet. They all gave me big hugs when I arrived.'

'Yeah, you're the cool auntie with the exciting London career.' Roisin picked up the teapot. 'More tea?'

'No, thanks. I think I'll get going and let you finish packing and organising.'

'I'm all packed and ready. Just the final details. I have another twenty minutes or so before the last panic sets in, which will happen just as my mother-in-law arrives. Poor woman, she doesn't know what she's let herself in for.' She leaned forward. 'As we won't have the weekend to catch up because of the change of plans, I need to know... What about your glamorous life? All those rich clients and their billion-dollar pads. And what about your love life? Any new man I should know about? You've been very quiet over there the past couple of months.'

Maeve laughed and sighed at the same time. 'Glamorous? I suppose it is, if you see it from the outside. I do get to rub shoulders with the rich and even a little famous. But you have no idea how difficult they can be. How they want everything done not yesterday, but last year. And men…' Maeve stopped as the image of Stephen Taylor popped into her mind. 'Nothing much to report, I'm afraid.'

Roisin's eyes narrowed. 'I see a glimmer of something there. You're thinking about someone. Come on, dish. You can't hide anything from your sister.'

'Oh, it's nothing really,' Maeve laughed. 'I met this guy just a few days ago. We had dinner and then I left. But it wasn't a real date. He was just lonely and I happened to be there.'

'But you liked him?'

'Uh, well, maybe a bit.'

'Cute?'

'Yes.'

'Rich?'

'Could be.'

Roisin laughed. 'Sounds perfect.'

'No,' Maeve protested. 'We only met the once – well, twice, actually. His dad is a client. But that's all. He didn't ask for another date or anything. He just said "maybe another time" and I said "who knows" and that was it. And now I'm just going to forget about it and have a lovely holiday with Auntie Phil. End of story.'

'Oh, Auntie Phil,' Roisin said, looking sad. 'Poor thing. I'm glad you're going to stay with her. She needs cheering up.'

'I know.' Maeve felt a pang of guilt. 'I should have come over for the funeral. And I should have been in touch more.'

'I'm sure she understood. Have you called her to tell her you're arriving tonight?'

'Yes. She was a little startled but happy I'm coming earlier.'

'I'm sure she is. She is so brave. The funeral was beautiful. We all cried buckets, except Auntie Phil. She was the picture of courage and strength. I bet she's been miserable in private, though. They were so happy and so in love all through the years.' Roisin sighed and got up. 'I'm glad you're going down there. It'll be good for you both.'

Maeve jumped from her chair to help her sister tidy up. 'I hope so. I need a rest.'

'I can tell,' Rosin said over her shoulder as she washed the tea mugs. 'You look really drained. I suppose you have been overdoing it as usual?'

Maeve put her arms around Roisin. 'So have you. Oh, Rozzie, why are we like this? Always striving and trying so hard?'

Roisin hugged her back. 'Because that's what we were brought up to do. Work hard and do well, just like our parents. They expected so much of us.'

Maeve sighed and let her arms drop. 'Yes, that's true. But it's thanks to them we were both top of our class. "The brilliant McKennas", the other girls called us, remember? I bet they all hated our guts though.'

Roisin laughed. 'Sure they did.'

'Thank God for Auntie Phil. She let us run wild during the summers at Willow House.'

'And she taught us about sex and boys and make-up and clothes and how to be bitchy in the most elegant way.'

'She saved us from being miserable.'

'And now you have to go and save her. It's pay-back time.' Roisin picked up the car key from the table. 'Enjoy the drive. And let me know how you get on. We can FaceTime every couple of days. I'll need someone sane to talk to when I get back and the mad rush starts.'

Maeve laughed. 'Sane? You're barking up the wrong tree, my friend. Just look at my life. Does that look sane to you?'

Roisin giggled. 'Then I need someone completely crackers to talk to. Much more fun.' She checked her watch. 'It's getting late. We'd better get going or we won't get to the hotel in time for dinner. Go and say bye to Cian and the boys, and I'll put things away and get my ass in gear. And you need to get going. Friday night traffic can be terrible.' She looked wistfully at Maeve. 'I miss you like crazy, you know. I wish we could stay in touch more. But life seems to come in the way all the time.'

'I know. We must try harder.'

'We will.' Roisin made a shooing gesture. 'Get outta here. We've said our goodbyes. Get in that car and drive.'

Maeve laughed and went to hug her nephews. All tall and good-looking, they were such grand kids. And Cian was a wonderful father and husband. Handsome too, with his thatch of brown hair and chiselled jaw. He gave Maeve a tight hug. 'Have a good one, sweetheart,' he said. 'And come and see us again, when we're not so disorganised. Maybe Christmas?'

'I'd love to.' Maeve hugged him back. It was only during these rare moments she wished she had a family of her own. Just for a minute or two.

'It's a date, then,' Cian said. 'Promise?'

'Yes. Absolutely.' She waved goodbye to the boys before putting her suitcase in Roisin's silver Golf, and driving off through the suburbs in the golden glow of the setting sun. Freedom at last.

*

When she reached the motorway, Maeve turned on the car radio and switched the setting to Lyric FM and the Irish music night. As a lilting tune played by a tin whistle filled the air, Maeve's thoughts returned to Roisin and their childhood.

Their parents had both had high profile media jobs which demanded a lot of hard work. Family time was part of the schedule, but often restricted to Sundays and long weekends. Growing up in a home where there were rules and schedules to follow had been hard. It wasn't until they had started holidaying at Willow House that the sisters had become free spirits. And that had all been Auntie Phil's doing.

Oh, the summers in Kerry, when they had run free and barefoot and had swum in the Atlantic warmed by the Gulf Stream, when they had stayed up all night reading Nancy Drew and Enid Blyton and then slept until lunchtime. When they had picked strawberries ripened in the sun and eaten them with a drizzle of cream and those shortbread biscuits Auntie Phil baked. When they had lain, wrapped in duvets, on the lawn looking at the stars, whispering secrets to each other…

Such precious memories when they had been carefree and happy. When they had grown a little older, they had fallen in and out of love with the local boys, which had resulted in a lengthy talk by Auntie Phil about men and their 'urges' and how to stay safe and how to 'never agree to sex unless you're sure you want it as much as he does'. But Auntie Phil had also taught them that sex between two people who truly loved each other was the most beautiful thing in the world. Maeve and Roisin had giggled, but her wise words had stayed in Maeve's mind ever since.

Uncle Joe had been there, in the background, doing his gardening, reading learned books and appearing at meals to entertain them with funny stories. He'd said he loved watching the three girls having fun together, and that it was a great rest from the world of international law. He usually popped up from time to time on the beach, or at teatime under the big sycamore, where Auntie Phil served Earl Grey and scones with strawberry jam. He always wore his white cotton hat and his glasses perched on his nose, a little like Henry Fonda in *On Golden Pond*, the girls told each other. Such mellow, happy days.

Their summers at Willow House had come to an end when the girls had started college and went on holidays with their friends or took summer jobs instead. But Auntie Phil would occasionally land in Dublin from some exotic place and take both girls out to lunch and 'a bit of shopping', which usually meant browsing in the elegant department stores and ending up with designer items that didn't match their student wardrobes. Roisin had at that stage met Cian, and they had already started planning their life together. Maeve was at design college and working hard to get a portfolio together. As a result she got a job as trainee at a well-known firm in Ballsbridge, where she was swiftly offered a permanent job. Things had seemed to be going well.

Roisin's wedding was a few years later and as the years went by, Maeve was dating Lorcan, a relationship that had seemed perfect until his betrayal. It had been like being stabbed by a dagger in her chest. It wasn't only the pain of losing him, but also the shame of everyone knowing and looking at her with pity, which had made her want to run away to a big city where no one knew her.

Uncle Joe and Auntie Phil had retired from their globetrotting life just over ten years earlier and were living permanently at Willow House. Life happened, keeping the girls away from that beautiful place in Kerry. Roisin was busy with married life and motherhood. Maeve had made a name for herself in interior design and moved to London to start afresh, which had taken all her time and energy, until she crashed and burned. And now she was finally returning to Willow House and all her cherished memories, and it felt good.

Maeve switched to a news station and concentrated on the road. Having passed the exit after Abbeyleix, she continued on the motorway to Cork, where she would take the road to Killarney. Then the winding roads of the Ring of Kerry and, finally, Willow House and Auntie Phil's loving care and attention. It would be close to midnight when she arrived and she should really have stayed in a hotel on the way, but the thought of waking up and looking out over the Skellig Islands and the glittering ocean kept her going. Maeve wondered if her aunt would make her a hot chocolate with marshmallows on top like she had when Maeve was ten. It seemed, at that moment, more enticing than a glass of champagne.

Chapter Four

It had been said about Philomena Duffy that if hosting dinner parties was an Olympic sport, she'd have several gold medals. Her parties had been the talk of any town her husband had happened to be working in. Unlike many of her fellow corporate wives, she didn't see entertaining as chore, but truly enjoyed organising anything from the simplest tea party to a gala dinner for twenty. Gregarious and outgoing, she could converse with the strangest and most outlandish people as if she had waited all her life to meet them. She was the perfect wife, taking enormous pride in her appearance, and – even on a shoestring budget in the early days – always looking like a model on a catwalk. Nobody could guess she teamed chain store dresses with accessories she found in outlet stores. She wore everything with such panache it looked as if it had been made bespoke for her by a top-notch designer. Nor would anyone have guessed she spent her holidays in a ramshackle house in the west of Ireland, barefoot, dressed in torn jeans and faded T-shirts.

She had been a true hippie when she'd met Joe Duffy at a rock festival in Dublin in the 1960s. A young solicitor with ambitions to carve out a brilliant career in international law, he had fallen for Philomena like a ton of bricks the instant he'd seen her. It wasn't so much her dark eyes, black hair, beautiful face and lithe figure, but more her lively personality and her talent for witty one-liners delivered in her deep, sexy voice that he had fallen in love with. She had been instantly smitten too, and they had spent that first night in each other's arms under a large oak tree, with the music drumming in their ears and the lights of the city a distant glimmer behind the trees. After that, they were inseparable, married after only three months and off to New York for Joe's very first job in international law, where Philomena had taken on the role of corporate wife with more gusto than anyone had expected. She'd ditched the flowing kaftans, the beads and the wild hair, and replaced them with a sleek hairdo and classic clothes. The Jackie Kennedy look was still in vogue then, and like a chameleon, Philomena had adopted the simple style and made it her trademark, telling a surprised but delighted Joe she had grown up and that they were a team.

Travelling the world to work for various multinational firms, they waited hopefully for a baby or two. But none had appeared and Philomena had tried her hardest to cope with the idea she would never be a mother – a lifelong dream of hers. But when Philomena's younger brother had married and had two daughters in quick succession, she had found to her delight that she was a much-loved and needed aunt. Her brother and sister-in-law were more than grateful to be able to park their daughters with Philomena and Joe at the family home in Kerry, which had become their summer residence after Phil had inherited it from her parents. The girls called her their 'summer-mammy' and loved their holidays in this wild part of Ireland, where they could run free in the garden and on the white sandy beach below. Joe took them surfing and fishing and taught them to swim. Philomena spoiled them with home baking, stories read in front of the fire every evening and star-gazing on the lawn. The house and the village were in a part of Kerry that had no light pollution and was later designated as a Dark-Sky reserve. The heavens and their constellations were beautifully visible.

Those were the best years of Philomena's life and she cherished the memories, missing the girls when they were grown up, too busy with life to come and visit. But she and Joe had been happily retired by then, residing at Willow House permanently. Those golden years of their life had been wonderful too, and they had enjoyed each other's company, pursuing hobbies such as hill walking, gardening, fishing, reading, yoga and looking at the stars through a telescope Philomena had bought Joe for his seventieth birthday. He, in turn, took her on fabulous holidays at expensive hotels, which she had adored. And then, suddenly, he had had a massive heart attack and was gone.

Philomena had found herself alone. The year after Joe's death had been the worst time in her life, and she had spent the first few months doing practically nothing, just sitting stunned and shocked in the study, or at night on the back steps, gazing at the stars and wondering if Joe was on one of them, looking down at her with his little smile in the way that he'd used to sometimes when he'd thought she wouldn't notice.

'Joe,' she would whisper into the darkness, 'why did you have to go? Why did you leave me here all alone?' But the only reply she got was the soft breeze and the eerie cry of an owl. Then she would go upstairs and lie down in the big, empty double bed and cry herself to sleep.

This sad routine continued for six months, until nearly Christmas. Philomena had dragged herself around the empty house, eating very little and doing next to nothing. One day, when the late autumn sun shone through the dusty panes of the windows, she'd caught sight of herself in the mirror over the fireplace in the living room. *Who is that sad, old woman?* she'd thought. *That bedraggled creature looking like death warmed up. Is that what I have become*? She walked closer and stared at her wan face and sad eyes, at the hair hanging limply to her slumped shoulders. Dressed in one of Joe's jumpers and a baggy pair of jeans, she was the picture of neglect and… slovenliness, she suddenly realised.

'Get a grip, ya auld bag,' she said aloud. 'What the hell is wrong with you?'

She stood there for a long time, slowly straightening her back, pulling in her stomach and trying a smile. It didn't look great, but she'd work on it. She simply had to get her ass in gear. What on earth would her girls say if they saw her now? And Jackie Kennedy, her idol? She'd be disgusted.

'Sorry, Jackie,' Philomena whispered. 'I think I lost it there for a while. But I'll get it back, don't you worry.' She winked at the framed photo of Jackie in a Chanel suit from the glory days. Philomena had been in her teens when Kennedy was shot, but she still remembered that day as if it were yesterday. The Camelot days were gone in a flash, over there across the ocean, and a whole world had mourned a handsome, brilliant man. But Jackie had soldiered on, always looking her best. Sad – yes. But always, always chic. Classy to the end.

Well, if she could do it after that calamity, then so can I, Philomena thought, and set to work. It took a lot more effort than she had thought to get her seventy-two-year-old body back to the suppleness and strength of the year before. And even more care and attention than that to get her face and hair back to the groomed perfection Joe had so admired. She stretched her new widow's pension to its limits, buying the very best creams and hair products online, splurging on a hairdressing session at a top salon in Cork, where her hair was cut and coloured to a soft, dark brown. She practised yoga for an hour every day and went on long walks on the beach. She sorted out her wardrobe and started to wear her favourite clothes again, even if Chanel shoes and Yves Saint Laurent trousers weren't quite what people wore in the wild west of Ireland. She loved them, so she wore them. Life was too short to be dowdy. And then she got Esmeralda, who became her constant companion. 'What do you think of the new me, then?' Phil asked her. But Esmeralda didn't reply, just stared back with her inscrutable blue eyes.

Having pulled herself back from her grief, Philomena slowly got back to life: a life without Joe. She joined the book club at the library, worked hard in the garden, looked after Esmeralda and, nearly a year after his death, finally started to sort out Joe's affairs. His laptop was one of the things she had shrunk away from during those early months of terrible grief, but now she felt ready to tackle it. And that was where she had found something she couldn't understand. Something that hinted at a shameful secret.

*

Maeve stopped off in Cork to have a bite to eat. She parked the car near Prince's Street and headed to Quinlan's, where she knew they had great seafood. Ordering a crab sandwich and a bottle of water, she decided to call Philomena to tell her she'd be arriving very late.

Philomena answered on the first ring. 'Good evening. Philomena Duffy here.'

'Auntie Phil, it's Maeve. I'm going to be a little late. No, very late actually. I'm in Cork and it's nine o'clock. Could be midnight before I arrive. Sorry about this and about arriving tonight instead of Monday.'

'That's no problem, darlin'. I'm happy you're coming tonight. I'll leave the key under the flowerpot on the front step as usual. Same pot, different flower.'

'Oh, great. Thanks. I'll just tiptoe up to bed when I arrive. I'm in Quinlan's and have just ordered a crab sandwich, so I don't need anything to eat.'

'Perfect. Just one thing… Would it be okay of we ditched the "auntie" bit? Don't know why, but I feel you're all grown up now, and I don't need a reminder of my age.'

Maeve laughed. 'Oh. Okay, of course, er, Phil. No problem.'

'Thank you, pet. Looking forward to seeing you tomorrow morning. We'll have breakfast under the sycamore as the weather is so lovely right now.'

'That sounds heavenly.'

'And then I hope you can help me solve the… the *mystery*,' Phil whispered and hung up.

Maeve looked at her slice of soda bread topped with a pile of fresh crab and wondered yet again what had Phil so agitated. She picked up her knife and fork and cut into the fragrant sandwich, forgetting the problem as she enjoyed the taste of fresh crab laced with lemon mayonnaise. There was nothing on this earth as tasty as fresh Irish seafood. She looked forward to fresh shrimps and mussels at the little pub near the beach in Sandy Cove, and sitting outside on one of the rough wooden benches, the salty air brushing her face and the feel of sand between her toes, just like years ago when she was a teenager.

She suddenly remembered a wild boy from her past, the one with the gorgeous eyes and sweet smile. He had danced with her at the open-air fete and kissed her behind the sheep-shearing shed. She had never been kissed like that before. She still remembered the soft feel of his mouth and how he had pulled her close, the smell of beer and sausages on his breath and the press of his slim, fit body against hers. She had closed her eyes and returned his kiss with all the fervour she'd possessed. As he'd pulled her closer, she'd thought she was going to faint with excitement. But then he had laughed and run off, and she'd never seen him again, and she had gone back to Dublin and her last year in school. The following summer she had applied for a job in a furniture shop and had then gone on to study design, and had forgotten all about the wild, beautiful boy with the soft lips who had kissed her and run away. But here he was, popping up in her mind all of a sudden. Where was he now? What kind of life had he lived these past twenty years or so?

Maeve sighed and drank some water, finishing the sandwich. She continued on her journey through the soft velvety darkness with the stars twinkling above, the road leading her west: back to Willow House, her childhood memories and her dear aunt. And that mystery that needed to be solved.

Chapter Five

It was well past midnight when Maeve pulled up outside the front door of Willow House. The light was on over the ornate oak door and she found the flower pot and the key under it easily. She glanced at the vintage Jaguar parked beside the door. What a fancy car. Probably something Joe had bought.

The door creaked open as she tiptoed onto the tiled floor of the hall, carrying her suitcase. The door closed behind her with a soft click. She hung her jacket up on the hallstand, which was covered in coats and jackets and bristling with umbrellas and walking sticks at the bottom. She stood for a moment, breathing in the smell of leather, beeswax and a whiff of woodsmoke – the same as ever. Nothing had changed in the past twenty years, obviously. Maeve laughed softly as she made her way through the corridor and up the wide stairs, which were illuminated by a lamp on a little table on the landing.

She crept down the corridor, past Phil's bedroom door, and found her own door open with the bedside light on, and a thermos, mug and a bowl with marshmallows on the table. There was a note that said:

Welcome to Sandy Cove, sweetheart. Had to go to bed as very tired. But I made you some hot chocolate to drink before bedtime. See you tomorrow morning, when I will introduce you to Esmeralda, who sleeps with me. Sweet dreams. Phil xx

Maeve frowned. Esmeralda? Had Phil taken up with some woman? She shrugged. Well, what if she had? As long as Phil was happy and had found comfort in someone's arms, wasn't that a good thing? She sat down on the newly made bed to enjoy her hot chocolate with a couple of marshmallows, feeling like a child again. Then she opened her suitcase and fished out her pyjamas and toothbrush. Once she had undressed and brushed her teeth at the sink by the window, she crawled in between the cool, lavender-scented linen sheets. She fell asleep to the sound of the waves rolling onto the beach below, dreaming of summers long ago and of a boy with beautiful eyes and soft lips.

Maeve woke up slowly as the sunshine glowed behind the curtains. She lay in her bed and looked up at the ceiling and the old alabaster lamp that had always hung up there, and at the bookcase by the window where, in the dim light, she could see the spines of the books she had read and loved. Maybe she should take up Enid Blyton again?

She smiled, stretched and got out of bed, walking on the smooth oak planks to the window, where she pulled back the chintz curtains. Squinting against the sunlight, she gazed out at the view of the ocean, the Skellig Islands in the distance and the boats riding on the high tide. The beach just below the lawn was as white and inviting as ever, with waves lapping the sand and seagulls circling in the blue sky.

Across the lawn, she could see that the wrought-iron table under the sycamore was laid for breakfast. Phil, in a paisley patterned robe, floated across the grass with a basket of bread and a teapot. Maeve looked at her fondly. Phil looked the same as ever – despite her hair cut into a smart new style – her shoulders straight and her body slim. From the back, she could be taken for a much younger woman. As Maeve watched, Phil turned and caught sight of her looking down from the window. She smiled and shouted: 'Maeve! You're awake. Good morning. Come down and have some breakfast, will ya?'

'Coming!' Maeve shouted back.

She grabbed the threadbare blue dressing gown that hung on the back of the door and ran down the stairs. Walking through the house, it seemed at first glance that nothing much had changed, except for a lick of paint here and there, a pair of new curtains in the study and some cushions on the living room sofa that Maeve hadn't seen before. Apart from these minor changes, the house was like a time warp. The years seemed to roll back as she walked through the rooms.

But as she began to look closer in the early morning light, she saw that time had not been kind to the old house. The window frames were warped, the walls had cracks she had never seen before and there was mildew on the curtains in the living room, which explained the musty smell. Was this because of rising damp? On top of all this, there were water stains on the walls and some of the floorboards, which had to mean the roof was leaking. The old house needed a lot of work to stop it deteriorating further. It would cost a minor fortune to repair the roof alone, apart from all the rest. But how could poor Phil get the funds for that?

Maeve stepped outside through the open French windows. The garden, with its herbaceous borders crammed with flowers and its rose bushes by the far end of the house, was a little less tended than when Uncle Joe had kept a strict regime with his secateurs. The weeping willow that gave the house its name had grown to double the size that Maeve remembered, its branches touching the ground. The shrubs had grown to gargantuan proportions, the rhododendrons nearly obliterating the view of the greenhouse and the cliffs beyond.

Phil had sat down and was pouring tea into two large rose-patterned cups when Maeve arrived. She got up and enveloped her niece in a warm hug. 'My darling Maeve,' she exclaimed.

Maeve sank into her welcoming arms, breathing in that hint of Chanel No. 5 that clung to Phil's hair and clothes as always. 'So happy to be here at last,' she whispered.

'Lovely to see you again, pet.' Phil pulled back, looking intently at her niece. 'Let's have a look at you. Gosh, you're awfully thin and pale.' She touched Maeve's face. 'Stressed out? London eating you alive? You busting your gut to be perfect as usual?'

'All of the above, I suppose,' Maeve replied, studying Phil surreptitiously in return. She was still beautiful, despite the lines around her eyes and mouth, and the slight sag in her jawline. To the casual observer she could pass for a woman in her late fifties, despite the sad look deep in her eyes.

Maeve jumped as something brushed against her leg. 'Oh! What's that?' She looked around and saw a brown tail disappear under the table.

Phil laughed. 'Esmeralda has decided to grace you with her presence.'

Maeve let out a giggle. 'Oh, so *that's* Esmeralda.' She bent to look under the table and discovered a sleek Siamese cat who met her gaze with haughty blue eyes. Then she laughed even more, remembering her theories about Esmeralda the night before.

'What's so funny?' Phil asked, picking up the cat, whose tail swished angrily while she looked at Maeve with hostility.

'I thought, well, when you wrote that someone called Esmeralda was sleeping with you…'

Phil let out a loud laugh. 'You thought I'd turned lesbian in my old age?' She paused, looking thoughtful. 'Hmm, not a bad idea to cuddle up with some nice girl my age. The only problem is, I still like men. Not that I want a new one. Joe was the love of my life and the only man I ever wanted. That hasn't changed.' She blinked and buried her face in Esmeralda's fur. 'Joe was unique. No man could hold a candle to him.' She looked at Maeve, her eyes shining with tears. 'I'm all alone now, girl. Alone with my sorrow and with this new worry.'

'I know,' Maeve whispered and touched Phil's arm. 'I'm so sorry. So very sad for you.'

'Thank you. Yes, I'm sad and I always will be; I have come to terms with that.'

'And this thing you're worried about?'

'I'll tell you about that in a little while.'

Maeve gave Phil's arm a squeeze. 'No hurry. Tell me when you can. I'll do my best to help.'

'I know. That's such a comfort.' Phil nodded and smiled through her tears. 'And Joe is here, all around, in the wind that cools my face, in the stars glinting above, in the rustling of the leaves on a stormy night and in the soft summer rain. I can feel his presence all the time. Do you?'

'I think I can.' Maeve sat down on one of the worn cushions of a wrought-iron chair. 'I saw his Panama hat on the shelf in the hall. And his wellies by the door. He'll always be here for me.'

'I'm glad you feel that way.' Phil pushed the basket towards Maeve. 'Have some bread.'

Maeve took a slice of soda bread, warm from the oven, and put it on her plate. 'Oh, this smells lovely. And homemade marmalade. You've gone to a lot of trouble, Phil.'

'Not really. That's Old Time Irish marmalade from Tesco in Killarney. I still like baking though, and soda bread takes no time at all in the Aga. A kind of therapy in a way. And it makes the house smell nice.' She lowered herself into the chair beside Maeve and let Esmeralda onto the grass, where she sat, her paws neatly together and her tail wrapped around them.

'A very elegant cat,' Maeve remarked. 'But I don't think she likes me.'

'She will in time. She just wants to make sure you're up to her standards.'

'I'm sure that'll take a while,' Maeve said, meeting Esmeralda's haughty stare.

'She's a bit of a diva. Just ignore her and she'll come around.' Phil held out the bread basket. 'Here, have another slice. And a peach. I should really have made you a full Irish. You need a little fattening up.'

'I know.' Maeve took another slice from the basket. 'I'll do my best. With your cooking, I don't think it'll be hard.' She eyed Phil's slim figure. 'How do you keep so trim?'

'Gardening, yoga, housework and walking.' Phil shrugged. 'You should have seen me a few months ago, though. I was a wreck. I think I'd been paralysed since Joe passed away. But then something gave me huge kick in the behind and I decided to try to live again. It was hard to pull myself out of the bog hole I'd been in, but I'm getting there.' She smiled fondly at Maeve. 'And now you're here to cheer me up.'

'And to help you with that… problem you mentioned?'

A look of pain flashed through Phil's eyes before she nodded and looked down. 'Yes. I got a message from the bank to say they have found an account in Joe's name that they had overlooked. An account named "Romance", with money going into it from a foreign account several times a year. All the other accounts were in both our names – all except this one. And it was opened over five years ago.'

'That's very strange.'

'Yes, but that's not all. There are some files in the laptop and some kind of email address I haven't had the courage to even look at. It's all there for you to sort.'

'I'll do my best.'

'I knew you would.' Phil paused, looking worried. 'I have a feeling it could reveal things about Joe he didn't want me to know. If he was up to something… bad, I'm not sure I could cope.'

Chapter Six

Maeve forgot to eat and stared at Phil. 'But who… I mean, where did this money come from?'

'Some firm or person in America, lodging through something called LLC. There are some very large sums. That's all I've been able to find out so far. The bank is looking into it.'

'How strange. Did you find anything in his computer to explain it?'

Phil's shoulders slumped. 'I haven't really looked yet. There is so much, and I'm not familiar with computers and such. I have an iPad for my emails and online shopping, and for looking things up here and there. Joe used his laptop for writing. He was working on his memoirs and on something to do with international law. That's what I thought, anyway. But who knows? He might have had one of those online affairs for all I know. Or even a real one.' Phil's eyes were full of tears. 'But how could he? We were so happy, so incredibly close, nearly reading each other's minds at times. And then it turns out he had this secret that he kept from me. It couldn't be another woman, could it?'

Maeve shook her head. 'Absolutely not. There must be another explanation. Something perfectly reasonable that we'll both laugh at when we find it.'

Philomena sighed. 'Oh, God, I hope so.'

I'll take a look at his laptop and then I'm sure it'll all be revealed.'

'Thank you, Maeve. I'm so relieved you're here to help me out. That money could turn out to be very useful for me.'

Maeve swallowed her mouthful of soda bread. 'You're having money problems?'

'Yes and no. My widow's pension is quite substantial, but a house like this eats money. I need to have the roof redone, and it hasn't been rewired since the nineteen thirties. The insurance company says they won't cover me if I don't have that done at least. And that'll cost around ten thousand euros with all the wires and switches and a new fuse board. Plus the window frames are cracked and need to be seen to.'

'I know.' Maeve nodded and looked up at the roof and the missing slates. It sagged alarmingly in the middle, meaning the timbers might need replacing. The pink stucco of the façade, so charming years ago, was stained and cracked. The house was in a sorry state. 'The whole house needs a makeover.'

I know.' Phil sighed and shook her head. 'I had no idea all this was going to have to be done when we retired here. Joe said he'd take care of it. But he seems to have been distracted by other things. I'm not that bad yet, but in the end, I might have to sell up and move to something smaller and more manageable.'

'Sell up? Oh, no. It'd break your heart to have to leave. And mine and Roisin's. And Dad's, of course, as this is his family home, too.' Maeve drained her cup and got to her feet. 'Let's tidy up and get dressed. I'll have a look at that laptop straight away.'

Phil rose and started to pile cups and plates onto a tray. 'I'll bring this in, if you take the bread basket and the teapot.'

Maeve did as she was told and together they walked across the lawn, towards the back door. Maeve noticed the herb garden in the little courtyard was sprouting rosemary, chives, parsley and thyme, which filled the air with a pleasant herby smell. The back door was ajar and she walked in behind Phil, stepping over a cat basket, a pair of wellies and assorted footwear in the utility room before arriving in the large, warm kitchen that still smelled faintly of newly baked bread.

She put the teapot on the draining board and the bread basket on the large old pine table where she had sat all through her summer holidays as a child, enjoying her aunt's excellent cuisine and wonderful comfort foods. She looked around the kitchen with its old oak cupboards, the Aga exuding warmth, the double Belfast sink and the old flagstones polished by many feet through the years. It was, despite its battered look, the most comforting room Maeve had ever been in; she often daydreamed about it at times when she felt lost and lonely. It was as if the kitchen put a pair of loving arms around her every time she entered it. 'I love this kitchen,' she said out loud. 'It's my favourite room in the whole world.'

Phil opened the dishwasher. 'Mine, too. Especially in the winter. Then the Aga is my best friend and this room is like a womb. But maybe it needs a touch of paint and a bit of redecorating?'

'I wouldn't change a thing,' Maeve said, to reassure Phil, even though she could see how run-down it was. 'It has to stay exactly the same. How on earth would you redecorate a womb, anyway?'

Phil laughed. 'Very true. It's not possible.' She put cups, saucers and plates away and closed the machine. 'All done. I'll go and have a shower and get dressed. See you in the study in twenty minutes.'

'Great. I'll just have to check my emails too, just to make sure none of my clients have had a meltdown about their shower curtain or something.'

'But it's the weekend and you're on holiday. Surely nobody will be rude enough to disturb you?'

Maeve laughed. 'You don't know rich people.'

Phil smiled. 'Oh yes, I've rubbed shoulders with some of them. And if any of your clients are like them, I see what you mean.'

'Exactly.' Maeve bent down to stroke Esmeralda, who had slunk in through the open door. But the cat moved away to rub herself against Phil's legs, meowing softly.

Phil picked up the cat and kissed the top of its head. 'Pretending to be hungry, again? But you've had your breakfast. We must think of our figures, my sweet. A fat Siamese is not an attractive sight.'

Maeve blew Phil a kiss and left, walking slowly through the house again, absorbing the atmosphere of the old place, breathing in the smell of fresh bread, old books, potpourri and beeswax. Even if the rugs were worn and the colours faded, they still added warmth and colour to the long corridor that ran through the middle of the house. Maeve ran her fingers over the antique chest of drawers beside the door of the study, and glanced at the intricate tapestry on the wall, still there after what must be over a hundred years.

Oh, how lovely to be back, and how wonderful that this house was still here, even if it was nearly falling down. It would be a dream job to redecorate it and Maeve knew exactly how she'd do it without ruining the period feel. Looking into the large living room, she mentally painted the walls a warm primrose, replaced the threadbare curtains with something from the William Morris collection and upgraded the sagging sofa and chairs to classic pieces. New Donegal carpets would look lovely on the parquet floor, once it was sanded and polished. She nodded. She could do the old place justice and return it to the gem it once was. If only they could find a way to pay for the more urgent work. The thought of it being sold and owned by someone else horrified her. This had always, at the back of her mind, been 'home': a kind of solid rock she knew she could always count on. If it was sold, she would have nowhere to go when life was rough. There must be some way to make the money needed to restore it and keep it in the family. Maybe, she thought, as she walked up the winding stairs, the mysterious money in Uncle Joe's account was the answer? If they could find where it came from, they might also find out if it would keep coming in.

Maeve quickly showered, put on jeans and a shirt and stuck her feet into a pair of sandals before she checked her emails. There was just one, from Ava. *Re: Taylor house Holland Street.* Oh no. Why was Ava emailing about that on a Saturday? Was there something wrong with the Holland Street house? Maeve opened the message, which read:

Hi Maeve,

Sorry to disturb you on your break, but I just wanted to tell you that the dreaded Belinda is back from India. She was looking for you but I said you were away. She now wants to do up the whole house like a yoga retreat type of thing, with bells and candles, fabrics from India and Buddha lamps and stuff like that. Pretty hideous, I have to say. But Rufus has been schmoozing her and is trying to steer her back to what you decided before you left. You might send her an email or a text message just to make sure she's still willing to negotiate. Not that I care about what she wants to do, but it looks like her future husband is losing his cool, not to mention the very glamorous but bossy son who keeps sticking his oar in, saying we have to stop this massacre of an old house or we'll end up with no clients. In short: help!

Have a fabulous holiday in the back of beyond.

Cheers,

Ava

P.S. Stephen Taylor wanted to get in touch with you for 'personal reasons' he said. But I didn't give him your contact details without your permission. Let me know and I'll send them to him. Gorgeous man despite being a little domineering…

A xx

Maeve blinked and read the message again. Stephen Taylor wanted to get in touch with her? She felt tiny butterflies at the thought. He must be more interested in her than she had thought. He had tried to kiss her on the cheek, but she had stepped back and she was afraid it had sent him the wrong signals. But could that have enticed him rather than put him off? Who knew? Men like him were hard to figure out.

She walked to the mirror over the fireplace and stared at her image. 'You have lovely eyes,' she said out loud. 'And you have a very good figure, and…' She sighed and turned away. She'd never set any man on fire. She just didn't have 'it', or whatever she needed to make men want to get into bed with her. That was why Lorcan had left in the end. No fire, no… Maeve sighed and fluffed up her hair. But maybe Stephen had been attracted to her despite all that? She smiled at herself. He was a very handsome man. Maybe, when she got back to London, they could pick up where they had left off? She knew he had at least enjoyed their conversation and laughed at her jokes, which was a good sign.

But that had to wait. She had more important things to worry about, reading Ava's message again. What a horror story. The house could turn into something a lot worse than the original plan. But she'd let Rufus sort that one out.

After firing off a quick email to Rufus, Maeve closed her inbox and put her phone away. Time to tackle Uncle Joe's laptop and find out what he had been up to behind Phil's back. She hoped she'd find out quickly and that it wouldn't turn out to be ugly. But those kinds of secrets were never pretty, were they? Poor Phil, how would she cope with the truth if it turned out to be something horrible? *Only one way to find out*, Maeve thought as she clattered down the stairs.

Dressed in a white shirt, jeans and Chanel ballet flats, Phil was waiting in the study, sitting in the old leather chair behind the big mahogany desk with a laptop open in front of her. The window behind her was open and the worn green velvet curtains moved gently in the soft breeze. Maeve could see the old apple tree outside, the rusty swing still attached to one of its lower branches. She walked across the Donegal carpet with its faded Celtic design and joined Phil at the desk.

'So this is the laptop?'

Phil nodded. 'Yes. I turned it on.'

Maeve sat down on the stool beside Phil. 'Do you know the password?'

'Yes. I have it written down here.' She showed Maeve a notepad on the desk. 'I only found it by accident in his wallet. There was a card that said: "lptp.FdAroma17", whatever that stands for. So I tried it and it opened. But that's as far as I got.' Phil looked at Maeve with something close to despair in her lovely eyes. 'Do you think you could manage all this?'

'Of course. No problem at all.'

Looking relieved, Phil got up from the leather chair. 'Please, sit here. I'll leave you to it. I'll go and make a few phone calls and then I'll be in the garden. Give me a shout if you need anything.'

'Okay.' Maeve sat down in the chair Phil had vacated and pulled the laptop closer, leaning her back against the soft leather, breathing in the faint smell of the cigars that Uncle Joe had used to smoke from time to time. She'd used to peep in sometimes and he would wink at her and whisper, 'Shh…' when he wanted to be left in peace. Then she would close the door softly and tiptoe away, knowing he'd read her a story later, when he had finished his work. She realised how much she missed him and how empty the house seemed without him. Poor Phil, it must be a thousand times worse for her.

Maeve turned her attention to the laptop. As she typed in the password, the screen came to life and she clicked on the little documents folder in the toolbar. When she opened it, she saw to her dismay that there were around thirty files, all with different names that consisted of a series of letters. This would be more complicated than she had thought. She decided to go through them one by one, starting at the top. After clicking on a few of them that contained drafts of articles about the EU and the consequences of the new political climate, she found a document labelled 'psws'. She discovered it was a list of passwords for different websites and social media accounts. *Not a great idea, Uncle Joe*, Maeve thought, shaking her head at how careless he had been. She scanned the list and found a password that seemed to belong to a different email, a Gmail account with the name 'FdA'. He must have had an account Phil didn't know about. Maeve decided to see if she could log into the account. This turned out to be easy. The password worked and the page came up with a whole string of messages dated just before Uncle Joe's death, and also a huge number of unopened emails received after his death, some of them with the subject *Fanny's latest*, others that said *Please reply* or *Where are you?*

Maeve's eyes widened. With her heart racing, she opened the top message and nearly stopped breathing while she read it.

Chapter Seven

Hi Joe,

I have been trying to contact you many times in the past few months about the stuff we discussed for my further adventures with you. I liked your ideas and agree that we need to make the 'sauce' even more piquant than before. How about going to Paris for this one? I'm sure you know many areas in that fabulous city that would be perfect for amorous trysts. I would also like to up the temperature with more details of sexy underwear and perhaps some sex toys from those shops you mentioned. Lots of new games to explore for your naughty Fanny! Let me know how we can make this next adventure even hotter than the last one!

All best wishes,

Betsy xx

The message was dated several months after Uncle Joe had died, along with many others, urging him to get in touch. Maybe the woman who sent it had never found out he had died? Strange that she hadn't heard the news, Uncle Joe being such a well-known and respected public figure. But maybe she had missed it? Maeve read the message again. Holy mother, this was shocking! Poor old

Auntie Phil, how would she cope with this? But… Maeve tried to figure out what had been going on. Who was this woman? And who was 'naughty Fanny'? Was Uncle Joe involved in some kind of sleazy threesome?

Bracing herself for even more shocking revelations, Maeve opened an earlier email. It read:

Hi Joe,

I LOVED your new ideas! Keep ramping up the heat! Please send me more details of how you see us continuing the affair. I don't want it to turn into Fifty Shades, as that was a little too aggressive for me. Let's keep it sweet, but with a little piquancy, like strawberry jam with chilli peppers, if you get my drift. Fanny is a tart with a heart and that's the way I want her to stay.

Until the next time,

Betsy xx

Maeve sat back, trying to take it in. Good, reliable Uncle Joe, who had been so revered and admired. The international lawyer without a blemish on his reputation. The devoted husband to a beautiful woman… Had he been involved with not one, but two women beyond his beloved wife?

Maeve sat back and stared out the window without seeing the view of the garden and the greenhouse. A hard knot of dread clutched at her stomach as all kinds of horrible ideas flitted through her mind. What had he been up to? She suddenly felt a searing rage at this man who had been her favourite uncle, a kind of summer dad to her and Roisin. Who were these women?

Betsy and Fanny… She looked at the sender's email address: *Betsymalone@redhothouse.com*. Red Hot House? Was that some kind of bordello? Or… Maeve turned back to the laptop and googled 'Redhothouse'. What came up on the first page made her gasp. Red Hot House was a publishing house for romance in all kinds of genres. What on earth had Joe been involved in? Searching the website, Maeve discovered that the woman called Betsy Malone was some kind of editor. So, that was one of the women. But who was this Fanny? Some other staff member? Maeve stared at the screen and put 'Fanny' into the search engine at the top of the website page. Then the page froze, and as she glanced at the modem, she saw that the light had gone out. She looked up as Phil stuck her head in the door.

'Any luck?'

Maeve hesitated. 'Er… uh, not yet. Just looking into something and then the modem died.'

'Oh. Well, I'm afraid they called to say the broadband connection will be interrupted for some kind of update, so you won't be able to do much more until they've finished. Could be sometime tomorrow, they said.'

'What? No broadband?' Maeve looked back at the frozen screen. 'Shit, I don't believe it! How can they do that?'

Phil shrugged. 'Welcome to the back of beyond, girl. It appears they don't think we need the Internet in this part of the world. "Sure can't you watch TV?" they said last time I complained.'

Maeve sighed and picked up her phone. 'I can try my hotspot, I suppose.'

Phil smiled. 'That sounds faintly suggestive.'

Maeve felt her face redden as she thought of what those emails had revealed. 'It's a term that means using your phone as a modem for the Internet,' she explained.

'But that might not work either. The phone signal is very unreliable. It all depends on the weather and if there are strong winds. And those feckers who run the phone company. Can't bless themselves as far as I know.'

Maeve couldn't help laughing. 'Must be frustrating.'

'Not really. I'm old-fashioned enough to use a landline. Phones are for talking to people and nothing else. Much less distracting.' Phil stood in the doorway as if poised to leave. 'Do you want to take a break and come with me to the nursing home?'

'I didn't know there was a nursing home in Sandy Cove.'

'It's not a nursing home as such, but a house that these old ladies share, looking after each other. I read to them there every Saturday. We're doing Jane Austen right now. Great bunch of women. All in their nineties. Salt of the earth kind of old birds. You'd love them.'

Maeve looked at the laptop screen. 'I should really go through all these files, but I'll leave it till later. I could do with a little Jane Austen right now. And I've always loved your voice.'

'As long as you don't go to sleep, like some of my audience.'

'I am a little bit younger than ninety,' Maeve quipped.

'So am I. But time flies when you get older and before you know it, you're sitting there in a nursing home trying to stay awake while some boring woman reads *Pride and Prejudice* to you for the fifth time.'

'Maybe you should try something more modern?' Maeve suggested.

'I would if I could find it. But our personal collection doesn't have much that would suit. Joe didn't read fiction much and I didn't buy novels myself; I went to the local library before it closed down. There is a small bookshop here but it isn't very well stocked. They sell nearly only second-hand books and it's either the classics or trashy romances.'

'I might pay it a visit. Maybe I'll find something you've overlooked.'

'I doubt it. But you should go all the same. The owner is very nice,' Phil said with a wink. 'Local chap. About your age. You might hit it off.'

'Are you trying to set me up?' Maeve said with a laugh. 'With the owner of a second-hand bookshop?'

'Well, why not? You have to go out there and mingle.'

'With a bookworm from the sticks?'

'You have better options?'

'I might,' Maeve said, thinking about Stephen Taylor. Quite a catch, some might think.

Phil's eyes lit up. 'Really? Some dishy Londoner?'

Maeve turned off the laptop and got up. 'Dishy, yes. Very posh and proper, like something from *Downton Abbey*. His dad's also very charming. And now I just heard he wants my contact details.'

'The dad?'

'No, the son. Stephen Taylor. Oxford graduate. Literary agent and very good-looking in that upper-class British way.' Maeve smiled. 'Speaks with a plum in his mouth, calls people "old sport" and wears rugby shirts from the good old days of playing for Oxford.'

Phil laughed. 'I see. Well, they're not all bad, you know.' She started walking down the corridor, picking up her keys from a bowl on the hall table. 'Are you going to let him have your email address?'

'He can look it up on the firm's website. Let's forget about him.' Maeve looked lovingly at the smooth oak of the hall table. 'I love all the old stuff in this house, and how nothing's changed over the years.'

'Oh, that's just because Joe wanted everything to stay the same. But I might shake things up a bit now. Get new curtains and do a few sorely needed repairs. If I can afford to keep it. I need to think of some way to make money. Like renting it out in the summer months, or getting into the B&B business.'

'I'm sure there's something like that we can do. Not that I like the idea of strangers living here,' Maeve said.

'Neither do I. But beggars can't be choosers.' Phil opened the front door. 'Let's go and shake up the old birds. They'll love to meet you.'

'Can't wait to meet them either.' Maeve fell into step with Phil as they walked down the drive, through the ornate gates and up the narrow lane, shaded by large mountain ash and rhododendron bushes. As they walked along the main street, Maeve noticed a few changes since she had last been there twenty years ago. Gone was the old village shop where you could buy anything from wellies and nuts and bolts to milk, cheese, homemade bread and cakes. It had been replaced by a health food shop with baskets stacked outside the plate glass doors. The newspaper shop where Maeve and Roisin had bought sweets and ice cream had turned into an art gallery, and the pub on the corner was now a fast food restaurant. Maeve noticed that the art gallery was full of customers, and there were people queuing for hamburgers and chips inside the restaurant.

'This village has really changed since I was here last,' Maeve remarked.

'Oh yes, it's all very swish these days. It's turning into quite a tourist spot. But only for a few weeks in the summer. Off-season is very quiet.'

'The beach must be packed on nice days,' Maeve said, feeling sad that their hidden paradise had turned into a popular seaside resort.

Phil laughed. 'Not our cove. Nobody seems to have the energy to climb down the rocks. But the main beach is very busy in the summertime. Not that I mind. I like seeing the village so lively and everyone doing well with their different shops and restaurants.'

'What about the pub in the harbour? Don't tell me it's been turned into the Ritz.'

Phil laughed. 'No, it's still there and still the same shambles. But that's what people like. Sitting on wooden benches outside, enjoying a pint and eating shrimps and chips with their fingers.'

'Oh, yes,' Maeve sighed. 'That's my favourite thing in the whole world.' She turned to Phil. 'Let's go and have our dinner there tonight. My treat.'

Phil smiled and put her arm through Maeve's. 'Why not? There's live music on Saturday nights. Sometimes it's a whole Irish band and sometimes just Mad Brendan and his fiddle, if you can call him live, of course.'

'He's still playing?' Maeve smiled at the memories of music sessions at the Harbour pub long ago, with songs in Gaelic, and Irish dancing on the floor strewn with sawdust.

'Sure, who could stop him? But it's all great craic, as they say. And he still has the donkeys that escape from time to time for a quick trot down the street so they have to call the Guards to round them up.'

Maeve laughed. 'That's brilliant. Looking forward to seeing that.'

'And to the night at the Harbour Bar,' Phil added.

'Terrific. We might need it after the stint in the nursing home.'

Phil threw Maeve a glance full of laughter. 'Wait till you meet them. Not the dull auld women you might imagine.'

'Really?'

'You'll see.'

Chapter Eight

When Maeve stepped inside the bright living room of the large bungalow and saw the four occupants, she knew exactly what Phil meant.

Sitting by the window that let in the sunshine, the four women were absorbed by a programme on the large radio that sat on top of a mahogany bookcase. As she and Phil stood in the doorway waiting for someone to notice them, Maeve had a chance to look around the room. It was large and square with bare wooden floors and light-yellow walls adorned with watercolours and a few oil paintings, all beautiful landscapes form various parts of Kerry. The large picture window, which had stunning views of the main beach and the ocean, was hung with sheer white curtains that moved gently in the light breeze. The sofas and chairs arranged around the large fireplace were strewn with cushions in vivid colours. It was a lovely, welcoming room that would be wonderfully cosy in winter with logs blazing and soft light from the many lamps dotted around the room. But it needed a bit of an update, Maeve thought, imagining how much nicer it would look with more contemporary furniture and less of a mish-mash of colours. 'Blue, with some white here and there,' she muttered to herself. 'A nautical theme. Cushions with a design of seagulls and shells…'

'What?' Phil asked.

'Nothing. I was just doing a little redecorating in my head.'

'I thought you were taking a break.'

Maeve laughed. 'I know. Just fooling around for fun.'

'I see. But let's meet the girls now.' Phil cleared her throat. 'Hello,' she called and clapped her hands. 'Here I am with my lovely niece to meet you. She will read for you today.'

'What?' Maeve protested. 'I never said I'd—'

She was interrupted by a tall, gangly woman with grey hair scraped back from her lined face, who had risen from her chair when Phil had spoken. 'Oh, hello, Phil, there you are. And your niece, too.' She strode forward, her Birkenstock sandals slapping the floorboards, and gripped Maeve's hand tightly. 'Hello there, I'm Mary Watson.' She peered at Maeve through steel-rimmed glasses. 'Which niece are you? The pretty one or the high achiever?' She was dressed in an ankle-length blue cotton dress and leaned lightly on a walking stick.

'Uh…' Maeve didn't know what to say. She eased her hand out of the tight grasp as the other women approached with varying walking abilities.

'I think she must be the pretty one,' a tiny, chubby woman in a knitted dress said as she reached Mary's side. She studied Maeve from below. 'Lovely eyes. And that hair, just like Maureen O'Hara.'

Maeve instantly liked the woman. She had tight, white curls, a round smiley face and a soft, pink complexion. 'Hi, I'm Maeve,' she said, and took the tiny hand offered.

'I'm Louise,' the little woman replied. 'So nice to meet you, Maureen. Any new movies we'd like?'

'Uh, no...' Maeve replied, looking to Phil for help.

'Oh,' Louise said, nodding wisely. 'I see. You're resting.'

They were joined by the two remaining women, both of whom were youthful and well turned-out in matching skirts, blue cardigans and identical pink sneakers. 'Hello,' one of them said, 'I'm Oonagh, and this is my twin sister Nora.'

Maeve smiled at the sweet faces and shook their hands. 'I'm Maeve, except your friend seems to think I'm a reincarnation of Maureen O'Hara.'

'You could be,' Oonagh said. 'You're very like her, actually, with that dark red hair and green eyes.' She turned to Louise. 'This isn't the real Maureen O'Hara, pet. She just looks a little like her.'

This didn't register with Louise, who winked at Maeve and whispered, 'Incognito, eh? I won't tell a soul, promise.'

Maeve had to laugh. 'Thank you. It'll be our little secret, okay?'

'Of course.' Louise made a gesture to zip her lips and smiled conspiratorially. 'It'll stay right here.'

Mary Watson rolled her eyes and sighed. 'Oh, Louise, that's enough of that. Let's go and sit down and listen to Phil reading. I think we were on chapter five?'

'Chapter seven,' one of the twins announced. 'I think you fell asleep after the end of chapter four, Mary.'

Mary looked flustered. 'Oh dear, I might have. I was exhausted that day, after the party with my grandchildren the day before.'

'Your grandchildren would wear out an army,' Oonagh remarked.

'I wonder who they take after,' Nora said. 'I remember how fierce you were on the county council. Never stopped campaigning.'

Phil smiled at Maeve. 'What did I tell you? These women are special.'

'I can see that.'

'But come and sit down,' Mary urged. 'I'll get Sinead to make us some coffee to keep us awake. We're not allowed to snooze until after lunch, and then only for half an hour.'

They all walked back to the chairs by the window, where the radio was still blaring on. Mary switched it off. 'Enough of Marion. She can be a little pompous at times.'

'Marion?' Maeve asked.

'Radio presenter,' Phil whispered. 'Popular, but full of herself. And don't worry, you don't have to read. I was only joking.'

They sat down and Phil brought an extra chair from the group by the fireplace for Maeve. Louise picked up a basket with yarn and knitting needles from the floor and glanced at Maeve. 'I'd say you're a size twelve. I think I'll knit you a cardie to wear in your next movie. A green one. What do you say?'

'Lovely,' Maeve whispered as Phil opened the book. Louise nodded and everybody settled down to listen to Phil's melodious voice reading the lovely prose of Jane Austen. Sinead, who turned out to be the kindly faced housekeeper, tiptoed in with their coffee and silently handed each of them a cup. She held out a sugar bowl to Maeve, who shook her head and sipped the strong brew, transported to another era, as Phil read on. She looked around as the old ladies listened with rapt attention, frowning and smiling as the story wore on. Louise snorted at Mr Darcy's acerbic comments and muttered, 'What a sourpuss,' while her knitting needles clicked. Mary frowned and hissed a 'Shh,' and the twins looked dangerously close to nodding off. Maeve felt quite drowsy herself and jumped as Phil ended the chapter and closed the book with a loud snap.

'So what did we think of that?' she enquired, looking around the little group.

'I've read it before, but I enjoyed it,' Mary replied.

'I don't like that Darcy fellow,' Louise grumbled. 'Elizabeth Bennett deserves someone better.'

'Like who?' Oonagh demanded, sitting up straighter.

'Like Morgan Hamilton in the book I'm reading at bedtime,' Louise retorted.

'One of those silly romances, I suppose,' Mary snapped. 'From those trashy books Paschal in the bookshop sells for fifty cents. I know you love them, Louise. I saw you come out of the shop with a whole pile of them.'

'There's nothing wrong with a little romance,' Louise stated, looking rebellious. 'And these ones are surprisingly well written. They're set in Paris. Madeleine, the heroine, is a policewoman who cracks all the crimes in no time and she has these handsome men buzzing around her. I think this author could give Jane Austen a run for her money, you know.'

'Ha,' Oonagh said with a snort. 'I doubt that very much.'

'You'd be surprised.' Her chubby little body erect and her cheeks aglow, Louise's eyes were suddenly full of passion. 'I know,' she exclaimed. 'We could read one of those books when we've finished *Pride and Prejudice*. Just to prove to you I'm right.'

Maeve laughed. 'You might be on to something. Could you show me one of those books, Louise?' she asked.

'Afraid not,' Louise said with regret in her voice. 'I threw the last one in the recycling bin. But I know Paschal has the next two in the series. I was going to pick them up later today. Maybe we could go there together after lunch?'

'Or I could go now and pick them up for you,' Maeve suggested.

Louise beamed. 'Would you? That's very kind. Then I can start a new one tonight. My eyes are getting tired, you see, so I don't know how long I will be able to see well enough to read books. That's why I love listening to Phil reading.' She sighed. 'If only we could read something a bit more…'

'…Racy?' Mary filled in, with a touch of scorn in her voice.

Louise glared at her. 'Yes, why not? What's wrong with a bit of… er, sensualism?'

Oonagh nodded. 'I would have no objection. Let's give it a go. What do you say, Phil?'

'But we haven't finished the Jane Austen novel,' Phil protested.

'We all know where that one is going,' Louise remarked. 'And we can always pick it up again if you all find the romance one too exciting.'

Oonagh got up and put her cup on a table near her chair. 'I think that's a very good idea. Come on, girls, we're not dead yet. Let's put a little spice into the readings.'

Phil laughed. 'Okay, then. We'll give it a go. I don't mind as long as it's not too explicit.'

'It isn't,' Louise promised. 'The naughty thoughts will be in your heads. And the stories are exciting and fast moving. Romance, danger, humour… and a dash of how's-your-uncle,' she added with a wink.

Mary looked as if she was desperately trying to keep a straight face. 'You're an article, Louise O'Sullivan. No wonder the nuns were always putting you in detention.'

Phil put her book into her bag and got up. 'Okay, then. We'll regroup next week. In the meantime, Maeve and I will go and get those books and take a look.'

That settled, they bid goodbye to the ladies and left for the bookshop, Phil leading the way down the main street. 'So what did you think?' she asked over her shoulder as she walked briskly along, Maeve trying her best to keep up. 'Aren't they a hoot?'

'Loved them. Especially Louise,' Maeve panted. 'Could we slow down a bit? I'm not as fit as you are.'

Phil stopped and laughed. 'It's all right. We're here.' She nodded at a shop window crammed with antiques and books. 'Ye olde book and antique shop.'

Maeve looked at the window where souvenirs, antique clocks, china figures, crockery and vintage jewellery were displayed against a backdrop of books stacked in piles, creating a charming old-world image that spoke of bygone days and stories read in front of the fire on cold winter nights. 'How lovely. I never thought a bookshop could look like this.'

'Paschal is very artistic. A real free spirit. Wait till you meet him.' Phil pushed the door open, making an array of tiny bells chime. 'Hello?' she shouted. 'Paschal? Are you there?'

'Right here, darlin',' someone replied from deep within the dim shop. The voice was male, melodious and laced with a strong Kerry accent. A lovely voice that left Maeve eager to meet the owner.

'I've brought my niece,' Phil called back. 'She just arrived from London. She's dying to meet you.'

'A young lady from London?' the voice said, with a hint of laughter. 'Must behave myself then. But come in and close the door. I'll be with you in a sec.'

Maeve smiled as she listened to the melodious voice. Who was he?

Chapter Nine

They walked into the dim interior and Maeve looked around. The shop was small with an old-fashioned look, selling a variety of things that were mixed together in an array of shapes and colours. Irish hand-knitted sweaters shared a shelf with scarves and hats, maps and postcards were displayed on carousels, and the books were arranged in ragged lines on an antique bookshelf. An old chest with the drawers pulled out was packed with scarves, shawls and rugs in a collection of colours, and tweed jackets hung from a rack near the window. It was all charming and inviting, Maeve thought, but she couldn't help rearranging the books so they were more colour-coordinated.

She jumped as someone landed beside her from a ladder with a thump. 'Oh!' she exclaimed and stepped back. 'Sorry. Didn't see you.'

'Of course not,' the man said and gestured at the shelves that covered the far wall. 'I was up there trying to stack some old books.' He held out his hand. 'Hiya. I'm Paschal.'

'Maeve,' she said and shook his hand. 'Phil's niece.'

'I can see that,' he remarked, his sloping brown eyes studying her so intently it made her blush. 'You two are the spit of each other. But we've met before, many moons ago, in the far-away land of teenage angst.'

Maeve couldn't help smiling. 'Have we? I can't remember much about those days. I must be in denial or something.'

'I thought the Nile was in Egypt,' he quipped. Then he slapped his forehead. 'Gee, what a bad joke. But hey, I don't meet such sophisticated ladies that often. You have me all flustered.'

'Sophisticated?' Maeve laughed. 'Nah, it's more like the small-town girl still trying to cope with big city life. I haven't become that polished yet. It takes three hundred years and a lot of patience before you're a real Londoner.'

She couldn't stop looking at him. With his sing-song voice and his curly black hair and dark eyes, he was handsome in a wild, Poldark kind of way. He looked to be around her own age and she wondered if they really had met before, when they were teenagers? But there had been a lot of teenagers around during those summers and she couldn't remember them clearly. Paschal's eyes met hers for a moment – then they were interrupted.

'Paschal, I'm going to leave you two to sort it out,' Phil announced. 'I have to go to the post office before they close for lunch and then I'm going to buy cat food at the supermarket. I'll see you back at the house in a little while, Maeve.' With that, she walked out of the shop, leaving Maeve and Paschal staring at each other in uncomfortable silence.

Paschal cleared his throat. 'So… where were we? What can I do for you?'

What he could possibly do for her flitted through Maeve's mind for a second, making her face red-hot. Then she came to her senses and remembered why she was there. 'I'm looking for some books,' she started.

'Then you've come to the right place. Any particular books? Or just books in general?'

'Something romantic,' Maeve replied. 'A romance series with a heroine called Madeleine, set in Paris. I believe you have the next two books of the series in stock.'

He lifted an eyebrow. 'Romance? I wouldn't have thought that would be your cup of tea.'

Maeve squirmed. 'It's not for me.'

He grinned. 'Oh, I seeee. You're asking for a friend?'

To her annoyance, she felt her face redden again. Why did he make her blush every time he opened his mouth? 'Yes. An old lady who loves romance.'

'It's Louise, isn't it? My very special customer.'

Maeve relaxed and smiled. 'That's right. I only met her today and I love her already.'

'She's a grand old girl. But a bit scattered, if you know what I mean.'

Maeve laughed at the old Irish saying. 'Yeah, a bit. She thinks I'm Maureen O'Hara in disguise.'

'Count your blessings. She thinks I'm Tom Crean and keeps asking me about the Antarctic.'

'You mean Tom Crean, the explorer who went with Scott to the South Pole?'

'The very man.'

'You do look a little like him, I must say,' Maeve remarked, remembering that handsome rugged face she'd seen on so many posters and in books.

'Yeah, sure I look well considering I've been dead since 1938,' Paschal retorted with a grin. 'She's stuck on that idea and nothing I say will convince her otherwise.'

'Ah well, not her fault she's a little confused. She must be well over ninety. And she loves romantic stories; what's wrong with that?'

'Kindred spirits,' Paschal said with a knowing smile. 'Romance fans unite, whatever the age.' He reached under the counter and placed two books on the counter. 'The last books in the series Louise is reading.' He smiled and looked at the cover of the book at the top. 'Gee, that guy sure is… talented. The heroine seems to have struck gold. Or maybe that's one of the baddies? One of those guys who breaks a woman's heart and runs off once they got what they want…'

'Looks interesting,' Maeve laughed and rummaged in her bag for her credit card. 'How much do I owe you for those?'

'For you, only five euros. But I only take cash. I don't do credit cards.'

'Why not?'

He shrugged. 'Never organised it.'

'In this day and age?' Maeve put a five euro note on the counter and picked up the top book, glancing at the picture of a busty, dark-haired woman, her hair cascading down her back, looking enthralled as she gazed into the eyes of a bare-chested blond man sporting a glistening six pack. Maeve mentally rolled her eyes. What a cheesy cover.

'Fabulous couple, eh?' Paschal quipped as he handed her the change. 'You want me to put that in a bag for you?'

'Okay. Thanks.'

'You're very welcome, darlin'.' Paschal took a brown paper bag from a pile on the counter. 'Plain package to save you blushing walking down the street.'

'Why would I?'

'Why would you not? Joe Duffy's niece reading trashy romance... They would have great fun talking about this in the pub.'

'They?'

'The locals,' he explained. 'They're all gossiping about you already. I knew you had arrived by nine this morning.' He leaned on the counter, his dark eyes puzzled. 'I never know how this works, but the moment anything happens in this village, it's all over the neighbourhood within an hour. Talk about the jungle telegraph. I've lived here all my life, apart from a break now and then, and still can't figure out how the word spreads.'

'Weird,' Maeve mumbled and took the bag with the books.

'Sure is.' He got out from behind the counter and accompanied her to the door, holding it for her while she stepped into the sunny street. 'Have a lovely day, Maeve McKenna. See you around.'

'I suppose that's inevitable.'

'As sure as the day is long.' He smiled, touched her shoulder and retreated into the shop, the bells chiming as the door closed behind him.

Dazzled, more from her encounter with Paschal than the sun, Maeve stood there for a moment getting her bearings. Then she remembered the books. She pulled one from the bag and looked again at the cover. The title was *Heart to Heart.* Maeve turned the book to read the short blurb about Madeleine Heart and how she had solved a murder case nobody else could crack, with the help of 'a devilishly handsome stranger'. Maeve snorted. Gee, what schlock. Her eyes caught the name of the publishing house at the bottom: Red Hot House. Her heart skipped a beat. That was the publishing house where that woman worked. The one who had been writing to Joe. Clutching the book to her chest, she ran all the way back to Willow House, vowing to do some more research into this mystery.

Chapter Ten

By some miracle, the Internet was back up when Maeve returned, and seemed faster than it had that morning. Maeve picked up where she had left off – the Red Hot House website. She typed the name 'Fanny' into the search panel and, sure enough, a photo of a pretty woman with dark hair emerged alongside a short bio.

> *Fanny l'Amour is the bestselling author of ten novels in the romance genre. She lives in a remote part of the East Coast of America with her cat and her partner, practising yoga and walking, when she is not writing sizzling stories set in exotic locations.*

Hmmm, Maeve thought, *that doesn't give much away*. She peered at the photo and wondered what was hiding behind that pretty smile. The woman looked familiar, a little like Philomena when she was in her early thirties, except for the big bust and low cleavage. Phil would never have dressed like that. So was this woman someone who'd had an affair with an elderly lawyer? That seemed highly unlikely, as Fanny lived across the pond. But perhaps Fanny liked to travel – or had Joe taken a little holiday from time to time?

Maeve gave a guilty start as Phil stuck her head into the study.

'Hello. Lunch is ready. Salad and fruit in the kitchen. That okay?'

'Perfect.' Maeve turned off the laptop.

'The Internet is working again?'

Maeve got up. 'Yes. Faster than before, too.'

'Long may it last.'

Maeve laughed. 'Amen.'

Over a delicious seafood salad followed by freshly picked strawberries for dessert, Maeve and Phil chatted idly, filling each other in on their lives. Many years of catching up gave them lots to talk about.

When Maeve had told Phil about Lorcan's heart-breaking betrayal and her non-stop job in London, and Phil had commiserated, Maeve paused. Then she asked the question that had been burning in her mind since she found those emails: 'Phil, I was wondering… Did Uncle Joe ever go away on his own?'

Phil frowned. 'You mean travel, apart from visiting family around Ireland?'

'Yes.'

'Why do you ask?'

Maeve shrugged. 'Don't know. Just thought he might have been bored staying in one spot after all his travels.'

Phil sighed and nibbled on a strawberry. 'He was. But then he was writing those articles about the EU and its legal history, so he had to go off to Brussels for research and to meet up with old friends who were still working there. I think there is some kind of club for retired European lawyers there, near the EU headquarters.

He always came back refreshed. And—' Phil winked '—very, uh, attentive in the bedroom.'

Maeve squirmed. 'Oh. I see.'

'Don't look so shocked. Sex doesn't die after fifty, you know.' Phil smiled dreamily. 'We had a lovely sex life right up to the last month or so, when Joe started to feel under the weather. He was such an old romantic. Always giving me flowers and little gifts, especially when he was back from his trips. "Absence made my heart grow so much fonder," he used to say, handing me a little package or a box of divine chocolates. And then he'd tumble me into bed, no matter what time of day it was. I felt those trips away stimulated his mind and made him happy.'

I bet, Maeve thought.

'I cherish those memories,' Phil whispered, her eyes brimming.

Maeve put her hand on her aunt's arm. 'Of course you do. I'm so sorry. I didn't mean to make you sad with my questions.'

Phil put her hand over Maeve's. 'You didn't. I love talking about him and remembering him with so much love. It makes me feel he's still here.'

'He is,' Maeve declared. 'He'll never leave you.' She felt a stab of guilt as she uttered these words of comfort that might be a lie. If Joe had cheated on Phil, Maeve hoped his spirit was getting some kind trashing in the next life.

Phil sighed and got up, tidying away the dishes. 'I know.' She dabbed her eyes with her napkin. 'Enough of that. I was wondering if you've been able to find any of the stuff he was writing? He said he was working on his memoirs.'

'I'll have a look this afternoon. I only just got started, so it might take me a while to go through it all.'

'Of course. There seemed to be a lot of files there.'

'Lots to go through.' Maeve handed her plate to Phil. 'Thanks for lunch. I think I'll go to the beach for a bit when I've done a little more work on the laptop.'

'Good idea. Do you want coffee in the study?'

'Yes, please. I need to wake up.'

'I'll make a good strong cup, so.' Phil hesitated, looking at Maeve for a moment. 'If you find anything… strange… don't hold back. I want to know everything.'

'What do you mean?' Maeve asked, alarmed.

Phil waved her hand. 'Oh nothing really. It was just a thought. Joe always said we all have secret gardens, parts of ourselves we don't share with anyone. Hidden thoughts, things like that. I just wondered what was in his.'

'I see. Of course I'll share whatever I find with you,' Maeve promised, mentally crossing her fingers behind her back. She knew she would never be able to share anything ugly she found in Joe's 'secret garden'. She didn't want to break Phil's heart.

Those women, she thought, as she walked back to the study, *what did they know about Joe?* What memories did they have of him? She shook her head. And what about all that money? It didn't make sense at all.

Phil and Joe, she reflected, had been her template for romance when she was growing up. The way they had spoken to each other with respect but still teased each other; the way they would exchange a glance even across a noisy dinner table and laugh at a private joke; the way they had held hands when they'd walked on the beach; and the way Joe had looked at Phil as if she was the most beautiful, precious thing on earth. They'd had a special connection with a kind of banter only they understood. Joe could say something that appeared banal but which made Phil blush and smile as if she had a delicious secret. They had seemed the closest, most loving couple around. Phil had often said, when she looked at Joe from afar, that their love story was written in the stars. Maeve hadn't quite understood what Phil meant back then, but now she did. Joe and Phil had truly been one, and now Phil was only a very sad half. Surely it wasn't possible that Joe could have carried on with someone else behind her back?

Maeve checked her emails before getting stuck back into Joe's files and folders. Nothing from work, so all must be quiet on the Holland Street front. She hoped Rufus was on the case and able to steer Belinda away from her Indian yoga ideas. That should keep Ava quiet over the weekend at least.

One new message popped up. Not from Ava, but from Stephen Taylor. Why was he writing to her?

Dear Maeve,

Sorry to bother you during your holiday. I just thought you should know that my father's so-called fiancée has gone completely bonkers and is now turning the house into some kind of yoga retreat. She's planning to rip out walls and those lovely parquet floors and put in mahogany planks, as well as adding some kind of glasshouse at the back for tropical plants, etc, etc. And that's just the start. It's going to cost more than my father can afford, not to mention what it's doing to his blood pressure.

But nothing I say has any effect, so I felt I should ask you to stop this madness. I am sure you are experienced in advising clients so they don't ruin fine old houses, so I urge you to talk to Belinda and make her see that what she's doing is not a good idea. It's very distressing to watch her wrecking the house – and what it does to my father – without being able to do anything about it myself, as I'm sure you can understand. I hope you might be able to at least prevent the annihilation of the house. The marriage is another matter, of course. I just have to grin and bear it if it does go ahead. But as I see it, the house is your responsibility and I'm sure that with your artistic flair and feeling for style and design you will understand how distressing it is to see an old house being disfigured in this way. It is costing my father a lot of money and he has been forced to dig into some of his savings to pay for it all, which is very worrying on top of everything else. But I'm confident you could handle the matter in sympathetic way. I apologise if this comes across a little aggressive, nothing personal I can assure you! I enjoyed your company very much during our evening together and look forward to many more when you come back from your holiday. I hope you are enjoying the break over there in that beautiful part of Ireland.

With best wishes,
Stephen Taylor

Maeve sighed. How was she going to handle this? It was a tough nut to crack and Belinda was one of those women who would not listen to reason. Stephen was right, the house would be completely disfigured if Belinda had her way. She felt sorry for Stephen, who was obviously distressed but the last lines in the message made her smile. The more she thought of him the more she was looking forward to seeing him again. His message had made her feel more confident and she suddenly looked forward to getting back to London, tanned and rested after her holiday. But in the meantime, how should she reply? How could he expect her to do anything about it if Belinda had made up her mind, especially from this distance? Maeve gritted her teeth and quickly wrote a short reply.

Dear Stephen,

Thanks for your email. So nice to hear from you. I'm very sorry you are so upset about what's going on in your father's new house. I'm aware of the situation and my assistant, Rufus, is dealing with it in the best possible way. As you know, I'm away on holiday at the moment and Rufus is looking after everything in my absence. But if, in the end, Belinda should stick to her latest plans, there is nothing I or anyone else can do, I'm afraid. But try not to worry. I'm sure it will all turn out well in the end. With very best wishes,

Maeve McKenna

P.S I enjoyed our evening very much too. Hoping to see you when I get back.

There. That should placate him a bit, and show him she was interested in seeing him again. He was right: the house was in danger of losing all its period features and charm. But maybe he was more worried about all the money his dad was spending on the house, leaving very little to inherit ? That was his business, though, not hers. Maeve shrugged, pressed 'send', and picked up her phone to have quick word with Rufus before she went back to her detective work. She knew he wouldn't mind her calling him on a Saturday.

Rufus answered at once. 'Hello, Maeve. Are you having a lovely holiday?'

'Wonderful, thanks. Sorry to disturb you at the weekend, but I just wanted to call you about—'

'The delectable Belinda? Don't worry, lovely. I'm on the case and I think I'm making progress. Had to join her yoga group yesterday so I could speak to her, and we had this lovely chat in the Jacuzzi. Her boobs were a bit of a distraction, the way they were bobbing up and down, but I managed to pull myself together and get to the point.'

Maeve laughed. 'You're a scream, Rufus. So what did you say to her?'

'Well, I complimented her on all her work and—'

'What work? On the house?'

'No, I meant the work she's had done on her body. The fillers and the Botox. I said it was all a work of art and nobody would guess she was a day over twenty-five. She lapped it all up without question.' Rufus drew breath. 'It's going to be okay. I told her that Indian yoga thing is so yesterday, and if she pursued it she'd end up being the laugh of London. So now she wants everything to be classic and timeless, she says. I think she'll stick with that, so don't worry about a thing. The two of them are going off on some kind of mini-break next week so all will be quiet around here. You can deal with her when you get back. Just relax and have a good time and enjoy the rest of your holiday.'

'Rufus?'

'Yes?'

'You're a brick.'

'All part of the job, you know. Have a fab holiday.'

As he hung up, Maeve shook her head and laughed. Thank God for Rufus. She turned her attention back to the laptop. She soon forgot all about Stephen Taylor, absorbing herself in sifting through drafts of articles for various newspapers, a whole raft of lists and research material, tax documents, and a few attempts at memoirs that Joe never seemed to have got off the ground. Then there was a folder marked 'Stories for F'. *Aha!* Maeve opened the folder. A long list of files with various names came up. She clicked on one named 'Fanny's first', discovering about ten documents inside. She opened the top one, named 'draft 6'. The first page said 'The Siren of Paris' with the name 'Fanny l'Amour' beneath it.

Maeve sat back and stared at the name. Here it was: the proof of a connection between Fanny and Joe. But what did it mean? The document was full of red lines and comments. She leaned forward and looked at one of the notes in the margin. The author of the comments was not Joe, but Betsy. Maeve blinked, her mind whirling. What was this all about? She tried to make sense of it. *The facts*, she thought. *Let's get them in order…* She pulled a notepad from the top of a pile of books, found the stub of a pencil in the top drawer of the desk and made a list.

1. *Fanny is the author of romantic novels published by Red Hot House*
2. *Several drafts of each novel are on Joe's computer*
3. *The editing is done by an editor called Betsy (Malone?), and maybe also Joe*

4. *Money has been deposited in an account in Joe's name at regular intervals*
5. *Betsy Malone has been writing to Joe's secret email address, mentioning Fanny and what she has been up to*

Maeve stared at the list, trying to figure it all out. Could Joe have been working as an editor, rather than having some kind of secret affair with two women behind Phil's back? She chewed on the pencil and thought for a while. How could she find out more? By emailing this Betsy Malone, perhaps? She nodded to herself. Yes. If this was simply a business arrangement, this Malone woman would reply with a confirmation. Another option would be to email Fanny through her website and ask a few questions. Why not do both, while she was at it? Feeling satisfied with her decision, Maeve googled 'Fanny l'Amour' and soon found her rather garish website, the home page of which was adorned with pink roses and red hearts. She clicked on the contact form, filled in her own email address and quickly tapped in a short message.

Dear Fanny,

I have recently started reading your lovely books and find them really exciting and well written. Very impressed with the editing too! Is this the work of the in-house editor, or do you have someone else helping you? In that case he or she is excellent! I'm so happy I found your books. Thank you for writing them.

With best wishes,

Your new Irish fan, Maeve

She sent it off before she could change her mind, feeling only slightly guilty about lying. That done, she composed a message to Betsy Malone.

Dear Betsy,

I hope this message won't come as too much of a shock to you, or cause you too much sadness. It has recently come to my attention that you had some sort of association with my late uncle, Joe Duffy, who sadly passed away last year. I wonder if you could confirm for me what the nature of this association was? I see that you work for a publisher, and that Joe may have perhaps assisted you with the editing of some novels? Please rest assured that if your relationship with Joe went further than just a business venture, I will not share this information with my aunt, as it would upset her. Looking forward to your reply.

With kind regards,

Maeve McKenna

Maeve sent the message and turned off the laptop. She hoped her email to this Betsy woman was correct and not too accusatory. Stretching her stiff back, she felt it was time for a break. The sun shining through the open window and the salt-laden breeze made her yearn for the beach and a swim in the ocean. Her eyes felt dry and her neck sore, and she realised she'd been sitting at the computer screen for over an hour. There was a cup of coffee beside her. Phil must have put it there while she was so absorbed that she hadn't noticed. Maeve swigged the lukewarm liquid, grimacing at the taste. Pure rocket fuel, but she needed a jolt.

Brighter and feeling more awake, Maeve climbed the rickety stairs to her room to change into a swimsuit. At the top of the stairs she stopped, looking down the stairwell into the hall. From here, she could see how badly the hall floor had been damaged by rain that had seeped in through the cracked window frames. Every part of the house needed to be repaired, or the house would soon not be fit to live in.

She sighed and continued, nearly tripping over Esmeralda, who was sitting on the landing in her usual Egyptian cat pose, her tail circled around her paws. She hissed as Maeve righted herself and shot her a glance over her shoulder with her piercing blue eyes.

'I'm so sorry, your highness,' Maeve muttered as the cat walked away, her tail high, nose in the air. *What a stuck-up snob*, Maeve thought, as Phil's bedroom door opened and Esmeralda slunk inside.

Phil stuck her head out. 'Maeve? I'm having a little lie-down. Everything all right?'

'Absolutely fine,' Maeve replied. 'I'm taking a break and going for a swim.'

'Good idea. The tide is in so it should be nice. The water is still warm.' Phil yawned. 'See you at teatime.'

'Sleep tight,' Maeve said, hurrying to her room and quickly changing into her blue swimsuit. Throwing a denim shirt over her shoulders, she grabbed a towel from the bathroom. She looked around for a book, but changed her mind. She didn't need any distractions. The beach would provide plenty of entertainment. Pushing all concerns about Uncle Joe out of her mind for the moment, Maeve skipped down the stairs and out through the French windows of the living room. As she walked across the lawn, she was at once overwhelmed by the bright azure sky and the wind in her hair. Seagulls screeched above her as she took in the glorious views of the deep blue ocean, the stunning coastline and the craggy outlines of the Skellig Islands shimmering in the distance. The beach – their beach, a curve of white sand separated from the main beach by an outcrop of rough rocks – was only accessible from the house by steps cut into the rock, and a path that ran along the steep cliffs on the other side that most people avoided. She knew people rarely visited this beach even though it was supposed to be public, and she couldn't wait to be there.

Maeve felt a dart of pure joy as she made her way down the steps, holding on to the thick rope Uncle Joe had put there years ago for support. This was truly paradise. Why had she been gone so long?

Chapter Eleven

The swim in the cool, crystal-clear water was heavenly. Maeve had forgotten how magical it was. She could see fish below her and gave a start as a stingray glided gracefully across the sand near the bottom. Why had she forgotten her snorkel and flippers? She made a mental note to find some, so that she could enjoy the rich underwater world of this part of the Atlantic coast. Turning onto her back and floating, she looked up at the fluffy clouds, taking deep breaths, her body relaxing for the first time in weeks. This was the best remedy for stress. And wasn't she lucky to have all this available whenever she wanted? She couldn't believe she had stayed away so long. It was like a free spa treatment and gym all rolled into one. She felt a stab of fear as she thought of Phil's financial problems. It would be heart-breaking to have to give up this paradise.

Maeve turned and swam slowly back to shore. She waded onto the beach and looked at the house perched above her on the hill, its pink stucco façade glowing in the sunshine. The bay windows glinted, and the lawn looked greener than ever. She knew it was just the light and the distance, but from here it looked like the graceful, beautiful house it had once been. But up close, it was a different story. Willow House had to be restored. It was too lovely to be allowed to just fall down and be forgotten. Maeve promised herself that she would do everything in her power to keep this unique place in the family. To save it – even if she had to steal, beg and borrow. It would be more than a pity to let it go: it would be a crime.

But the sun warming her back and the pristine blue sky made her forget her these gloomy thoughts. Sighing happily, she spread her towel on the soft white sand and lay down, closing her eyes to the sun, telling herself to only stay a few minutes as she hadn't put on sunblock. She put sunblock on her mental list, along with the flippers and snorkel, and gave herself up to the heat of the sun on her skin, the salty smell of the air and sound of the waves lapping on the beach.

Only minutes later, she sensed someone standing beside her, casting a shadow on her face. She looked up, momentarily blinded, and squinted at the figure. 'Phil?'

'No. Me, Paschal,' he said, and squatted in the sand beside her.

She sat up. 'Oh. How did you get here?'

His teeth gleamed in his tanned face. 'You mean what the feck am I doing on your private beach?'

'No, uh…' Maeve pushed her tangled hair back. 'I was surprised to see anyone here. Most people don't even know about this beach.'

'Except the locals.' He pointed at the cliffs. 'You know the cottage up there?'

She looked up at the thatched roof sticking up behind a hillock. 'Yes. I thought it would be falling down by now.'

'I'm doing it up. My uncle owned it and used it as a fishing hut, keeping nets and lobster pots and stuff like that there. And we lived there during the summer holidays. He used to anchor his little fishing boat in the bay here.'

Maeve nodded. 'Oh yes, I remember. There is a tiny pier and slip just below it. We used to dive from there at high tide when we were kids. A whole gang of us. Where you there then?'

He laughed. 'Yeah. I was the skinny little kid who used to be pushed in all the time. But then I got my own back when I grew to over six feet by the time I was fifteen.'

She ran her gaze over his tanned chest and broad shoulders. 'You're not so skinny now.'

'I work out.'

'You go to a gym?'

He shook his head and laughed. 'Nah, there's no such thing in this village. I swim a lot and then I repair the beach hut and lift rocks out of what I hope will be a garden one day. I help your aunt out with hers, too. Then I row the currach with some of the other lads to train for the regatta later this autumn. Nothing like real work to keep you fit.'

'The currach?' Maeve asked. 'I didn't know they were still in use.'

'Not for fishing, of course. Now we use them for rowing in races.'

'I used to love seeing them out there in the bay when I was young. They looked so graceful, especially when they were rowed by a good team. But I'm sure the modern ones aren't made with animal hides any more.'

'No. Now they're made with tarred canvas. But they still look roughly the same.' He got up. 'I must go for my swim while the tide is in. See you around, Maureen, *mo stór*.'

'Bye for now, Tom,' she said, laughing.

He made a mock military salute and walked away across the sand, his skin bronze against the bleached green cotton of his swimming trunks. Maeve watched him throw himself into the water and swim away, his superb crawl barely making a splash in the blue water as his arms and legs moved in perfect sync. She laughed at herself, mesmerised by this outdoorsy type, so close to nature and so sure of his own destiny, happy in his own skin. *It must be nice*, she thought, *to live out your life in the place you were born and know that this is enough to make you happy.*

She looked up at the old cottage again. She could see now that the thatch had recently been renewed, and the shutters were newly painted. A quaint little place. Was this his permanent home, she wondered, or just a base for the summer? She looked at him swimming far out into the bay, and laughed at him calling her Maureen. Then she wondered what he had meant by those words in Irish. *Mo stór*, he had said. What did that mean in English? She racked her brain, trying to remember the little bit of Irish that was left from her schooldays. Then it came to her. It meant 'my darling'.

Cheeky thing, she thought, getting up and brushing the sand off her. But the words and the way he had looked at her stayed in her mind while she slowly headed back to the house.

After a cool shower, Maeve slowly got dressed and dried her hair, feeling refreshed. Her shoulders tingled and her nose glowed pink, slightly burnt by the sun. She dabbed on a cooling face cream and went back downstairs to join Phil on the little patio outside the kitchen, shaded from the later afternoon sun. It was unusually hot for September.

Phil, looking rested, was already at the small wooden table with Esmeralda curled up at her feet, the cat's eyes opening and then closing as Maeve arrived, as if she couldn't be bothered to stir for such a lowly person. Just to annoy her, Maeve stroked her head, making Esmeralda press closer to Phil.

'She hasn't accepted me yet.'

'She will,' Phil assured her. 'She's just playing hard to get.' She lifted the teapot. 'Tea? I know it's quite warm this afternoon, but I love a cup of tea even on a hot day.'

'Me too.' Maeve eyed the bread basket. 'Buns; how yummy.'

'Cinnamon. From the bakery. I was too lazy to bake. And in any case, why would one when there is Murphy's bakery practically next door? Did you have a nice swim?'

'Wonderful.' Maeve bit into the warm bun, its rich cinnamon flavour filling her mouth. 'What a beautiful day this is.'

'Back-to-school weather, we call it. We often get warm sunshine at the beginning of September, before the autumn storms arrive. Anyone on the beach?'

'I met Paschal. God, can he swim!'

'He's part fish, that boy.'

'A real natural. Like a kind of Robinson Crusoe, the way he lives in that little cottage.'

Phil snorted. 'In the summer, yes. In the winter he puts on a suit and tie and lectures in Marine Biology at Cork University. He's a full professor, you know.'

'Really?' Maeve stared at Phil, trying to imagine Paschal all suited and booted, but failing. 'You're joking.'

'No, I swear. He's very smart behind that wild image. And he's not quite a boy any more, at his age. I think he's just turned forty.'

'Ancient.'

Phil smiled. 'Young to me, of course. But at forty you'd expect a man to be settled with a wife and a few children.' Her face took on a sober look. 'Well, that could have happened if it weren't for—' She stopped and picked up her cup.

'If it weren't for…?'

'Not for me to talk about it. Something terrible happened to him a few years ago. I'll let him tell you when you know each other better.'

'Maybe that's best,' Maeve agreed, even though she was dying to know. It had to be something sad. Maybe some woman broke his heart? Maeve took another bite of her cinnamon bun and sipped her tea. 'So, are we going to the Harbour pub for dinner tonight?' she asked, changing the subject. She didn't want Phil to think she was interested in Paschal. Or guess how he made her feel.

Phil brightened. 'I'd love to. You'll enjoy it. Lots of singing and dancing. Most of the locals here are very talented. We had TG4, the Irish television channel, here in July recording some of it for their "Music Around Ireland" series. It'll be broadcast in November, they said.'

'Then we have to go. I love Irish music, even if most of it makes me cry. Especially those laments on the tin whistle. Must be because I'm homesick.'

Phil sighed and put down her cup. 'Ah, yes. I know. I was homesick most of the time when we were abroad. Not desperately, but it was always there, a little sadness deep inside.'

'Exactly.'

'So,' Phil said, after a moment's silence. 'How are you getting on with Joe's laptop? Find anything yet?'

Maeve squirmed. 'A few bits and pieces,' she replied. 'I have some ideas, but I need more proof.'

Phil frowned. 'Proof? Of what?'

'Of where that money came from. Could you get me a bank statement for the account?'

'I could ask the bank to send me one. Why?'

'I need to know when the money was lodged. Was it always the same sum?'

'No. It varied. Sometimes it was several thousand, sometimes just a few hundred. There's still money going in, but very little.'

'I see.' Maeve thought for a moment. Should she tell Phil that Joe had been connected to a romance author and her editor in some way? No. Not yet. She had to discover the nature of that connection first, and get an answer from Betsy and, of course, Fanny.

'What do you think it was? That money from America?' Phil asked, sounding worried. 'Something illegal?'

'God, no. Not at all. I'm sure it was all very correct. You know how Uncle Joe was always so honest and truthful.'

Phil laughed. 'Gosh, yes. I always thought that was such a yawn. I was the direct opposite, lying through my teeth if I could get away with it. And most of the time I did.'

'Lying about what, exactly?'

Phil made an airy gesture. 'Well you know… Stuff. White lies, just to be polite. Looking interested when I wanted to scream with boredom. I built up a well-painted façade that didn't show the cracks underneath.'

'You're the epitome of the brazen hussy.'

'I take that as a compliment.'

'It is. But back to this bank account. When did he open it?'

'The bank said it was ten years ago. It would have been just after he retired. He was very sad then. Bored. Missing his job, his status. He said nobody wanted him. He hated growing old.'

'What about you? Do you miss the glamour and the travelling?'

Phil shrugged. 'Some of it, yes. I used to love entertaining, organising dinners and inviting people over. I took great pride in laying a beautiful table with the best Irish linen and crystal during the glory days, when Joe was doing so well. And I was bloody good at it, too. But it had got a little tired by the time I turned sixty. I thought I was too old to swan around in ball gowns and kiss people I'd rather slap. All that smiling and "so nice to see you" was getting on my nerves. I stopped paying attention, drank a little too much and mixed people up at dinner parties. I once mixed up a German with a Frenchman and put my foot in it. Long faces all around, especially Joe's. We had a big row after that. I tried to pull myself together, but the fun had gone out of it. Then we went to Brussels, where he spent most days and some of the nights locked in meetings and negotiations, leaving me all alone in a big house in the suburbs. When he had to retire at sixty-five, we came home. I'd never been happier.'

'But he wasn't?'

'Not at first. But about six months into his retirement he cheered up, and got stuck into the garden here. We made friends with the locals. He contacted his old friends in the EU and started writing documents and reports. He spent hours in the study with the radio on, writing away. And his little trips to Brussels and Paris to meet up with his former colleagues cheered him up.'

Maeve nodded. 'Yes. So you told me. And that was around the same time he opened this secret account?'

Phil thought for a moment. 'Yes. Around that time. I thought perhaps it was something to do with a political column he was writing for the *Irish Times*. But the lodgements are from the US, as I told you, so…'

'What makes you think they were from America?'

'It's from Western Union. That's American, isn't it?'

'I think so.' Maeve nibbled absentmindedly on her bun. 'Anyway, the bank will be closed by now. Why don't we leave this until after the weekend?' She suddenly felt this was the right thing to do. She needed a break and time to think. She'd pick it up again on Monday. And there would probably not be a reply from either of the women she had emailed during the weekend in any case.

Phil brightened. 'Yes, let's leave it all alone for now. We'll put on our glad rags and go to the pub.' She picked up Esmeralda and got to her feet. 'It's nearly six o'clock. I'll go and get myself dolled up. Then we'll walk to the pub, have something nice from their menu and listen to the music. Everyone will be there and they're all dying to meet you. Paschal will be playing the tin whistle with the band. Wear something pretty.' Phil gathered the tea things on a tray and went into the kitchen, Esmeralda tucked under her arm.

Maeve remained on the patio for a while, musing over what Phil had said, trying to fit the pieces of the jigsaw together. Joe had been over to Brussels and Paris at regular intervals. But… had it really been to meet up with former colleagues? And what on earth were those payments all about? The answer must be there, somewhere among the many files and folders. She sighed and got up. Enough about that. It was time to have a little fun.

She went into the house, looking forward to the laughter and music. And, if she was being honest, to seeing Paschal again.

Chapter Twelve

The pub was situated at the edge of the little harbour, where small fishing boats were anchored with their colourful hulls glowing in the golden light of the setting sun. The water of the bay was as smooth as a mirror, reflecting the pink clouds in the darkening sky. Maeve stopped and looked at the view, breathing in the sweet air, and the smell of grilled steaks and Irish stew from the pub. 'This is a heavenly spot.'

'Gorgeous,' Phil agreed, looking quite gorgeous herself, Maeve reflected as she looked at her aunt. She was dressed in an unusual combination of a paisley print Emilio Pucci silk shirt in dark green and blue, teamed with a khaki flared linen skirt she said she had picked up for five euros in a sale. She wore her usual scuffed Chanel ballet flats and sported an old handbag that had belonged to her mother. 'Waste not, want not,' she'd said gaily as they'd set off from the house, having approved of Maeve's outfit with a nod and a smile. 'Love the denim shirt. Goes well with those white trousers. Perfect for an evening at the pub.'

'That's a relief,' Maeve had said, laughing. 'One wouldn't want to let the side down here in the back of beyond.'

'Not as backward as you think,' Phil had remarked, which Maeve saw was very true as they now entered the pub. The cramped space was packed with mostly locals and visitors from Cork, all dressed in trendy casual clothes of one kind or another. The bar at the front was crowded, with double lines of guests ordering drinks. To the side was a small desk, where a waitress was trying to organise tables for dinner at the restaurant on the other side of the pub. It seemed you had the choice of sitting inside at the large window, or outside at long tables that were filling up fast. Maeve feared they would end up having to eat standing up, but she hadn't reckoned with Phil's talent for getting attention, even in this packed space.

'Nuala, darling,' Phil called, in her deceptively sweet, sing-song voice that momentarily silenced the pub as everyone turned to look at the tall, elegant woman. 'A table for two, when you have the time.'

Nuala, a large woman with short brown hair who Maeve vaguely recognised, looked up from her list. 'Philomena, nice to see you. Yes…' She consulted her list, then looked into the restaurant. 'There's a free table by the window. Is that all right? Or you can sit outside if you want. We'll turn on the heaters out there later.'

'The one by the window will be perfect,' Philomena replied.

Nuala nodded. 'Seán Óg!' she yelled into the back of the pub. 'Show Philomena and her—' She peered at Maeve. 'Good lord, if isn't Maeve! Hi! Remember me? Big fat Nuala from Cahersiveen. We used to be friends when we were teenagers. I was twice the size then,' she said, sticking out her chest. 'And now I'm thinner, older and married to Seán Óg, who inherited this pub after his dad died.'

'Of course I remember you,' Maeve said and shook Nuala's hand. 'You look great!'

Nuala squeezed Maeve's hand in an iron grip. 'Not as great as you. Holy Mary, look at you. Like a film star. I hear you live in London now. Must be fantastic.'

'It's grand. A bit stressful. So glad to be back.'

'But you're only here on holiday, like?' Nuala said. 'I mean, who'd choose to live here permanently if they didn't have to?' She looked wistfully at Maeve. 'Wouldn't I love to go to London, even for a short break? But all we've ever managed was a weekend at the Galway races. Nice, but there wasn't the same buzz.'

'Hey, Nuala,' a woman complained behind them. 'How about getting us sorted? You're holding up the whole queue with yer yakking.'

'I am talking to a friend. From *London*,' Nula said, looking important.

'Big deal,' the woman said. 'Get us a fecking table, will ya? We're starving.'

'We can chat later,' Maeve whispered to Nuala, and followed Seán Óg, who had just appeared to usher them to their table. *Another childhood pal,* Maeve thought as she looked at Seán Óg's broad back. He turned around as they reached the table and beamed a smile at her. 'Hiya, Maeve. Welcome back. Long time since we swung our hairy legs at the teenage disco, eh?'

'Sure is,' she said with a laugh. 'You have really grown since then.'

Seán Óg, a handsome man with bright red hair, laughed and flexed his biceps. 'Didn't I just? Played rugby for my school and then worked out like mad. Now I just row the currach here and do a bit of running. And three kids, a wife, the pub and all of that keeps me out of trouble.'

'I bet.' Maeve was amused that this big man still had 'Óg' attached to his name, a term in Gaelic meaning 'little', used for small children. The name had obviously stuck.

'Thank you, Seán Óg,' Phil said as he pulled out her chair for her. 'Could we see the menu, please?'

'I thought you might know it by heart by now,' he replied. 'It's the same as always, except for tonight's special, which is hake in a white wine sauce.' He winked at Maeve. 'I did a stint at Ballymaloe, you know.'

'The five-star cookery school?' Maeve asked. 'Wow.'

'That's why he's such a great chef,' Phil said. 'I'll have the special, please.'

'Me too,' Maeve cut in. 'And some white wine. Pinot Grigio, if you have it. '

'We do, indeed. And for the lovely Philomena?'

'A pint of Guinness for me,' Phil announced. She laughed at Maeve's surprised expression. 'I was never into wine like your uncle. I had to pretend I was, and ooh and ah about vintages and stuff. But that was an act. I love a pint now and then, so shoot me.'

'Nothing like a pint of the black stuff,' Seán Óg agreed. 'Pinot Grigio for Maeve and a Guinness for Philomena. Coming right up. And I'll get you some crab claws on the house for a starter. Just because we're so happy to see you.'

The crab claws were delicious. Maeve closed her eyes as she chewed the succulent flesh, sucking on every little claw and piece of shell. 'Messy but heavenly,' she declared, rubbing her fingers with the wet wipe that had been provided along with the napkin.

'Nothing like them,' Phil agreed, dabbing her mouth.

The hake was just as good, served with new potatoes, sugar snap peas and a salad on the side. Home-made ice cream with chocolate sauce rounded off the meal perfectly.

Maeve looked out at the terrace, where the long tables were crammed with guests digging into their steaks or seafood with gusto, chatting and laughing or just admiring the stunning view. 'This restaurant is a true gem,' she declared. 'It should be in the Michelin guide.'

Phil shook her head. 'No, it shouldn't. Then we'd be even more overrun by tourists and poor Seán Óg and Nuala would have to hire more staff and they'd have to work even harder themselves besides.' She leaned forward and stared at Maeve. 'Why can't things stay the same? Why not enjoy things as they are, without wishing for more? Look around you. Everyone is having a good time. And now we'll have music and dancing. Isn't that enough?'

Maeve nodded. 'You're so right. Isn't it stupid, the way we always want more and more and are never happy with what we have? That's an important lesson. I wish I was more like you, just being thankful for what I have.'

Phil sat back and put her napkin on the table. 'Comes with age, I suppose. When you're young, you're always striving and working toward goals that seem important. I feel happier now at my age than I ever did before – except for missing Joe, of course. My only goal is to keep my house from falling down, so I don't have to sell it.'

'I know. It's in a bad state, I'm afraid.'

'So it is.' There was fire in Phil's eyes as she met Maeve's gaze. 'But it has to stay in the family and I'll do whatever it takes to keep it. I will find a way to pay for the upkeep somehow. Maybe turn it into a B&B, like I said.'

'But then you'd need to redo the bedrooms and have en-suite bathrooms,' Maeve remarked. 'And that costs money, too.'

'Your dad has said he and your mam'll help out a bit if I need it. If your mam agrees.' Phil sighed. 'But you know me and your mam. Never got on. She was the successful one. I was the dosser who became a housewife instead of having a career. But in those days, that's what women did. Your mother was the exception.'

'Is this where I'm supposed to say she was Superwoman?'

Phil laughed. 'No, this is where you're supposed to say life's not about achievements, but about love.'

'But it is.' Maeve paused. 'Maybe I'm growing old, too. But I'm beginning to think life is about a different kind of achievement. Like falling in love, staying married until death do you part; like coping with a rootless, globetrotting life. Like speaking half a dozen languages and always smiling and being cheerful; like giving elegant dinner parties in foreign countries; and like being there in the background for your husband, who would never have had the career he had without you.'

Phil kissed Maeve on the cheek. 'Thank you, darling. Nobody's ever said anything like that to me before.'

'But it's true. You're a superstar, Phil.'

'So's your mother. In a different way. And she loves you, too.'

'I know.'

'I'm very grateful to her. It made up for not being a mother myself. Between all of us, we were a family.'

Maeve put her hand on Phil's arm. 'A fantastic family. It was like having four parents instead of two.'

They were interrupted by shouts and cheering from the pub area. Maeve could hear string instruments being tuned and a sound system being tested. She glanced into the pub and saw that the floor had been cleared for dancing. 'I think the music session is starting,' she said.

Phil jumped up. 'Oh, great. Let's go and sit in the pub. I thought we'd watch the show from here but we'll see better inside. I hope Paschal's arrived. He's a wonderful singer.'

Maeve scanned the pub for a place to sit. She spotted Paschal on a high stool at the bar counter, a pint of Guinness in his hand. He was laughing at something Seán Óg had said. He was wearing a faded checked shirt and jeans, his dark curls damp, looking as if he had only just got out of the shower. As he stopped laughing, he looked around and caught sight of Maeve, shooting her a slow smile that made her heart beat faster. She smiled back. He got off the stool and walked across the room, his pint in his hand.

'Hi,' he said. 'Nice to see you again. Hope you'll like the music tonight.'

'I'm sure I'll love it,' Maeve replied.

'Hello, Paschal,' Phil said, beside them. 'We were looking for a place to sit.'

'There are two chairs over there at the round table,' he said, after a quick search around the room. 'The Murphys won't mind if you join them. They're a noisy bunch but I'll tell 'em to shut their gobs. The music is about to start, anyway.'

They followed his advice and joined the happy group at the round table near the open window. 'This way, you'll have some fresh air,' Paschal remarked. 'I'll get you a drink. What'll you have? Another pint, Philomena?'

'God, no,' Phil protested. 'I'll be on my ear if I drink any more. An orange juice, please. But Maeve should have at least a glass of Guinness. She hasn't had any yet.'

'I'll send one of the lads over with the drinks. See you later, girls.' With that, Paschal walked away to join the musicians, picking up a tin whistle from one of the band members.

'Ooh, he's going to play,' Phil said with a happy sigh. 'He has a great musical talent, you know.'

'Really? But as far as I remember, so do most people in this village.'

'They do. I think it's because of the music teacher in the all-Gaelic school in the old days. She started a tradition that is still so alive today.'

'I think I remember her. Wasn't she the one who was so strict?'

Phil laughed. 'Yes. Good old Mrs Madigan. I'm sure some of her more famous students are happy she whipped them into shape in Irish dancing classes. That drill got some of them into *Riverdance*. She died two years ago and they came back and performed at her wake. Mrs Madigan would have loved it. Best funeral in years, they say.'

'What a nice send-off,' Maeve said. 'And so typical for here.' It was true, she thought. There was an acceptance of death in this part of Ireland that made it easier to bear. Still sad and tragic, but a natural part of life. The person's life was celebrated rather than wept over, and friends rallied around and helped out in any small way they could.

Their drinks arrived and the band started to play a lovely slow ballad, with Paschal on the tin whistle. Maeve sipped her Guinness, a drink she hadn't tasted for years. The bittersweet flavour and the traditional music brought her back to her teenage years, when a pint of Guinness had been drunk from cans bought in the shop as a dare while they listened to Irish tunes coming from pubs along the main street of the village. What had felt so daring seemed innocent now. In her mind, those carefree days seemed suddenly so vivid. She tapped her foot when the music transformed into a lively jig, and smiled back at Paschal as he looked across the room at her. He put away his tin whistle and walked across the floor until he was at their side again, holding out his hand. 'How about a dance, my lovely?'

Chapter Thirteen

Maeve was about to protest that she hadn't danced a jig in years, when she realised he wasn't talking to her.

Phil jumped up from her chair and took Paschal's hand. 'I'd love to, darlin'.' As if joined by the hip, they glided through the throng and stopped in the middle of the floor.

Awestruck, Maeve watched as they started to dance, their feet tapping the floorboards in time with the music. Phil moved and jumped with the others on the dancefloor, who had to be more than half her age. Her skirt twirled, her hair bounced around her pink cheeks and her eyes glowed as she danced, as light-footed as anyone around her. The music ended and the dancers stopped abruptly, all breathing hard. The applause rang out and Phil laughed and took Paschal's proffered arm, letting him lead her back to her chair, where she sank down, dabbing her hot face with a napkin.

'Whoa, that was hard work.'

'You've still got it,' Paschal said, laughing. 'You certainly showed everyone you're still a contender. Let's do another one.'

'Aw, gee, no,' Phil protested. 'Nice of you, but that was enough for tonight. For the whole week, actually. I'll be feeling the pain tomorrow. But it was worth it for the fun.'

Paschal wiped his forehead with the back of his hand. 'I enjoyed it too. It's not often you get to dance with someone so in tune with the music.' He glanced at Maeve. 'You might like to do a twirl.'

Maeve took a swig of her Guinness. 'I'm not much of a dancer.'

'But it's easy,' Phil cut in. 'You just listen to the beat and it becomes part of you. You know the steps. I taught you myself.'

'Yeah, when I was seven,' Maeve said, laughing.

'It'll come back to you,' Phil argued. 'Just like riding a bike.'

'I'll probably fall off and break something,' Maeve replied, feeling like a big chicken. But she didn't want to make a fool of herself in front of everyone. 'Maybe another time. I think I'll just watch and listen tonight.'

Paschal shrugged. 'Fine with me. I'll ask Nuala. She loves doing the auld twirl now and then.'

Before Maeve had a chance to say anything, Paschal had marched off and pulled Nuala from behind the bar, blushing and laughing. Maeve looked at them as they started to dance, with Nuala light on her feet, dancing as if she were born to it, smiling at Paschal, her face pink and her eyes sparkling.

'He's such a lovely lad,' Phil remarked, still fanning herself. 'But now I feel like wandering home and getting into my bed.'

'Me too,' Maeve said, suddenly tired of the music, the charged atmosphere she felt whenever Paschal was around and the noise and heat of the pub. 'It's not late but I'm sleepy and hot. It's been quite a busy day. What with the work on Joe's laptop, meeting your old ladies and swimming, I packed so much into my first day here. A walk in the cool air and then bed will be good.'

Getting up, they waved to Nuala and Paschal and went outside, where the ocean lay silent and calm. The night sky stretched endlessly above them, the stars glinting, looking close enough to touch.

Maeve took a deep breath and stuck her arm through Phil's. 'Oh, how I love the nights here. The sky is like a velvet canopy that someone sewed diamonds all over.' She pointed up. 'Look at that star glimmering and glinting. Maybe it's a spaceship?'

'Or someone we loved, trying to say hello,' Phil suggested, sighing wistfully.

'What a lovely thought.'

They walked down the village street where the cottages were quiet, the odd light in a window here and there. A small dog sniffed at them, then trotted across the street and into a front garden, barking at a door that opened and let him into a warmly lit interior. The door closed again and then all was silent and still, the only noise their footsteps on the pavement.

'How do you feel about Paschal?' Phil asked, as they turned into the lane that led to Sandy Cove.

'How do you mean?' Maeve said, grateful that the darkness hid her blushing face. 'I only met him today.'

'You seem a little tense around him. And he…' She paused. 'I think he's attracted to you.'

'If he is, I'm the last one to know about it. He didn't pay me much attention tonight.'

'Oh, he wouldn't make it obvious in front of everyone. The whole village would be gossiping about it in ten minutes. But oh, I wish he could find someone like you.'

Maeve sighed and pulled her arm away. 'Please, Phil, don't try to matchmake. All I want is to have a holiday and to help you solve the mystery of Uncle Joe's money. I'd like to find out what it was. He might be owed more than what was in that account.'

'Oh,' Phil exclaimed. 'I never thought of that.' She squeezed Maeve's arm. 'Please do your very best to find out.'

'I will, darling auntie,' Maeve said, and hugged her aunt. She thought she could see a tear glinting on Phil's cheek and it broke her heart. Phil didn't need this worry on top of her grief and loneliness. Something had to be done to help her.

Later, as she opened the window in her room, Maeve prayed to the dark heavens and all the glimmering stars that something – anything – would happen to make Phil happy again. Nothing was more important to her at that moment.

A star winked at her in the nearly purple sky at the same moment as her phone pinged. Who could that be at this late hour? Looking at her phone, she discovered a text message that said: *Hey Maureen, I'd like to know you better but without an audience. Come down to the cove tomorrow at ten and we'll have a swim. Your friend Tom C.*

Paschal. How had he got her number? Probably from Phil. Maeve smiled as she switched off her phone. Should she feel miffed that he didn't want anyone to know about their budding friendship – if that was what it was…? But at the same time, she understood completely where he was coming from. This village was a tight-knit community, and if she so much as sneezed right now, here in the privacy of her bedroom, everyone would ask if her cold was better the next day.

That was just the way it was. In any case, she didn't want anyone, not even Phil, to know how drawn she felt to Paschal already, even though they had only just met.

Funny, how life threw things at you when you least expected it. Here she was, having had no luck or even interest in men while she pursued her career, and now she was developing a crush on this man from the west who she had only just met, and getting emails from a dishy man in London.

Suddenly exhausted, she climbed into bed and pulled the duvet over her, looking forward to her swimming 'date' the next day. She'd take a break before she had to resume the search for Uncle Joe's dirty secret on Monday. She stared into the darkness with an eerie feeling that something would be revealed that would change Phil's life. And maybe even her own.

It was only six o'clock when Maeve peered at the clock on her bedside table the next morning. The pale sunshine poking through a slit in the curtain and the sound of birdsong made her feel instantly awake. She had slept like a baby all night and now felt ready to get up and tackle whatever the day would bring. Pulling back the curtains, she opened the window, peering into the garden, where a shower of rain had left drops on the leaves of the trees and shrubs. The air smelled of wet grass and earth, mingled with the scent of late summer roses. It was hard to believe it was late September. She listened to the waves crashing onto the rocks beside the beach and wondered if Paschal was also up and enjoying this special time of day. Maybe he was wandering across the wet lawn in his pyjamas with a cup of steaming coffee, looking out at the view of the Skelligs from his cottage. Or maybe he slept naked? With a tiny shiver, she pushed the thought away and threw on her dressing gown. Tea, toast and the laptop were at the top of her agenda, not naked men walking in the sunshine, she told herself sternly.

After letting a sour-looking Esmeralda out into the garden, Maeve padded into the study with a mug of tea to look for clues to Uncle Joe's secret life, or at least glance at it before she got cracking on Monday.

As the laptop booted up, she sipped her tea and looked around the study, still feeling Uncle Joe's presence. Despite the fact that the study was now more run-down and damaged by damp, she could still imagine him sitting in the chair at the mahogany desk, a glass of wine at his elbow and one of the long, thin cigars he used to smoke perched on the edge of the cut-glass ashtray. The worn Donegal carpet was soft under Maeve's bare feet and the cracked leather of the chair cool and smooth on her back. The leather-bound books in the bookcase beside the fireplace and the table with knick-knacks by the window added to the timeless elegance of the room. She had spent so many happy hours here, sitting on a little stool by the fire, listening to Uncle's Joe's deep voice as he read them stories from long ago. Entranced, she and Roisin had listened, even when they had grown old enough to read themselves. Uncle Joe had made the stories come alive in a way that had been too enchanting to miss.

Maeve turned her attention to the laptop. First, she must check if either Betsy or this Fanny woman had replied to her emails. She saw a flag on the inbox of Joe's account, and, her heart beating, she held her breath while she opened it. Two messages. One was an 'out of office' reply for Betsy's address. She was on vacation and would be back two weeks later. The other one was from Fanny – but it was not what Maeve had expected. It was not a reply, but Maeve's own email, coming back to Joe's address with the subject: *New message from Fanny l'Amour's contact page.*

Maeve stared at it. But… But… What was going on? Why was her message to Fanny's website coming back to… Joe? Then the answer dawned on her. Fanny's contact address was automatically directed to this email account. Fanny l'Amour couldn't tell her anything about Uncle Joe. Because Uncle Joe *was* Fanny l'Amour. Or had been.

Chapter Fourteen

Oh my God. Maeve looked at the screen. The solution had been staring at her all this time. Her mind reeled. Could it be true? Uncle Joe, writing saucy romances under a pen name? Unbelievable. The Betsy woman had to be his editor, then, rather than his clandestine lover. Well, that was a relief. So…

Forgetting her decision to leave it all until Monday, Maeve went to the Amazon book page and typed in the name 'Fanny l'Amour'. At once, a whole row of colourful book covers appeared, all with swooning women pressing their nearly bare breasts onto the swelling six-packs of lightly clad, handsome men. Maeve looked at a series about what appeared to be the romantic adventures of a woman called Audrey Swann. She checked the rankings and noticed that some of the books were sitting quite high in the bestseller chart. The publication date of the last book was a little over a year earlier. Then – of course – nothing. The reviews were mostly glowing, apart from a few nasty one-stars. Most of them mentioned the amazing writing, the sensuality and humour.

Intrigued, Maeve clicked on the 'look inside' feature of one of the books and started reading. The first few paragraphs were so vivid and enchanting, she was instantly pulled into the story. It was all about the character Audrey Swann coming to Paris in the 1960s to work at a bank. Beautiful, innocent, and clueless about the sophisticated Parisian way of life, she was soon in the claws of a sexy Lothario called Yves, who had seduced her by page six. Then he left her on page eight, leaving poor Audrey heartbroken and determined to hate men forever.

Maeve laughed as she read on, enjoying the slightly tongue-in-cheek undertones in the excellent prose, nevertheless feeling sorry for poor Audrey and cheering her on until she reached the end of the sample, hoping Audrey would find true love with someone more worthy as the story unfolded. She was still reeling with the shock of her discovery as she turned off the laptop and sat there, staring at the blank screen. What should she do next? Should she tell Phil? How would she react? This would shock her to the core. Maeve would have to think carefully before she broke the story to her aunt.

Still trying to solve the problem of what to do about telling Phil, Maeve got up and left the study to get ready for her swimming date with Paschal. She checked her watch. Half past seven. Phil wasn't up yet, and Esmeralda was hovering around, meowing and whipping her tail angrily… Maeve decided to bring Phil a cup of tea in bed before she went out, and see if she was in a fit state to learn some startling news.

Minutes later, Maeve knocked on Phil's door, carrying a tray with a cup of tea and a slice of buttered toast. No reply. Maeve slid the door open and stuck her head into the dim room. 'Phil? Are you awake?'

'Yes,' Phil replied, her voice hoarse. 'Come in.'

Maeve walked in and found Phil not in bed, but sitting in an armchair by the window, wrapped in a cashmere shawl, her hair tangled and her face white. She turned and looked at Maeve with a haunted expression. 'Didn't get much sleep,' she said hoarsely. 'It started to rain, so I had to put out the buckets on the far side of the landing and in the spare bedroom for all the leaks. Then, when I did sleep, I had bad dreams. Woke up to awful thoughts.'

Maeve put the tray on the bedside table and flew to Phil's side. 'Darling Phil, what thoughts? Feeling sad?' She pulled back the faded curtain and handed Phil the cup. 'Here. Tea. Drink it while it's hot.'

Phil took the cup with hands that shook slightly. 'Sad? Oh, yes. The whole black dog thing. It hits me sometimes.' She drank the tea in deep gulps. 'Lovely. Thank you so much.'

'You're welcome.' Maeve pulled up one of the spindly little chairs beside the chest of drawers and sat down beside Phil. 'Do you want to talk about it?'

Phil sighed. 'I don't know. What's the use of talking and making you sad, too?'

'I don't mind. Just seeing you like this breaks my heart. If you tell me, it might help us both.'

'You're a sweetheart.' Phil sipped her tea and patted Maeve's hand. 'I'm so glad you're here. It means a lot.'

'Happy to be here,' Maeve said, feeling suddenly guilty about her long absence. 'Is it about Uncle Joe?'

'Yes. And no. Lots of things. Growing old all alone. Missing the glory days and all the glamour. And yes, of course, Joe. I still can't believe he's gone and that I'll never see him again, or hear his voice, or see his muddy footprints on the carpet that I used to give out about. I'm missing being young with him and all the adventures we had. And how proud he was of me, and how we were a team and...' Phil stopped and let out a loud sob. 'Sorry.'

Maeve took the teacup from Phil's shaking hand. 'No need to be sorry. Of course you must be desperately sad and lonely. But...' She stopped. 'I thought you said yesterday that you had become fed up with the high life and the entertaining...?'

Phil shrugged. 'Yes. But I loved the excitement, even though I started to hate it as I grew older, I was relieved when it ended. I just miss having people around me, that's all. And I miss— him. But...' Phil turned her pale, tear-stained face to Maeve. 'I had some terrible thoughts during the night. That money... What if Joe was blackmailing someone? Maybe he knew something and tried to make money out of it? We were a little strapped for cash as we were putting money aside for our old age in case of illness, but then he told me he had made investments that gave dividends. So we suddenly had some extra money and could go on holidays, and he could buy that stupid car. Fun-money, he called it. But that was a big lie. There were no investments. So who was paying him – and for what?'

'Oh, God.' Maeve put her arms around Phil. 'No, there was nothing like that, I swear.' She pulled back and looked into Phil's eyes. 'I have just discovered something I was afraid might shock you. But nothing as bad as blackmail. I wasn't going to tell you this morning, but I think you should hear it right now.'

'Hear what?' Phil exclaimed, her eyes wild. 'Tell me!'

'Well...' Maeve paused. 'It's about that secret garden of Joe's. I have just found the way into it.'

Phil gasped. 'What?! Jesus, Mary and Joseph, girl, spit it out!'

'Okay.' Maeve clasped her hands in her lap. 'It appears Uncle Joe had a string to his bow we never knew about. He wrote novels.'

'Novels?' Phil asked, looking confused. 'What kind of novels?'

'Romance,' Maeve said. 'Under the pen name "Fanny l'Amour". That's where the money came from. It was royalties paid into his account from a publisher in America. Red Hot House. I'm pretty sure the bank statements will confirm it.'

Phil gasped and stared at her. 'Romance?' she whispered. 'Fanny l'… Are you pulling my leg?'

'No,' Maeve assured her. 'It's true.'

'Oh, holy feck!' Phil put her hand on her chest as she looked at Maeve. 'Dear Lord in heaven, what a…' She straightened up, her eyes blazing. 'I could kill him if he wasn't already dead.' She stopped and looked at Maeve. 'Royalties? And how many of these awful books did he write?'

'Ten or so. They seem very popular. And they're not awful, but well-written and kind of tongue in cheek. He had a website, too. I mean, she does. Fanny. With a photo.'

'Of… him?'

'No, of a woman that looks suspiciously like you when you were younger. I think he must have had an image of you Photoshopped, now I think of it.'

'Shit,' Phil said with passion, her face red and her eyes flashing angrily. 'The sneaky bastard. Sorry, but it makes me absolutely furious.'

'I can imagine,' Maeve said, feeling slightly guilty to have given Phil this strange news out of the blue. The sad look in Phil's eyes was gone, replaced by red-hot fury, mixed with shock.

They both gave a start as Esmeralda jumped onto Phil's lap. Phil relaxed and hugged the cat to her chest. 'Darling Esmeralda. She knows when I need her.'

'Maybe I shouldn't have told you. But I felt…'

Maeve was interrupted by her phone pinging. A text message. From Paschal, saying he was already at the beach. 'It's Paschal. He asked me to go swimming with him this morning. How on earth did he get my number, anyway?'

'I gave it to him,' Phil said with a cheeky grin. She made a shooing gesture with her hand. 'Go on. Out of here. Go swimming with Paschal. I need to think. And I will take a peek at the laptop while you're out. I need to see what was going on.'

'But I…'

'Go,' Phil ordered and got up, letting Esmeralda jump onto the floor. 'I'll be fine. All this was like a shot in the arm. I'm suddenly full of energy. But now I need to digest it and think.'

'I know. I'll let you alone, so.'

'Enjoy the swim. And Paschal,' Phil said, smiling.

'Thanks. I will.' Maeve walked out, deciding to leave it all to Phil for the moment while she went out to swim with a very sexy man.

Paschal was sitting on a large piece of driftwood when Maeve made her way down the steps and across the soft white sand. He was in his swimming trunks, looking across the bay through binoculars.

'Hi,' Maeve said, spreading her towel on the sand. 'I would have come earlier but Phil was in bad shape this morning so I was trying to cheer her up.'

'No worries,' Paschal muttered without moving. 'Thought you'd forgotten.'

'I had, but your text reminded me,' Maeve confessed. 'What a lovely morning for a swim.'

'It's perfect. Is Phil okay?'

'She's a little better now. What are you looking at?'

'Dolphins,' he said, still looking out to sea. 'A whole pod of them having fun out there.' He turned and handed her the binoculars. 'Here. Take a look.'

'Thanks.' Maeve took the binoculars and looked through them out at sea. 'I can't see anything.'

'There. To the left.' Paschal took her shoulders and turned her slightly in the right direction, looping the strap of the binoculars over her head.

The brief contact with his hands on her bare shoulders made Maeve shiver for an instant. Then she looked again out to sea through the glass, and gasped as she saw the dolphins at play. A whole group of shiny backs jumping out of the water. One of the dolphins leapt up into the air and disappeared again, followed by the others. Maeve couldn't take her eyes off the graceful creatures playing out there in the blue ocean. 'They look like they're having a ball.'

'Sure they are. Great craic out there. It's not often there are so many of them. You're lucky to get to see it.'

Maeve handed the binoculars back to Paschal. 'Wonderful. Here, you have another look.'

Paschal resumed looking out to sea. 'They're going further out. Maybe following a shoal of fish. Fantastic animals, aren't they?'

'Incredible.'

He lowered the binoculars and peered at her with his sloping brown eyes. 'Phil having a rough time?'

'Yes. I think she had a bad night.' Maeve pulled up her knees and wrapped her arms around them. 'She seems to cope so well most of the time. Always cheery and smiling and cracking jokes. But then I'm sure she's bleeding inside.'

'Haemorrhaging at times, I suspect,' Paschal said, frowning. 'It's only been a year. She and Joe were such a close couple. It'll be years before she recovers, if ever.'

Maeve buried her toes in the sand. 'I don't know how to help her.'

'You're here. That's a good help for a start. Nobody can make it better, but being there and listening is a great comfort.'

Maeve glanced at him. 'You seem to know about grief.'

He looked down at his feet. 'Perhaps I do. But this isn't about me.' He looked at her again. 'Phil's grief is still so fresh. I think she needs something to do. Some kind of project.'

'Yes. You're right. Like a job, or something that'd give her a purpose.'

'A reason to get up in the morning,' Paschal agreed. 'I know she's worried she might have to sell the house. The repairs would cost a fortune so she might have to.'

Maeve looked up at Paschal. 'I know. The roof needs to be replaced, and the house rewired or the insurance company won't cover her, or something, she said.'

'That, too.' He rose from the log and stretched. 'How about a swim? The water's getting colder but it's a great way to shake the blues.'

Maeve followed him to the water's edge and waded in, wincing as the cold water hit her warm skin. But Paschal raced ahead and dived in and she followed suit, gasping at first at the chilly shock, but then relaxing as she got used to it. She followed in Paschal's wake as he swam ahead towards a rock sticking out of the sea. She swam hard, and was exhausted by the time she reached him. He was sitting on the rock, and pulled her up to sit beside him, smiling as she tried to catch her breath.

'A little out of shape?' he asked.

'More than a little,' Maeve had to admit. 'Haven't swum like that for years.'

'You'll soon get the fitness back. You have a good technique. All you need is stamina. But it's late in the season. The water will get quite cold, fast. You should get yourself a wetsuit and then you can swim all winter.'

'Oh, but I'm only here for two weeks.'

'There is only now, you know, this time, this moment. Who knows what the future will bring?'

She laughed, trying to lighten the mood that had suddenly become charged with emotion. 'You're right of course. I should try to do as much as I can while I'm here. But I'm going back to London at the end of next week.'

'That's what you say now.' He winked. 'I bet you'll still be here at Christmas.'

She moved away, his hot gaze unnerving her. 'What makes you say that?'

He shrugged. 'Don't know. Wishful thinking? I wouldn't mind if you stayed, Maeve McKenna. You make the place look a lot more interesting.'

She stared at him, strangely mesmerised by his eyes on her, not knowing what to say. Then he leaned forward and touched his lips to hers in a feather-light kiss, before sliding back into the water and swimming back towards the shore. She sat there, staring at him for a moment, her heartbeat increased, not from the cold or the swimming but from the feel of his lips against hers. Why had he kissed her? She shrugged. He was probably just flirting for fun. Whatever the reason, she had enjoyed it. There was nothing wrong with a bit of a flirt. As long as you didn't take it seriously.

She got back into the water and made her way slowly back to shore. Paschal was gone by the time she waded onto the beach. She sank down on the towel, closing her eyes, letting the sun warm her chilled body and her thoughts drift.

I bet you'll still be here at Christmas, he had said, and she suddenly wished he was right. Oh, to leave all the hard slog and the stupid clients and the sofa cushions and the fancy loo seats and stay here in this tranquil, beautiful place... She sat up and mentally slapped herself. What was she thinking? She loved her job, and when she got back she'd crack it and London and get her mojo back. Of course she would.

Chapter Fifteen

Showered and dressed, Maeve checked her email before she went back to the study. Only one, from Stephen. More problems with the house?

But the message had nothing to do with the Holland Street house. Maeve's smile widened as she read it.

Dear Maeve,

I hope this finds you well. I apologise for my rather abrupt message earlier. Didn't mean to sound like such a grump. All is well with the house now thanks to your excellent colleague Rufus, who managed to persuade Belinda to stick to the original plan and do as little damage as possible. Can't tell you how relieved I am. Belinda and my father might be a match made in hell, but what do I know? I'll leave them to sort it out – or not. Whatever, as my daughter would say.

But I was thinking of you, and wondering when you're coming back. Despite us only meeting that one time, I find myself missing you. You were such a breath of fresh air in my otherwise dull life, making me laugh and teasing me, in that wonderful Irish way.

I'm looking forward to hearing that lovely lilting voice and seeing that gorgeous smile again.

The real reason for this message is that I received tickets to the premiere of a play in the West End on the fourth of December and I immediately thought of you and how much I'd like you to come with me. The play is based on a book by an author I represent. We'll go backstage to meet the actors and there'll be a reception at a hotel nearby afterwards. Black tie, etc. Thought you might accept to be my date? I know it's a long time away, but time flies, as they say. Should be a fun evening, even more so with you there.

Hoping to hear from you soon.

Stephen

Maeve's heart beat faster. What an exciting event. And she'd be going with a very glamorous man who appeared to be very attracted to her. She suddenly couldn't wait to see him again. He probably looked amazing in black tie. She loved the holiday season in London, with the glittering lights, the seasonal music in all the shops, the parties and drinks and all the fun of dressing up and going out. And this invitation topped them all. She was tempted to reply at once, but held back. No need to sound too eager. She'd email her reply tonight.

Still excited, Maeve skipped down the stairs and into the study, where she found Phil at the desk, the laptop open, Esmeralda on her knee. She looked up as Maeve walked in.

'This,' she said, pointing at the screen, 'is very, very strange. Not to say shocking. Joe had a secret life inside this computer. He was a different person – a… a woman,' she ended, her face pale.

Maeve pulled up a chair and joined Phil. 'I know. Incredible.'

'It's as if I never knew him at all. It's like discovering he was a cross-dresser or something.'

Maeve nodded. 'I know. I have to say I was pretty shocked too. But... well, although it is pretty weird, it's kind of amazing too. I mean... He was imagining how a woman would feel and then he hit on something that he was good at and could make money out of. I have a feeling it happened by accident and then he was on a roll. Those books are not at all bad. And written with a large slice of humour.'

'I know. I read a bit of one of them online. I ordered a few too. I want to read them. It's like a message from Joe.' Phil's eyes suddenly filled with tears. 'I can't get over it. All that hard work writing those books. And all that money.' She wiped her eyes. 'He tried to tell me, you know.'

Maeve stared at Phil. 'He did? When?'

'A few months before... before he had that fatal heart attack. We were laughing and running up the stairs, and he said he had something exciting to tell me. But then he had some kind of turn and nearly stopped breathing. I helped him into bed and was about to call the doctor, but then he looked fine again and told me not to fuss. And when he'd rested, he asked me if I read romance novels. I said no – of course I didn't read such trash; words to that effect. So he kind of clammed up after that. I should have asked him what he meant, but I was more worried about his health and getting him to go and see a doctor, which he refused to do. He said he felt fine and to leave him alone. So I did. But I shouldn't have.' Tears ran down Phil's cheeks as she looked at Maeve. 'I felt so guilty about that for a long time. And now I feel even more guilty. If I hadn't sneered like that, he would have told me. Maybe it caused him so much stress that he…'

'Stop it,' Maeve ordered and gripped Phil's hand. 'It wasn't your fault he died. And he should have had the courage to tell you, even if you looked down your nose at romance. What use is it to blame yourself?'

Phil sighed and dug in her pocket for a tissue. 'I suppose you're right. But oh, I wish…' She shook her head and blew her nose. 'No use wishing for what never was.'

'No.'

'Okay.' Phil sat up. 'Back to the present and the money. I'll look at the bank statements tomorrow. I have a feeling there was a lot coming in at some stage. '

'But what did he do with it?' Maeve asked.

'He spent it.' Phil sighed. 'I was so stupid. I never asked how we could afford that lovely car, or the holidays in the south of France at expensive hotels when we were living on his pension and putting away a large part of it for a rainy day. I felt we needed to make sure we could afford private health care should we need it, not to mention a top-notch nursing home. I just closed my eyes to it all and accepted his explanations of being "careful with the pension" or "some back-payments of expenses and great dividends".'

'But you had fun.'

Phil smiled wistfully. 'Oh, yes we did. Suddenly we had the time to laze around and to see all the places we'd always wanted to visit. Joe called it our golden years; it was as if he wanted to pay me back for all my hard work during his career. He became more cheerful and seemed to stop missing his career. We had never been so happy.' She smoothed Esmeralda's fur. 'I suppose it was all worth it. I have such happy memories of those trips. He could have been sensible and spent the money on the house, but he was the kind of person who lived for the moment. And wasn't he right? We only live once. He used to say that all the time when I was worried about bills. He'd say something about how you shouldn't take life for granted, and that in the blink of an eye, everything can change, that you have to grab opportunities to have fun and enjoy life while you can. And of course, he was right.'

Maeve looked at Phil in silence as the words sank in. It was so true. She felt a pang of something shifting, something important and earth-shattering that she couldn't quite put her finger on. 'Paschal said something like that this morning.'

Phil looked at Maeve with an odd expression. 'Yes, he would. He has reasons to think along those lines. He's a very brave man, you know.'

Maeve frowned. 'How do you mean?'

Phil hugged Esmeralda. 'He has a lot to cope with, poor boy. But this is not the moment to talk about that. I'll tell you about him later.'

'I'll hold you to that.' So Paschal had something sad in his past…

Phil looked at Maeve over the cat's head. 'What do we do now?'

Maeve woke up from her trance. 'About what?'

'All this?' She gestured at the laptop.

'I emailed that editor and told her Joe passed away. I asked about the nature of their relationship. I thought it was something completely different. I might call her when she's back from her holiday to make sure she got it.'

'Oh.' Phil paused. 'But… what if she's still around? Fanny, that is.'

Maeve blinked. 'How do you mean?'

Phil leaned forward with a new fire in her eyes. 'I mean, if we pick up where Fanny – I mean Joe – left off. We could write those stories and keep Fanny's name alive. She was very popular, you said, and her books are still selling even years after they were first published. There's a fan base already up and running, a website, and all the other stuff. Why let it die? Why not keep going?'

'You mean you want to write romance novels?'

'No, I want *us* – you and me – to do it together. Just think about it, Maeve! It could be fun, and this way we could make money, do up the house and keep it in the family. Joe would have loved that.' Phil sat back and looked at Maeve expectantly.

Maeve laughed. 'Phil, you're a nutcase. We can't do that. It'd be… it'd be some kind of fraud.'

Phil's eyes narrowed. 'Well, Joe used my face for that website. Isn't that fraud, too?'

'I suppose. But… well, we can't tell that Betsy woman a pack of lies and pretend to be Joe. In any case, she must know he's dead by now.'

Phil nodded. 'I know but… We could still pretend he wrote it.'

'What do you mean?'

'I mean we'll write a bit of the novel first. Make it really good, and then send it to her and say it was his last oeuvre. Something we found in his computer after he passed away. And then, when she's read it we'll tell her the truth with the proposal to continue Fanny's work and success.'

'You're mad.'

Phil smiled wistfully. 'I know. But I think it'd be wonderful to continue his work. Inspirational in a way.'

'I suppose. But how do you know we'll produce something that's as good as Joe's stuff?'

'I don't. But I want to try all the same. Joe must have found it a great balm to his soul. Maybe I will too? And who knows? It might turn out to be even better. Maybe a new *Fifty Shades*.'

'That'd be a miracle.' Maeve thought for a moment. It was a crazy idea, but if it worked, it could be just what Phil needed. A project, Paschal had said. And here it was, right in front of them. She looked at the screen and the cover of Fanny's latest. With a bit of effort, it could be possible to put together a similar story. 'Okay,' she said. 'Let's give it a lash. What do we have to lose?'

'I knew you'd come around. And you know what? We could test the book on some readers before we send it off. We have the perfect audience right here.'

Maeve glanced at the cat. 'You're going to read to Esmeralda?'

'Don't be silly,' Phil said with a snort. 'I mean the old ladies at my reading group. They'll tell us what they think of our book. I bet they'll even suggest plot changes and character flaws. We don't even have to tell them what we're doing. We can pretend it's a romance by… Fanny l'Amour… and say we're reading it for fun. I mean, we agreed to try something like this anyway.'

Maeve let out a giggle. 'You're one crafty woman. Mother of God, this is completely nuts. I can't believe we're sitting here talking like this.'

'So? Did you ever think you'd discover that Joe was masquerading as a female romance writer?'

'Not in my wildest dreams.'

'There you go, then.' Phil let Esmeralda down on the floor. 'Life is full of surprises.'

Roisin called just before lunch. Maeve was tidying up the kitchen and jumped as the phone rang.

'Hi, it's me,' Roisin said. 'What's new in the sticks? Tell me something fun and exciting. It's all slog here.'

'Exciting? In the bog of beyond?' Maeve laughed. 'Well, the sun is shining and I went swimming this morning and met…' She stopped, not wanting to talk about Paschal just yet.

'Who?' Roisin asked.

'Just a local. But… I got some exciting news from London.'

'Oh? Mr Posh called you? The one you had dinner with last week?'

'No, he emailed me. With an invitation to a premiere in the West End in December. He represents the author and we'll go backstage and meet the actors, and then there is a party in some swish hotel. It's black tie too, so I'll need something glam to wear.'

'Oh my God!' Roisin shouted. 'How fabulous. Some people have all the luck. And here I am with my job and three kids. The bloody teachers have decided to go on strike, just at the start of a new school term. So now I'll have them at home on top of everything else. And you get to go to fancy parties in London with a gorgeous man. How unfair life is. I *knew* you fancied him, even if you tried to hide it.'

'Calm down. I'm not sure I fancy him, but… Let's say I'm getting interested.'

'Interested? You're just being cautious.' Roisin sighed and lowered her voice. 'Maeve, all men aren't Lorcan. It's time you started to trust a man again, and go with the flow. If you like him, show it. And let him take you out to all the fab places in London and have fun.'

'I'll try.'

Roisin groaned. 'Tough job, isn't it? Going out with a rich hunk who is dying to give you a good time at the hotspots in London. I pity you, darlin'. But do it for me and then I want all the details, and I mean *all*.'

'It's not until December.'

'That gives you plenty of time to prepare. I'll send you a list of things to do to make the best of yourself.'

'Yeah, I know you will. Exercise, diet, skin care, massage. With bullet points. As if you do all of that.'

'I would if I could. Have you replied?'

'Not yet,' Maeve admitted.

'Then please send that man a nice reply and say yes.'

Maeve laughed. 'Okay, darling sister. I will. Just for you.'

'Brilliant. Got to go. Talk soon.'

Maeve said goodbye and went back to tidying up, thinking about what Roisin had said. She was right. All men weren't Lorcan, and it was high time Maeve had a go at trusting someone again. What was that Uncle Joe had said? That you had to grab every chance to have fun, because life was short and you didn't know when it would be over. So true. Maeve decided there and then do just that, starting with a nice reply to Stephen. She picked up her phone and typed the email:

Hi Stephen,

Many thanks for your message and the invitation to the premiere. My calendar for December is filling up already, but I see that the date you mentioned is free, so I'm happy to accept your invitation and look forward to the event.

Best wishes,

Maeve

She felt a little spark of excitement as she thought of the event. It would be amazing. And to go with such a handsome man was the cherry on the very delicious cake.

Maeve sent off the message, satisfied that it was friendly but not too gushy. The event seemed to shine like a bright star on the horizon of the future and her return to London. Who knew what it would lead to?

Phil didn't hang around. She started work on the new book the next day and stayed in the study until the early evening, tapping away at the laptop, only taking a break for lunch. This continued for the rest of the week while Maeve spent the days relaxing, reading and walking on the beach, enjoying her time off and simply doing nothing. The bank confirmed that the payments into Joe's bank account did indeed come from Red Hot House, which made all the pieces of the puzzle come together. Maeve began to feel much better and by the end of the week, she was nearly back to her old self.

The following Saturday, Maeve drove to the supermarket in nearby Waterville, a charming little seaside town famous for its golf course.

The mild, sunny morning had turned into a wet and windy afternoon, with black clouds gathering over the steep mountains of MacGillycuddy's Reeks in the distance. Carrauntoohil's jagged peak stuck up in the middle, looking less than inviting, even though it was one of the most popular hiking areas in Kerry. *The middle of September already*, Maeve thought. *And only a week left of my holiday.* The realisation that she would have to go back soon gave her a stab of sadness. She didn't feel she could leave Phil just yet. She needed to see their mad scheme through and make sure it was going to work. Then there was this lovely time of year, when the village and the beach were at their best. Walking on the beach, just enjoying the view, picking up shells, watching the seabirds and maybe seeing the dolphins were things she had come to cherish. She hadn't spoken to Paschal again, only seen him in the distance on the beach and through the window of his shop, where he smiled and waved. She had regained her energy and felt nearly ready to get back to the busy life in London. But not quite yet. She just needed a little extra time, more than what was left of her holiday. Maybe she could ask Ava for yet another week off? If things were ticking over at the firm and Rufus was handling things well, that might be possible. But then what? Maeve pulled up outside the supermarket and sat there thinking, while the rain smattered against the window and the wind shook the car. What a day.

This was only the first of the many autumn storms that would batter this coast, mixed with calm days full of golden sunshine. Autumn in Kerry was always spectacular in one way or the other. Pity she wouldn't be here long enough to experience it. Maeve sighed, fished her rain jacket from the back seat and put it on, ready to brave the elements. It was like being slapped in the face with a wet facecloth as she walked across the tarmac and wrenched open the supermarket door against the strong wind. She slipped inside and pulled the door closed behind her, breathing hard as she stood in the warm, bright interior.

The shop was full of customers: a mixture of locals, and tourists looking at postcards and maps. Maeve pushed her rain-sodden hair out of her eyes, grabbed a trolley, pulled her list out of her bag and started along one of the aisles. She was taking a carton of milk from the fridge when someone bumped into her from behind, painfully scraping her heel. Whipping around, she came face-to-face with someone horribly familiar.

Chapter Sixteen

Maeve stared at the woman, who was dressed in a shiny pink raincoat, her perfect blonde hair only slightly ruffled and her face made up as if she was on the cover of *Vogue*. It was Belinda, Oliver Taylor's fiancée: the woman who was causing so much trouble with the Holland Street house.

They looked in shock at each other for a moment, until Belinda said in her grating baby voice, 'Oh, it's you!'

Maeve nodded. 'Sure it's me. But what are you doing here, of all places?'

Belinda smoothed her hair. 'I know. It's so weird. This place is *so* not me. I wanted to go to Marbella, but Oliver wanted to do the Ring of Kerry. I had no idea it would involve such a long drive around this peninsula looking at green hills and a load of *sheep*. Then we stopped here so Oliver could do a bit of golf. Thank God for spa hotels, eh? Which one are you staying at?'

Maeve let out a giggle. Willow House, with its leaky roof and flaking paintwork, was almost as far removed from a spa hotel as a mud hut in the African bush. 'I'm not in a hotel; I'm staying with my aunt in a village nearby.'

'I see,' Belinda said. 'I'm sure that's a lot of fun.' She glanced into Maeve's trolley. 'Shopping for food? You have to do your own cooking?' she said with a shudder. 'That's very brave of you. I wouldn't know where to start.'

'But I thought you were doing a cordon bleu cookery course in London?' Maeve couldn't help remarking.

'It hasn't started yet. And that's for entertaining, not for making porridge.' She glanced over Maeve's shoulder. 'But here's Oliver now. He must have given up on the golf.'

Maeve smiled at Mr Taylor as he approached. 'Hello, there! Fancy meeting you here.'

Mr Taylor returned her smile and shook her hand. 'Why, hello, lovely lady. This is a nice surprise. Are you staying here in Waterville?'

'No,' Maeve replied. 'I'm staying in Sandy Cove about half an hour's drive away. In an old house called Willow House.'

Mr Taylor nodded. 'I see. I've dragged poor old Belinda here to do the Ring, but we've stopped here for a couple of days so I can hit a few balls.' He put his arm around Belinda. 'She's been very brave.'

'The weather was nice yesterday and this morning,' Belinda said with a pout. 'But look at it now. Absolutely horrid.' She darted a sour look at Maeve, as if it was her fault.

Maeve smiled and shrugged. 'It's what we call "a nice, soft day" around here.'

Belinda sighed and rolled her eyes while Mr Taylor laughed. 'I love the Irish way of taking everything on the chin,' he said.

Maeve shrugged again. 'Well, what can you do about the weather other than take it as it comes? How are the plans progressing with the house since I last saw you?'

'Going well,' Mr Taylor replied. 'But we had a few changes of direction since Belinda returned from India which is why we took this break away from it all.'

'We decided on a different look and had to start again,' Belinda cut in.

'I heard when I was in touch with Rufus,' Maeve replied. 'I know there were a few... er, alterations. Maybe I should have delayed my holiday to make sure everything was going as planned.'

Mr Taylor put his hand on her arm. 'Don't worry, dear lady. It wasn't your fault at all. Belinda changed her mind and decided she wanted something completely different. But I think we're back on track again. Except with a slightly different kitchen – isn't that right, darling?'

Belinda studied her nails. 'Yes. I saw this wonderful kitchen in a house in the Cotswolds when we were there for a weekend break. Granite worktops are much classier, I think. And then that Shaker style I thought I liked before is a bit... stark. So we went with this Cape Cod look instead. It'll be fab; I just know it.'

Maeve let out a sigh of relief. No more yoga retreat. 'Oh, I see. Well, whatever you're happy with.'

'Until she changes her mind again,' Mr Taylor remarked dryly, a glimmer of weariness in his bright blue eyes. 'We're not going with the paint you suggested for the living room. Belinda insists on wallpaper.'

'It'll look divine,' Belinda interjected. 'I found this cute shop in Chelsea where they do their own designs. And I picked the perfect shade of green with little blue dots. And that cute man in your office was a great help. He even came to my yoga class.'

Mr Taylor glanced out the window as the sun shone in. 'The weather seems to be improving. I might even have time for a round on the golf course before tea.'

'And I can get back to the spa and that amazing indoor pool,' Belinda said, looking relieved. 'Then we're off to do the rest of the ring-thing tomorrow, and then back to London, thank goodness.'

Maeve raised an eyebrow. 'So Ireland wasn't really up to scratch?'

Belinda shrugged. 'Not my thing, really. Charming, I guess, and all that. And the music is kind of fun.'

'And the stunning scenery, the ocean, the wildlife, the castles and the fresh, unpolluted air…?' Maeve felt a rising anger bubbling inside her but she knew she shouldn't show it. After all, Belinda was a client and they were always right. But here she was, looking at her nails and practically yawning, drawling on about spas and pools in what was one of the most beautiful places on the planet. Maeve shot a look at Mr Taylor, who shrugged behind Belinda's back. Maeve caught a sudden glint of annoyance in his eyes, gone as soon as it appeared. What a strange relationship. The gold-digging bimbo with the wealthy older man was a classic scenario, but Maeve found it odd that a man of such intelligence and class should have been caught by such a woman. Sex was probably the driving force behind this. That, and a fear of loneliness. Even Maeve could relate to that. She could write a book about being lonely.

'Oh it's all very nice,' Belinda said politely. 'But I'm more of a city person, really. And this part of the world is a little short on shopping.'

'I see. Well…' Maeve pushed at her trolley. 'I'd better get going. My aunt is expecting me back for tea at five, so…'

'Is your aunt's house far away?' Mr Taylor asked, while Belinda wandered off to browse in the souvenir section. 'I think you said it was called Willow House?'

Maeve nodded. 'Yes, that's right. It's in a village called Sandy Cove. Half an hour's drive from here.'

'Lovely sounding name for a house.'

'Yes, I love it too. It was built in 1912 by my great-great-grandfather as a summer house. But now my aunt lives there permanently. It's a real gem of a house, but a little run down.'

Mr Taylor smiled. 'That would add to its charm, I'd say. Nothing wrong with a bit of patina.' He leaned forward. 'But don't tell Belinda I said that,' he whispered conspiratorially in Maeve's ear.

Maeve laughed. 'Except a leaking roof loses its charm very quickly on a rainy day.' She smiled apologetically. 'Now I really have to go. But... You know what? If you want to see the house, why don't you drop in later today? Around five o'clock? If the golf doesn't take up all of your time, of course.'

Mr Taylor smiled again. 'Golf is nice, but I'm not an addict. Thank you for your invitation. I think I'll take you up on that. On my own, of course. Belinda wouldn't appreciate it. I believe she needs to have her toenails seen to. Or was it some kind of exfoliating? I never get those treatments right. And I never see any difference, even after she has spent hours at some salon or other. I pretend I do, of course.'

Maeve giggled. 'I know what you mean. I cut my own toenails, so I wouldn't know. Anyway, I'll see you later. The house is right at the edge of the village, overlooking the beach. It's quite big and pink, with a large weeping willow beside it. You can't miss it. My aunt will be delighted to see you, too.'

*

Phil was still in the study when Maeve arrived home with the shopping. The roof had leaked as usual during the heavy rain, and buckets of water stood in the hall where it was still dripping from the ceiling. Maeve could hear muttering and laughing as she put everything away in the kitchen. She frowned and went to see what was going on. The study door was half-open and Phil's voice floated out into the corridor.

'Veronica,' she muttered. 'Hmm, would she say that?' She looked up from the laptop as Maeve walked in. 'Back already?'

'Already? I've been gone two hours. I met a friend in Waterville and I've invited him for tea. What are you doing?'

'Tea?' Phil looked confused. 'Is it that time?' She put her hand to her cheek. 'I had such a good time with Veronica, I forgot what time it was.'

'Veronica?'

Phil nodded. 'Yes. The heroine in the novel we're writing. I started it last Monday, just to see what would happen. And lots did. I'm calling her Veronica, didn't I tell you?'

'No, you said you would tell me when you had written a few chapters. But I like the name.'

'Yes, me too. She has just gone on board a cruise ship. I think she'll fall in love with the captain. He's French and very handsome. What do you think?'

'Uh, okay.' Maeve resisted an urge to feel Phil's forehead. She looked slightly feverish, with red cheeks and shining eyes, and she was still in her gardening clothes with her hair a mess. 'Sounds good. I'll take a look later. Have you written much?'

'An outline and five chapters, which makes it—' Phil consulted the screen '—fifteen thousand words, it says here. Is that a lot?'

'It's amazing. Truly. Dad usually writes about a thousand a day when he's working on an article. He says that's his record.'

'Woohoo, I've beaten my baby brother, the whizz-kid,' Phil exclaimed laughing. She rubbed her eyes. 'But I'd better stop now. My brain is cooked. Tea, you said?'

'Yes. With a guest arriving in about half an hour. Nice man your age.' Maeve winked. 'Very handsome. English. Lots of dosh.'

Phil shot up from her chair. 'You invited a complete stranger to my house for tea?'

Maeve shrugged and smiled. 'I'm afraid I did. Seemed like a good idea at the time. But I do know him. He's a client from London who's here to do the Ring and play golf.'

'Yes, but *I* don't know him.' Phil walked to the door and pushed past Maeve. 'I wish you had asked me first.'

'And then you'd have said "no, I'm not equipped", or "I don't look my best" or "the house is a mess", or whatever excuse you'd come up with. And you love entertaining, so here's your chance to be the perfect hostess.'

'There is that, of course,' Phil had to admit. 'But all of those other things you said I would say are true, too.' She walked ahead, along the corridor and up the stairs. 'And we don't have *anything* to offer for tea.'

'How about scones and strawberry jam with whipped cream?'

'From the supermarket?' Phil asked, as if Maeve had picked those items from a garbage bin.

'Yes, but they looked fine. The scones are from Hartigan's in Cork.'

'Probably stale,' Phil shot over her shoulder from the top of the stairs.

'No. Freshly made today. Do you want me to help you change?'

'I think I can manage that, thank you,' Phil snapped and slammed her door shut. Then she opened the door again and peeked out. 'This man… Is he married? Bringing a wife?'

'No. But he has a fiancée half his age.'

'I see.' Phil nodded, still glaring at Maeve. 'Why are you standing there? You'd better go and get tea and scones ready. And straighten up the drawing room. Nobody's been in there since the dawn of creation. It's probably smelly and dusty. But what can I do, when you invite people willy-nilly like this without giving me a chance to prepare?' She closed the door again with a bang.

Maeve sighed and went down to the kitchen to whip cream and place the scones in the oven of the Aga to warm up. 'She's in a bit of a snot,' she said to Esmeralda, who sat up on her cushion and glared at her. 'But she'll enjoy herself all the same. Just wait and see.'

Esmeralda turned her back on Maeve and started to clean her face, as if she was also getting ready for afternoon tea with a guest.

'I'm going nuts. I'm talking to a cat,' Maeve muttered and took out a bowl from the cupboard over the sink.

When she had put the best china on a tray and the scones in a basket, Maeve went to inspect the drawing room, bringing a cloth for dusting. Phil hadn't exaggerated the disrepair of the room, but despite its dilapidated state it looked lovely with the afternoon sun streaming in through the tall sash windows. The Donegal carpet, faded but still beautiful with its Celtic design, and the sofa and chairs with their worn, pale green velvet upholstery, piled with embroidered cushions, made the room inviting and cosy. The walls were hung with watercolours and there was a big oil painting over the fireplace of Maura McKenna, the very first lady of this house, wearing an exquisite gown of yellow silk, beautiful with her brown hair and hooded hazel eyes. She had been like something from a fairy tale to Maeve and Roisin as they'd grown up. They had often tiptoed in here and stared at the gorgeous woman, making up stories about her going to balls and having adventures. Probably not true, given the fact she had been the mother of five children and quite the matriarch, ruling the house and gardens with an iron fist, and dying at the age of ninety-seven. But now her lovely eyes looked down at Maeve and, as always, Maeve smiled back at her. 'Hello, lovely Maura. I see you're still here, looking after the house.'

Maeve quickly wiped the antique mahogany table by the fireplace and straightened up the books in the bookcase, giving the photos in silver frames a quick flick with the duster as she went along. She had just opened the windows to dispel the slightly musty smell, and was plumping up the cushions and turning them around to hide the moth holes, when the doorbell rang. Running down the corridor to the hall, she saw that Phil had beaten her to it. Not only that, she had also managed to transform into Jackie Kennedy and Grace Kelly rolled into one. Mr Taylor was in for a treat.

Chapter Seventeen

Dressed in wide black trousers and a crisp white cotton shirt, Phil looked fresh, youthful and chic. Her hair was tamed into a perfect shining bob and her minimal makeup was just enough to make the most of her beautiful eyes and full mouth. *Demure yet sensual*, Maeve thought, knowing that this was exactly her aunt's intention. Dressing up was hardwired into her after all the years as a hostess.

Phil swung the door open and smiled at Mr Taylor, who was standing there looking up at the façade of the house. 'Hello,' she said and held out her hand. 'Welcome to Willow House. I'm Philomena Duffy, Maeve's aunt.'

'Oliver Taylor,' he said, and shook Phil's hand. 'I hope I'm not barging in on you unexpectedly.'

'Not at all,' Phil protested, stepping aside to let him in. 'Maeve told me she had invited you. Please come in, and don't trip over the buckets. Tea is ready in the drawing room.' She was an expert hostess – she sounded as though she received guests for tea every day, Maeve thought, and Mr Taylor was just one of her many visitors.

Mr Taylor stepped inside, looking around the hall. 'Such a treat to see a house like this that hasn't been touched since…' He stopped.

'I'm sorry. I didn't mean that as a criticism. I meant that I love to see all these original period features just like this. Untouched.'

'Except by the wear and tear of time,' Phil said with a laugh. 'Some people call it bohemian chic, but it's really just neglect because of a lack of funds. If I had the means, I'd certainly do it up.'

'I'd prefer to call it "restore",' Mr Taylor said as he looked up at the ceiling. 'Look at those cornices. So lovely.'

'And this is just the hall,' Phil remarked. 'Lots more wreckage to inspect. Thank God it stopped raining. I was getting tired of emptying the buckets. We need a new roof.'

'And new gutters,' Maeve filled in.

'But we still love this old place, despite the flaws,' Phil said with a sigh. 'Tea, please, Maeve.'

'Right away.' Maeve ran to the kitchen and Phil led Mr Taylor into the drawing room. She checked everything on the tray while the kettle boiled, then made the tea and carried it through, where she found Mr Taylor and Phil on all fours looking into the fireplace. 'You can just make it out,' Phil said. 'The crest of the McKenna family. The back of this fireplace was taken from their castle near Kenmare, which was their seat in the twelfth century.'

Mr Taylor peered at the back of the fireplace. 'Yes. I can see it now. Three lion's heads on a shield and… something above it.'

'The head of a suit of armour. The McKennas were quite fierce in their day. They came originally from County Monaghan, but a branch of the family ended up here for some reason.'

'Very interesting,' Mr Taylor said, his voice echoing inside the fireplace. 'I'm discovering more and more about Ireland on this trip.'

'There's a lot more to us than meets the eye.' Phil, still on her hands and knees, looked into Mr Taylor's face. 'Before we get up, if we can manage that without calling an ambulance, may I ask you something personal?'

Mr Taylor looked slightly nervous. 'Uh, yes?'

'The Stones or The Beatles? Which were your favourites?'

'The Stones, without a doubt,' he replied at once.

Maeve smiled at the two of them, sharing memories from their teenage years, that to her seemed like so long ago, but to them probably felt like yesterday.

Phil smiled. 'Right answer.'

'Phew,' he said with mock relief.

'And Elvis? You liked him?'

'Very much, but I have to confess to a penchant for Frank Sinatra. I suppose that makes me a real fuddy-duddy in your eyes.'

Phil beamed. 'Not at all. I adored Frankie, and still do. Elvis was okay, but there was nobody like Frank for a romantic evening under the stars.'

'Very true.' Mr Taylor let out a grunt. 'Can we get up now?'

'Of course.' Phil backed out of the fireplace and got up, brushing her hands. 'Are you all right? Do you want a hand?'

'I can manage, thank you.' Mr Taylor scrambled to his feet, grinning. 'I'm not that old yet.'

'I'd say we're the same vintage,' Phil said with a laugh. 'Creaky bones and all that. But still alive and kicking.'

Mr Taylor shot her one his dazzling smiles. 'Very much so in your case, if I may be so bold.'

'You may indeed,' Phil said graciously.

Maeve put the tray on the table. 'Tea for two,' she said. 'I'll leave you to talk. I have… some work to do in the study.' She winked at Phil. 'Must read that… report.'

Phil smiled and grabbed the teapot. 'Tea?'

'I thought you'd never ask.' Mr Taylor held out one of the cups. 'Tea, please, and plenty of it. Nothing like a cuppa this time of day.'

'Couldn't agree more,' Phil chortled, and swished her hair while she filled his cup.

Maeve smiled at Phil's flirtatiousness, although she could still see the lingering sadness deep in her eyes. She was just having fun, a break from the darkness. It was nice to see that she hadn't lost her touch all the same. Mr Taylor would be enchanted in no time. Belinda might even find herself with a formidable rival. But it was early days, and Phil was still grieving. It was enough that she was enjoying Mr Taylor's company and was coming alive again, even if only for an afternoon.

With Phil's warm voice floating down the corridor, Maeve went to the study to read the first chapters of the new book. She didn't believe for a second that it would be anything other than drivel, and she wondered how she would break it to Phil that her mad scheme would never work.

But it turned out that Phil's attempt at writing a romance novel was a lot more than just drivel. Maeve read the chapters Phil had written, her heart beating and her mind whirling. She had been quickly drawn into the story of sultry Veronica Fairchild, heiress to Irish whiskey millions, who had rebelled against her father and stormed out of the family mansion in Kinsale to marry the man of her dreams – a surfer dude she had met on the beach in Biarritz. But having had all her money cut off, the dream soon ended, and Veronica found herself alone and penniless. Maeve felt tears well up as she read how Veronica, destitute but proud, found a job as a stewardess on a cruise liner sailing around the Mediterranean.

Maeve shook her head in amazement. This was a hell of a story. The grammar was a bit off and the text was riddled with typos, but the core of the writing was excellent and the story riveting. When Veronica met the captain, the sexual attraction between them was sizzling. Maeve couldn't wait for the next instalment. Or… Maeve thought for a moment. Maybe she could have a go at the next chapter herself? Why not? She was smitten with the sexy captain herself already, and Veronica seemed anxious to get to know him a lot better, too. Maeve stopped reading and listened for a moment. There were voices and laughter from the study. Phil and Mr Taylor were obviously having a good old chinwag and wouldn't need a third wheel. She typed 'Chapter Six' at the top of the new page and got stuck in.

Veronica looked into the captain's flirty eyes and smiled. 'You know my name,' she whispered, 'but what's yours?'

'Jacques,' he said and lifted her hand to his lips. 'Enchanté, mademoiselle. You have made this ship a lot more interesting.' His eyes drifted to her cleavage, where a rosebud nestled in the swell of her bosom. 'I like your… little rose. Very pretty.'

Veronica felt her face flush. His eyes promised so much more than his words, and his lips on her hand had made her yearn for more. But they were in the receiving line, and there were passengers waiting to be greeted and helped to find their cabins. She was working here, she had to remind herself; she was not one of the rich passengers. 'I must get to work,' she whispered.

'Me too. Good luck on your first day. I will be in touch.' With that he winked, saluted and, when they had greeted all the passengers, was gone, leaving Veronica trying not to swoon and pull herself together. She was sure the captain would contact her later, and that they would... She smiled dreamily as she imagined what they would do. Then she straightened up, turning her attention to the last passenger in line.

'Whoa,' Maeve said to herself, fanning her face. What fun to write. She suddenly understood how Uncle Joe, tongue in cheek, had written similar stories while idling away the dark winter days here in this ramshackle house. The rain would have lashed against the windows, but in his imagination, he would have been transported to exotic sunny locations with his sexy heroines, making up adventures and romantic trysts galore. Maeve laughed and shook her head. 'What a dark horse you were, Uncle Joe,' she said out loud. She suddenly realised what a huge gift he had left Phil. If Phil continued writing as Fanny, she too would be transported to exotic locations and find solace in the creation of these stories, this coming winter and many more to come. If only he had explained it all in a letter. But he had not known he would leave so suddenly. He had planned to tell Phil one day but lost his nerve when Phil dismissed romantic fiction. What a pity.

Voices floated through the open window from the garden, where Phil was showing Mr Taylor the pink and yellow roses, the greenhouse and the stunning view of the ocean from the edge of the lawn. Maeve couldn't help but notice Mr Taylor looking at Phil with wonder.

Maeve sighed and drew her head in. Such a pity Mr Taylor was stuck to Belinda. And Belinda surely wasn't about to let him go, as long as he continued to splash his cash on everything she wanted. But it was still nice to see Phil enjoying a man's company.

Maeve left the study to make herself a fresh cup of tea and to tidy up the cups and plates left in the drawing room. She put her phone in her pocket, but pulled it out again as it pinged. There were a number of messages from various people – the first one from Ava, then Rufus, and finally one from Paschal. Maeve stopped to check through them. Ava's message was long, rambling and annoyed, something about a client complaining about the bathroom fittings and how Maeve would have to handle that when she got back. Rufus wondered if she could call him, and Paschal… Maeve forgot all about Ava and Rufus as she read the short message: *Dark skies tonight with meteor showers. Should be spectacular. I'm barbequing at my place, playing some music and stargazing. Bring sleeping bag, warm clothing and your good self at around eight p.m. Let me know. P x*

Maeve felt nearly as hot as Veronica in the story as she read the message. It seemed like an invitation to something a lot more intimate than a dinner date. *See you then*, she quickly typed, stomach fizzing, and sent it before she could change her mind. Not a glittering event in London, but something even more magical. Who could resist such an invitation?

Chapter Eighteen

'Sleeping bag?' Phil asked, her voice bubbling with laughter. 'Sounds suggestive.'

'Stop laughing,' Maeve ordered. 'I want your take on this. You know Paschal better than I do.'

'But I bet you want to get to know him better.' Phil winked as she sat down at the desk in the study.

'Yes, I would. I find him interesting. Different. And…' Maeve hesitated. 'A little…'

'Intriguing?' Phil looked quizzically at Maeve.

'Something like that. Not sure how I feel about him to be honest.'

'You're behaving like a sixteen-year-old just out of the convent school. You're a grown woman, for God's sake! Take a walk on the wild side for once, Maeve. If he likes you enough to invite you for an evening's stargazing, you should be so lucky. He's very hard to please.' She stopped and peered at Maeve over her glasses. 'But maybe it's not him you're afraid of, but yourself?'

Maeve squirmed. 'Yeah, well… You know. Once bitten and all that.'

'Sit down,' Phil ordered, gesturing at a chair opposite her. 'You're flitting around. It makes me dizzy.'

'Sorry.' Maeve replaced the little bronze figure she had been fiddling with and sat down. 'So, how did the tea party go?' she asked, changing the subject. 'Nice man, don't you think?'

Phil looked thoughtfully at Maeve. 'Yes. Nice. And sad. Can't cope with the death of his wife. And now he has some young thing to keep happy. He's obviously terrified of being alone, so he picks someone half his age to make sure he dies before her.' She sighed. 'Men are all grown-up babies who're looking for a mammy.'

Maeve laughed. 'I think you're right. But Oliver Taylor doesn't look as if he's suffering, does he?'

'No, he's all smiles and charm. He enjoys life and the girl he's with seems to make him feel young and virile. As long as it lasts. But during our little walk in the garden, we talked. About grief and being alone.' There was a sudden flash of pain in Phil's eyes. 'We both know how hard that is.'

'Of course you do.'

'But enough about that. We have to turn our minds away. This writing lark could be a nice distraction.' Phil switched on the laptop. 'So… Let's see what we should do… You had a go at the next chapter, you said?'

'Yes. Just for fun. Your first chapters were great. I love Veronica already.'

'Me too.' Phil looked at the screen as the document came up. 'Let's have a look, then…' She read in silence for a while with an expression of deep concentration while Maeve waited.

'It was only a bit of fun,' Maeve said to break the silence. 'You can delete it all if it's rubbish.'

Phil suddenly laughed. 'I love this. I think we can keep it all and press on with the story, don't you?'

'Yes,' Maeve said with a sigh of relief. 'I hope so.'

'But we need a little more zing, I think. We need to make Veronica a girl who is heartbroken after what happened . Her first love was only after her money and that was a huge blow to her. So she doesn't trust men and is afraid to let anyone get too close. But at the same time, she's sensual and wants to be loved for herself. She flirts for fun, not allowing herself to invest her emotions, and then…' Phil paused for effect.

'Then…?' Maeve whispered.

'She meets Mr Right. And he refuses her advances, even when she practically strips in front of him.'

'So she has to work hard to win his heart?'

'Exactly.' Phil looked at the screen. 'A long way to go. We need inspiration. And I know where to get it.'

'Where?'

'I'll tell you tomorrow. Now get your sleeping bag, go on your stargazing date and I'll keep going here.'

Maeve checked her watch. 'But it's only seven o'clock.'

'Yes, but you need to make yourself beautiful. And I want to be alone with Veronica for a while.'

Maeve laughed and got up. 'Okay. In any case, I have a few calls to make. My boss is lining up work for when I come back to London early next week.'

Phil looked alarmed. 'Next week? But I thought you might stay longer.'

Maeve smiled and shrugged. 'I can't, I'm afraid. I only have the two weeks off. Ava needs me.'

'Not as much as I do.' Phil's expression changed. 'But there might be a way…'

'A way to what?'

'Never mind,' Phil muttered.

'Beautiful,' Maeve said to her image in the mirror. 'How do I do that?' Her face, rosy from the run up the stairs, her green eyes staring back at her and her auburn hair, curly from the damp air, were all quite fetching. But hardly beautiful. And how on earth did one dress for an evening looking at the stars? She turned away from the mirror and went through her meagre collection of clothes. Well, this wasn't exactly a gala evening at the Ritz, but she had to make a little bit of an effort all the same. First, underwear. She wasn't planning to sleep with anyone, but nice undies always made her feel attractive and sexy.

After her shower, she wriggled into a champagne-coloured lacy set she had packed on a whim, the way you might bring an umbrella to go for a walk. *Just in case*, she had thought at the time. After spraying herself with a light mist of Shalimar perfume, she pulled on a soft green cashmere sweater and her best jeans, the ones that were maybe a little snug but showed off the curve of her hips and her trim waist. She ruffled her curls, brushed her teeth, applied mascara and lip gloss and pinched her cheeks. Winking at herself in the mirror, she picked up the sleeping bag she had found in the wardrobe and ran down the stairs, grabbing her anorak before she opened the door and peered out. It was already dark and the evening stars shimmered above her.

'Have a magical evening,' Phil said behind her. 'You look so lovely.' She kissed Maeve on the cheek and handed her a torch. 'Don't fall over anything on your way back. Good night and good luck.'

'Thank you. Will you be all right?'

'Of course. I have Veronica to keep me company.' Phil smiled. 'I have great plans for her. You're not the only one with a hot date.'

Maeve laughed. 'Can't wait to find out what happens.'

'Go on,' Phil said and shooed Maeve out the door. 'Go forth and get wild. It's that kind of night.'

Maeve stopped and stared at Phil. 'What do you mean? What kind of night?'

'The kind of night when anything can happen.'

Chapter Nineteen

Phil's words rang in Maeve's ears as she made her way across the garden, through the gap in the hedge behind the greenhouse and onto the path along the edge of the cliff. The sun was dipping into the blue waves of the Atlantic, the craggy outlines of the Skellig Islands were black shadows against the sky, which was streaked with orange and pink. A seagull let out a shriek above her and birds swooped down to the beach from the cliffs to catch the last insects. The air was becoming chilly with a slight whiff of smoke. *Autumn smells and sights*, Maeve thought with a shiver. She would soon have to go back to London and her clients. It all seemed as far away at that moment as the pale moon that rose above the pines on the edge of the village. She knew she would be tempted to stay if she could. But it was impossible, she thought as she walked along. She had to return to London. Back to her life, but also maybe to a less lonely existence, if Stephen's interest in her meant anything at all.

But she forgot about Stephen and London as she looked at the thatched roof of the little cottage ahead. She knew the house well, but it had been a wreck when she was here last with Roisin. They had climbed up from the beach and gone to investigate, finding the house a near-ruin and the garden overgrown with weeds. But now, in the golden light of the setting sun, Maeve saw that it had all been returned to its former glory, with roses climbing up the whitewashed wall beside the newly painted green half doors, and a neat little vegetable garden at the side of the house. The tiny lawn ended in several large boulders, probably to stop the sea eroding the garden during winter storms. How amazing that this cottage had been turned back into what it once was, only more charming, Maeve thought as she stood there admiring the house, its neat garden and the stone fence that surrounded it.

'There you are,' a voice said in her ear, giving her a little fizz.

Maeve turned and discovered Paschal in a white fisherman's sweater and jeans, carrying a bag of charcoal.

'Hi,' she said, feeling a little self-conscious. Would he notice her efforts to look beautiful yet natural? 'Lovely evening.'

He peered at the sky. 'Yes. And it will stay clear so we can see the stars. There'll be meteor showers tonight, so it should be spectacular from here. The darkest skies in Europe, they say.'

'I've read about that somewhere.'

'I'm going to light the barbeque so we can start grilling the meat in about an hour.'

'Oh. Great.' She looked around. 'Where is the barbeque?'

'On the beach. Just below the rocks. I've put everything down there. I just have to light it and then I'll get the meat from the fridge. Come on down with me.'

'Okay.' Maeve followed Paschal across the grass, around the boulders and down the steep path to the beach, where he had made a barbeque by balancing a steel grid across two rocks in the shelter of the cliffs. It was mild here, with the sand still warm from the sun, and the boulders providing ample shelter from the wind.

Paschal lifted the grid and poured a heap of charcoal onto the base, sprinkling a little paraffin over them and lighting a match. He watched as the coals started to burn and placed the grid back. 'Should take about an hour to get really hot.'

Maeve nodded. 'Do you want me to help with anything?'

'Could you come with me to get the meat and sausages? I have some aubergines and courgettes I thought we could cook on the coals as well. And then there's salad and bread. Not to mention beer, wine and other bits and pieces.'

'Gosh,' Maeve exclaimed. 'You've gone to a lot of trouble.' She was touched that he had organised such a feast just for her. She had thought this would just be a few sausages and a beer. But here he was, putting together what seemed like a banquet. She scrambled up the path in Paschal's wake, looking forward to the evening with him. Food, music and then gazing at the stars on the beach. How romantic. She smiled dreamily as she reached the house, then gave a start as someone came around the corner. It was Nuala and Seán Óg, carrying a crate of beer and a bottle of whiskey.

'Hi, Maeve,' Nuala said, smiling. 'Are you here early to help out? We've brought some beer and a bottle of Bushmills. I think the others are bringing stuff too. Paddy will bring his guitar, of course, and we'll have a bit of a sing-song.'

Maeve stared at them. 'Uh, that's nice,' she managed, while her heart sank. So this was not a romantic date on the beach after all. It was a party, and she was just one of the guests, invited at the last minute. How stupid of her to think otherwise. 'I didn't bring anything. I didn't know it was that kind of…' She stopped and smiled, trying desperately not to show her disappointment. 'Well, great to see you both again. I was just about to help Paschal carry the food to the beach. The barbeque is lit and should be ready for grilling in about an hour.'

'Fabulous.' Nuala beamed at her. 'Some of the gang from the old days are coming as well. The teachers' strike gave the kids a break from school so a lot of them came down this week. Such a pain for the parents but the kids are delighted. Do you remember Finola? Used to date Seán Óg before he fell head over heels in love with me.'

Seán Óg laughed. 'Yeah, she couldn't compete with your soda bread and chocolate muffins. Nobody could. I knew I had to have you from the very first bite.'

Nuala winked at Maeve. 'My mam made them but he didn't find out until it was too late. Go on, Seán Óg, get your arse in gear and help Paschal carry all the stuff down. We're going to make salad and gossip.'

Nuala looked pretty tonight, Maeve reflected, with her dark hair curled around her face, the light blue sweater and wide trousers making the most of her generous curves. With her friendly face and hearty laugh, she was the kind of woman anyone would instantly warm to. Maeve remembered how Nuala had been the very same in her teens, a true friend and a shoulder to cry on. Maeve imagined she would be a wonderful wife and mother. Seán Óg seemed to think so anyway, judging by the way he looked at her. Maeve felt a pang of envy. Nobody looked at her that way. How lucky those two were to have each other.

*

The party swelled to about twenty people as the evening wore on. Down on the beach, they lit torches and feasted on the delicious meat and vegetables, which had been expertly cooked by Paschal and passed around with the help of Nuala and some of the other women. Maeve swallowed her disappointment and enjoyed catching up with her former teenage pals, most of whom had now left the village and lived in Cork or Dublin, only visiting the village for the summer, or when, as during this week, there was an unexpected break from school because of the teachers' strike. 'No better place to spend the holidays,' one of the women declared. 'You can keep Marbella and the Costa del Sol. This is where it's at'. And she was right. With the stunning coastline, the clear waters of the Atlantic, the surfing, Kerry had everything. Another woman mentioned that they brought their children here, so they could grow up connected to a place where their parents and grandparents had their roots.

Maeve told them about her work and life in London, which sparked off a lively discussion about city life versus country life. She shot a furtive glance at Paschal, who was busy looking after everyone. He met her gaze with an expression that was hard to decipher, but she saw something in his eyes that made her pulse race and her face flush. She was the first to turn away, and she was afraid to look back at him after that, but still she felt his eyes on her all through the evening.

Paddy started strumming softly on his guitar. Maeve sat on a piece of driftwood, staring out at the black, shiny surface of the sea, the islands in the distance and the deep blue sky, where the stars and moon shone brightly over the white sand and rugged cliffs.

Nuala sat down beside her. 'Gorgeous evening.'

'Wonderful.'

'Paschal is a great host. He throws this party every year at the end of the summer. A bit late this year, but then we got this gorgeous week.'

'I didn't know this was some kind of tradition.'

Nuala looked at Maeve in the dim light from the torch beside them. 'Did you think you'd be on your own with him?'

Maeve hugged her knees to her chest. 'Yes, I suppose I did. Silly of me.'

'Not at all. Paschal likes you. I've seen how he looks at you. But...' Nuala leant closer. 'He can't have a relationship with a woman right now,' she said softly. 'Or even a friendship. It's too close to... You know.'

Maeve pulled back. 'No, I don't know. Phil hinted at something, but she didn't tell me what it was. I wish everyone would stop tiptoeing around and spit it out.'

'Oh?' Nuala stiffened. 'So you don't know what happened to him?'

'No.' Maeve put her hand on Nuala's arm. 'Tell me,' she pleaded.

Nuala got up. 'Paddy is about to play and there'll be singing in a minute. Help me carry some of the plates and stuff to the house. We can talk there.'

Maeve helped Nuala carry a pile of plates and cutlery to the house, carefully picking her way on the path, the darkness making it more difficult. When they were finally in the little kitchen and

Nuala had poured hot water into the sink and rolled up her sleeves, she turned to Maeve. 'Grab a towel and dry, and I'll tell you the story while we work.'

Maeve took a towel from the stack on the counter. 'Right. Now tell me. What is this big secret everyone is hinting at?'

Nuala turned off the tap and turned to face Maeve. 'No big secret,' she said, her face grim. 'Just the most awful tragedy that could happen to anyone.'

Chapter Twenty

'What happened to him?' Maeve whispered, dreading the answer.

'Four years ago,' Nuala started, 'Paschal was married to a girl called Lorna from Cahersiveen. Very pretty and fun. The two of them were such a popular couple around here. Her mam was born here and her dad owned a pub in Cahersiveen. I don't think you'd have known her because she went to school in Tralee and she was ten years younger than Paschal.'

Maeve nodded. 'Okay. Go on…'

'Lorna was killed in a hit-and-run accident two months after the wedding. She went for a walk on the main road. It wasn't normally busy at that time of year, so I suppose she felt safe enough. She loved walking and keeping fit. The car sped around the corner and the driver probably didn't see her. She was killed instantly.'

Maeve gasped. 'Oh my God. How terrible.'

'Tragic,' Nuala agreed. 'And even more tragic: she was pregnant with their first child. So two people were killed by that gobshite, who just drove off and left her there on the road.'

Maeve's hand flew to her mouth. 'Oh, no. How awful for Paschal. I can't even imagine how devastated he must be.'

Nuala nodded. 'He is. But he is also a very brave and positive person. He wants to go on living, he says. Not to me, but to Seán

Óg. They're as close as brothers. Seán Óg is the only one he talks to. Paschal has been a bit of a hermit since the accident. During the summers he lives here, doing the place up and running the shop. But he goes back to teaching in Cork every October – so he's only here at weekends over the winter – and I'm not sure he has much of a social life in Cork. It's very sad.'

'What about the shop?'

'Over the winter it only opens three days a week. He usually finds someone to run it when he's not here. Don't know if he's found anyone for this winter, though.' Nuala glanced at the dishes in the sink. 'I suppose we should finish these. But I just wanted to explain what was going on with Paschal and why he might appear a bit... weird, around you. I think he's scared to get into something new with a woman. I expect he feels it might hurt Lorna's family if he were to start seeing you openly. It's been four years, but they're still grieving. Seeing Paschal happy with someone else could make them even sadder.' Nuala sighed and turned to the sink. 'Well, that's my take. Sorry to upset you. I'm sure you'd be very good for him, but then you'd be going back to your glamorous life in London sooner or later.'

'Hardly glamorous,' Maeve said, more to herself than to Nuala. 'But yes, of course I have to go back.' She picked up a plate and started to dry it. 'It will be hard to leave, of course. Sometimes I feel I want to chuck in everything and live here for good.'

Nuala glanced at her over her shoulder. 'Are you serious? You'd give up London for a small village in the bog of beyond? Why? Because of Paschal?'

Maeve felt her face flush. 'Not because of him. We hardly know each other. Lots of other things. Peace, for a start. And the beauty of this part of Ireland. And Auntie Phil, who is so lonely, despite all her bravado. I can't let her sink into old age, living with a cat. And then the house – Willow House. We have to find some way of making money to restore it. And we might have stumbled on something that could save our bacon. I've actually been fooling around with the idea of working from here – online or something. Might not be possible though.' Maeve drew breath and stared at Nuala, feeling she had finally said out loud what she had buried inside ever since she arrived over a week ago. She would love to stay. Life here seemed more rewarding than fiddling with curtain fabrics and bathroom tiles, and living in a dingy flat. If she had been able to start her own firm and do real designs, it would be different. But there was little chance of that, and it was beginning to look as if she'd always be playing second fiddle to someone like Ava. Sooner or later she'd have to try to break free. It was time to try something new and take a few risks.

'What have you stumbled on?' Nuala asked. 'Something great that would make you money?'

'Yes, but I can't tell you about it yet. I have a feeling it could be something fabulous.'

Nuala nodded and smiled, and was about to speak when Paschal walked in.

He looked at the two of them. 'So what's going on here? You look as if you've just discovered the meaning of life, or maybe found that crock o' gold.'

Maeve laughed, her spirits soaring. 'Yes,' she exclaimed. 'I think I've found it. The crock o' gold. Or something very like it. At Willow House.'

Paschal smiled and shook his head. 'Did you take a swig of Paddy's poitín?'

'No.' Maeve laughed at the idea that people still drank the nearly lethal homemade spirit. 'Does he have some? I've never tasted it.'

Paschal winked. 'Now that's not something I should be telling you, my sweet colleen.' There was a flash of something in his eyes as he looked at her, gone as soon as it had appeared. But she knew she hadn't imagined it.

Returning to the beach, they sat around the fire. The temperature had dropped further and they all put on their jackets, some even slipping into their sleeping bags. Paschal strummed his guitar and Paddy and Nuala sang a beautiful ballad in Irish. Then they all settled down to look at the stars in their sleeping bags or wrapped in blankets. Snuggling into her own sleeping bag, Maeve lay on the sand, her head on a small pillow Paschal had given her, looking up at the Milky Way stretching across the velvet sky like a wide belt studded with glimmering diamonds. She could see the constellations quite clearly. The moon lit up the water of the ocean with an eerie light.

'It's glorious, isn't it?' Paschal whispered beside her.

Maeve gave a start. 'Oh! I didn't know you were there.'

Paschal zipped up his sleeping bag. 'Just got here. Had to put out the fire.' He looked up at the sky. 'Look, a meteor. The show has started.'

And what a show it was, Maeve thought as she watched the meteors streaking across the black sky, leaving trails of sparks behind them. It was like fireworks on New Year's Eve, only better. 'What if one of them hit us?' she said with a shiver.

'Nothing to worry about. What you're actually seeing is the meteors burning due to the friction when they move through the earth's atmosphere. Spectacular, isn't it?'

'Incredible.'

'Did I hear you say you were going to stay?' Paschal suddenly asked. 'To Nuala, just now in the kitchen. I thought I heard you talk about finding the crock o' gold? Does this mean you're not going back to London?'

'No it doesn't. It might just mean that Phil will able to keep the house and get it fixed up. I have to go back to work next week. But even when I do go back, I'll be coming here very often.'

Paschal was silent for such a long time, Maeve thought he'd gone to sleep. But then she felt his hand under her chin, turning her face around. 'Does this help you make up your mind, Maeve McKenna?' he murmured, kissing her softly on the lips. His stubble scratched her face, but his mouth was soft and he smelled of the sea and smoke from the fire, which triggered a memory from long ago. She was suddenly fifteen again, being kissed for the first time by that wild boy. Oh, how sweet it felt, just like that kiss on a summer's evening that had forever stayed in her memory. She forgot about the meteor showers and the Milky Way, wanting the kiss to last forever. But then a smattering of raindrops hit them. They broke apart and looked up to see that clouds had suddenly obscured the starlit sky. Within seconds, heavy rain started falling, making everyone around them swear and scramble out of their sleeping bags, racing up the path to the house. The show was over and the spell was broken. *But not the feelings*, Maeve thought, as she met Paschal's gaze just before she left to go home. He could smile and talk and pretend to be cool. But the look in his eyes told a different story.

Chapter Twenty-One

'So,' Phil said, looking at the group by the fire during the extra reading time they had organised that Wednesday. 'What did you think?'

The women stared back at her in silence. Then Mary Watson spoke. 'Ooh,' she said with a sigh. 'That was lovely. I've never read romance before. I used to think it was a load of rubbish. But this story is… well… it's…'

'It's bloody fecking good, that's what it is,' Louise interrupted. 'That Veronica is a sassy broad.'

'Louise!' Oonagh chided. 'Please mind your language. What on earth will Maeve think?'

Maeve lost her composure and burst out laughing. Listening to Phil reading the saucy passage in her melodious voice and then seeing the old women blushing and swooning had been priceless. 'It's okay,' she said, still laughing. 'I've heard worse language from the swishest people in London.'

'And those actors you work with, I bet,' Louise interjected.

'That too,' Maeve replied with a wink.

'Do we want to continue reading this story?' Phil asked. 'Now that you've got a taste of it?'

'Yes, please,' Mary said, pushing her glasses up her nose. 'I like it a lot.'

'Not too vulgar?' Phil asked.

'Not at all,' Oonagh declared. 'Sexy but subtle, I'd say.'

'Good.' Phil closed her Kindle with a satisfied smile. 'Then perhaps I should reveal that this is not a book I bought, but one that's being written by a… friend.'

The women stared at her. 'You know a real writer?' Mary asked, looking impressed.

Phil nodded. 'Yes. But I have to confess I'm using you as guinea pigs – or beta readers, as it's called among writers. This… friend of mine asked me to help out and get feedback from readers.'

Louise clapped her hands. 'Ooh, that's lovely! We can decide what happens to the heroine, then, is that right?'

'Exactly,' Phil confirmed. 'I take it you like her?'

'Yes, I do,' Oonagh piped up. 'But I'd like Veronica to be a little more assertive. I find her too much of a doormat at the moment. I know she's sad because that cad let her down, but that should make her angry. I want her to get her revenge. Maybe this man could come back at some stage and ask forgiveness?'

'And then she gives it to him,' Mary cut in. 'In a big way. But can we have a little more of the sexy captain, please? I know he's just an interlude before she meets Mr Right, but he's very *interesting…*'

'Oh yes,' Louise agreed, her eyes twinkling. 'He's very like a man I knew once. He was very… hot. I was nearly tempted to go… *all the way,*' she ended in a whisper. 'That was before I met my husband, of course,' she ended, looking prim.

'I should hope so,' Mary snapped.

Oonagh's twin sister, Nora, who hadn't uttered a word since Phil stopped reading, started to laugh. 'Haha, Louise, remember when you went to the doctor for a check-up and he asked if you'd ever been bedridden?'

Louise giggled. 'Yes, and I misunderstood him and said: "Many times, Doctor. Once even in a canoe."' She sighed wistfully. 'My husband was a very lustful man.'

Maeve laughed. 'That's hilarious. I bet the doctor was a little embarrassed.'

'He laughed.' Louise smiled at the memory. 'He knows I get confused sometimes.'

Phil got up. 'I have to go and do some work now, ladies. I've taken note of your suggestions. I'll be back in a few days when I have a few more chapters to share. Thank you so much for listening and for all your help.'

'It was a lot of fun,' Mary assured her.

'I can't wait to see what happens next,' Oonagh said.

They left the old ladies discussing Veronica's further adventures.

Phil stopped outside the newsagent's. 'That went well.'

Maeve smiled. 'They loved it. Their suggestions were spot-on. Louise is a hoot, isn't she?'

'She always makes me laugh.' Phil pushed at the door of the shop. 'I have to get a few things here and then I'm going to the garden centre to see about flowers for Joe's grave.'

'Oh.' Maeve suddenly realised she hadn't been to the grave since she came. 'I'll go with you, Phil.'

Phil smiled and patted Maeve on her arm. 'Yes, I'd love that. I'll go and see about flowers and then you can join me in the graveyard.'

'Great. I'll go on home to check my emails and see if my clients are behaving themselves and then I'll see you over there.'

'Oh.' Phil looked at Maeve with concern. 'You'll be going back to London this weekend.'

'Yes,' Maeve said. 'I will.' She glanced across the street where she could see Paschal in the bookshop window, arranging the display. He looked up but didn't smile and quickly turned his attention back to his task. Was he embarrassed about what had happened between them? She hadn't spoken to him since the night on the beach had ended in that spectacular kiss. What might have happened if it hadn't started to rain?

Phil followed her gaze. 'But maybe you should try to stay on a little longer?'

'I'm not sure,' Maeve said. 'Going back to work could be the best thing to do. Before I get too… fond of this place.'

'A little more time?' Ava asked, her voice cold. 'I gave you a whole two weeks off when I couldn't really afford it. Thank God you were able to work online and that Rufus is proving to be such an asset to the firm. He even saved that house in Holland Street from the brink of disaster. But your other clients are beginning to get very snotty about you not being there to oversee the jobs you started. That woman in Mayfair with the penthouse has threatened to pull out and get someone else if you don't show up soon.'

Maeve sighed, suddenly pulled back to London and the bitchy world of interior design. 'She could probably do it all on her own. Her and her stinking poodle that keeps peeing on my shoes.'

'I know she's a total nightmare, but just think of the money we're charging her. She's paid half of it already and if she pulls out we'll have to pay it all back, not to mention the workmen.'

'Yeah, that's a possibility.' Maeve sat down at the kitchen table where she had just finished her breakfast. 'I'll pop over at the end of next week to sort things out and then see what I can organise to do online from here.'

'What are you talking about?' Ava suddenly shouted. 'Online? From there? You can't mean what I think you mean, that you'll be doing some kind of mad *commute*!'

'Well… yes, I thought maybe…'

'Not possible,' Ava snapped. 'All the jobs are very hands-on, with clients who need constant schmoozing. You know that, Maeve. Please say you'll come back to pick up what you left hanging. And then we have all the new clients and the trade fair in ten days and…' Ava paused to draw breath. 'I wasn't going to tell you this until you came back, but we have a new client who asked for you especially. She wants you to do up her office near Covent Garden. Lovely period building and a very nice woman. She said she'd give you carte blanche to do what you feel would be best.'

'Oh.' Maeve realised this was some kind of carrot Ava was dangling to make her come back. It sounded like a dream job, she couldn't deny that. 'I'll book a flight for the end of next week,' she said. 'If you'll give me that extra week off.'

'Fabulous. See you then,' Ava said and hung up.

Maeve sank down on a chair and stared out of the window at the view of the garden and the trees starting to look decidedly autumnal, their leaves turning yellow. Time had flown since she'd arrived with so much happening; writing the book with Phil, getting to know this lovely village and then Paschal… She hadn't had a chance to speak to him since that evening, when he had kissed her under the stars and looked at her with such longing it had made her heart ache. She had felt such a pull towards him ever since, whenever she saw him from afar, in the window of the shop, and at the weekend with a group of children on the beach when he was taking them on a tour of the flora and fauna of the seashore. She watched him collecting shells and showing them how delicate the marine ecological system was and how everything was connected to each other, from the tiniest insect to larger fish and mammals. The children flocked around him, listening intently. It made her sad to think of the child that had died that day with its mother. What a wonderful father he would have been.

But she had a feeling he was avoiding her. Whenever their paths crossed, in the street or on the beach, he seemed busy and not eager to exchange more than a polite 'hello' or 'lovely day' or something banal about the weather. Did he regret kissing her like that, or had he forgotten all about it? Or was he unable to have feelings for a woman after the loss of his wife? He must be more troubled than she'd realised and maybe she was better off not getting involved with a man who carried such heavy baggage.

But she couldn't dwell on that right now. She had to go back and pick up her career again. That new job Ava had mentioned sounded wonderful. And it could be the beginning of making a name for herself and maybe even getting started on realising her dream of running her own firm. She could start small, and then make it grow in time.

Stephen Taylor was another light on her horizon. Maeve felt a dart of excitement as she thought of the possibilities waiting for her in London.

But right now, she had to go and visit Uncle Joe's grave. It would bring a kind of closure to her feelings about Uncle Joe's death and create a further bond with her aunt. Writing the novel with Phil was proving to be such fun, and now they had read the first ten chapters to the 'old birds', as Phil called them. The ladies' pithy comments had surprised and delighted them, and some rather saucy suggestions on how to make the sex scenes even more sizzling had been hugely helpful. Who knew that ninety-year-old women had such a modern take on sex? But then, they had all lived and loved and experienced things they had never dared talk about. Now, suddenly they could talk about them – and they weren't shy about doing so. It was all such a laugh. And Phil had sent off what they had written to Betsy Malone. Maeve hoped with all her heart the response would be positive. It could be the start of a new phase in Phil's life.

The graveyard beside the old church was quiet. The grey sky and the still air added to a feeling of sadness, but also of peace and tranquillity. The gravestones stood in silent rows, some of the graves well-tended, others neglected and forgotten. Phil walked down the gravel path carrying pots of cyclamen and a small spade. She would dig up the geraniums that had died after the light frost the night before and dig in plants better suited to this time of year. Later, after Christmas, she would put in heather that bloomed even in cold temperatures. She reached Joe's grave and saw that Maeve was already there, standing with her head bent, her hands clasped, her lips moving.

She looked up as Phil approached. 'I'm having a little chat with Uncle Joe,' she said, her voice breaking. 'I told him I was sorry I didn't come to the funeral. I should have, but…'

Phil put her burden on the grass and joined Maeve and kissed her on the cheek. 'Don't worry. I knew you were busy. In any case, funerals are for the living. I'm sure he understood.'

'I hope so.' Maeve sighed. 'I was busy, yes, but I was also staying away because I find it hard to face death and grieving. I'm such a coward when it comes to things like that.'

'It can be hard to see people you love suffer.'

Maeve nodded. 'Yes.'

'But you came now, when I needed you the most. Much better. I was surrounded by people after the funeral, but they stopped coming after a while. And then you arrived, when I was beginning to think my life would always be empty and without meaning. I can't thank you enough for that. I'm sure Joe is smiling down at you too.'

Maeve looked at the granite slab. '*Joe Duffy*,' she read out loud. '*Born in Killarney 1942. Died in Sandy Cove 2018.* His name is right at the top.'

'Leaving space for me, when my time comes,' Phil said gently.

Maeve shivered. 'How eerie, to look at your own grave.'

Phil shook her head. 'Not at all. I find it comforting to think we'll be together forever.'

'The two of you were so happy,' Maeve said with a sigh. 'And he was such a lovely uncle to me and Roisin. He was so funny, always telling jokes and teasing us and making us laugh.'

'How lucky we were to have had him in our lives.' Phil sank to her knees and picked up her spade. 'I found some lovely flowers,' she said, trying to shake off the sad thoughts.

'Red and white cyclamen,' Maeve said picking up the pots. 'I think he'd love that.'

'He would.' Phil dug out the geraniums and put them in a pile. 'Could you put these in the bin over there?'

Maeve took the dead flowers and threw them in the bin. When she came back, Phil had already planted the new flowers and stood up, brushing earth from her hands. 'I should have worn gloves. But it looks nice, don't you think?'

'Gorgeous,' Maeve agreed. 'You keep the grave looking so nice. I'm sure it's sad for you to come here.'

Phil nodded. 'Yes. Sad and happy at the same time. I feel he's here with me. But right now, I would like to have a word with him about that secret he kept all these years. If he were alive, I'd give him hell.'

'Me too.'

Phil suddenly chuckled. 'I have a feeling he is laughing up there in heaven. He must have meant for me to find it, with your help.'

'I wish he'd left a letter or something to explain,' Maeve said.

'Yes, so do I. He did try to tell me, but I sneered at his suggestions of my reading romance novels. He might have told me later but he probably didn't dare. He might have held off and waited for the right moment. It never came because…' Phil stopped and looked at the flowers. 'Well, you know. But maybe I was meant to find out this way.'

Maeve shook her head. 'I'm not sure I believe that things are meant to happen. I think they just do, out of sheer coincidence. And in any case, nothing might come of your idea of writing those books.'

'I think there's something…' Phil looked at Maeve, trying to find a way to explain her feelings. 'You know, when I started to read what Joe had written, I felt a strange jolt. It was as if someone was shining a light down a path I hadn't seen before.' Phil put her hand on Maeve's shoulder, willing her to believe. 'I suddenly wanted to try to continue Joe's work and follow in his footsteps and make him proud. It *will* happen. I can feel it.'

Maeve nodded. 'I hope you're right.'

They looked at each other and for a fleeting moment, Phil felt it stronger than ever – a kind of force or simply the power of her own wish. Whatever it was, she knew that something good would come out of all this.

The following morning, Maeve was making breakfast in the kitchen when an excited Phil ran in, her dressing gown flapping behind her. 'She replied!'

Maeve took the toast out of the toaster. 'Who?'

'That woman. Betsy. Said she loved the chapters we sent. Loves Veronica and wants to send a contract for a four-part series. With an offer of an advance of twenty-five thousand dollars. She must have sent the message last night when we were asleep.' Phil sat down on a chair and fanned her face 'Whoa, this is so exciting.'

Maeve blinked and stared at Phil. 'Are you serious? She wants to sign already?'

'Yes. Only…' Phil sighed. 'She thinks it's Joe who wrote it.'

'But I sent her an email to explain that Uncle Joe…' Maeve stopped. 'It must have got lost. But we have to tell her the truth.'

'Do we?' Phil stared at Maeve, panic-stricken. 'What if she says the deal is off? Sues me for fraud or something?'

Maeve looked sternly at Phil. 'You can't go on pretending to be Joe, Phil. That's not possible. And she obviously loved the book and thinks the writing is great and that it will sell by the bucket load.'

'Yes, I suppose. But…'

Maeve got up. 'You know what? I'll call her. There was a contact number on the website.'

'But it must be the middle of the night in America right now.'

Maeve checked the time on the clock over the dresser. 'It's ten o'clock here. She's in New York, so five hours behind us. I'll wait until after lunch. She should have just arrived in her office then.'

'You'll call her? And tell her everything?'

'Yes. Even if she didn't get my email. We have to. It wouldn't be fair to keep up the charade. '

'That's true.' Phil sighed. 'I wish Joe had had an agent. Then we could get help sorting it out and go through a contract, should there be one. I haven't a clue about stuff like that.'

'Neither do I. Maybe we should try to get one?'

'Let's sort this out first and see what this Betsy woman says.'

They both jumped as the phone rang in the study. 'That's the landline,' Phil said. 'Could be the old birds wanting the next instalment.' She got up. 'I'll get it.'

She came back at once. 'It's for you. Paschal wants to talk to you.'

'Oh.' Maeve flew up from her chair, nearly tripping over Esmeralda. 'Sorry, girl.' She laughed and dashed to the study. 'Hello? Paschal?'

'Howerya this fine mornin'?'

Paschal's sing-song Kerry accent sent a shiver of joy up Maeve's spine. 'Great, thanks. What can I do for you?'

'Sorry to have been a bit distant the past week. But things have been hectic with the shop and then preparing to going back to the university and my lectures for the next academic year. And—' He paused. 'I'm trying to resolve something in my head. I won't go into it now. Just some personal stuff.'

'I see.' Maeve was touched by the strain in his voice. He probably meant the grief he must still be struggling with. 'You don't have to tell me if you don't feel like it.'

'I will. But later. When we know each other better.' He paused again and then took a deep breath. 'I'm calling to ask about two things: one, the shop. Do you think you could mind it for me for a couple of days while I'm in Cork? I have to go back and forth a bit for meetings before the term starts. The lad who runs it for me in the winter season is off sick.'

'Of course. When are you going?'

'Tomorrow morning. Back on Saturday evening. That okay? You could pop in later today and I'll show you how things work.'

'Okay.'

'Great. Then, on Sunday, I'm going to Valentia to pick up some stuff. You might like to come for the spin.'

'I'd love to,' Maeve replied, feeling excited as she remembered the lovely island further up the coast. Cian had come down from Dublin on the bus to collect Roisin's car that she needed now that the boys were off school because of the strike, but she could borrow Phil's car. 'Haven't been there since I was a child.'

'About time you did, then. See you later.' Paschal hung up, leaving Maeve standing in the study with a big grin on her face. He wasn't into the niceties of saying goodbye or even thank you, but the warmth in his voice said more than a thousand polite words. While it was true that they didn't know each other that well, she still felt a strong pull towards him and she had a feeling it was mutual. That kiss had told her so. But his behaviour afterwards had confused her. What did he want from her? Friendship, or something more than that? And what did she feel for him? Was the attraction just physical, or something more? In any case, she was going back to London soon, so they couldn't possibly get into something deeper, unless a quick fling was all they wanted. Was that what she was after? Maeve asked herself. She found she didn't know the answer.

And London beckoned, with all its new possibilities, one of which was Stephen Taylor's interest in her – something she had to confess to herself she kept returning to. Maeve sighed, trying to sort out her feelings. On the one hand, she had Willow House and its beautiful surroundings, the lovely village with its friendly people, and this handsome man wanting to make friends; on the other, her life in London, which was taking a huge turn for the better. The two different worlds seemed to clash with each other, leaving her more torn than ever.

During lunch in the kitchen, Phil was on edge, picking at her scrambled eggs and ham. 'What will she say when we tell her? Betsy Malone, I mean. What if she pulls out of the offer?'

'Then we'll go to another publisher,' Maeve said and pushed the bread basket at Phil. 'Go on. Eat. You can't think straight on an empty stomach. We have to sharpen our brains and think of what exactly we're going to say. You're right though, I wish we had an agent. I really, really do.'

'Do you know any?' Phil asked. 'Didn't you tell me that handsome man you had dinner with was a literary agent?

Maeve gasped. 'Of course! Why didn't I think of him immediately? I suppose I didn't put him into this context.'

'You never told me much about him.'

'Not much to tell. Yet. But he seems interested in me for some strange reason.' Maeve leaned over the table. 'You remember Oliver Taylor, who came to tea?'

Phil's face turned a becoming shade of pink. 'Of course. Charming man.'

'Stephen is his son. Top London literary agent. Terribly posh and intellectual. And I'm going to a premiere with him in December. Maybe he'd agree to take us on?'

'Were you nice to him?'

'Yes, I suppose I was. We had fun.' Maeve smiled. 'But now I will be even nicer. ' She sat back. 'But first things first. I have to talk to Betsy in New York.'

'Do you have to tell her the truth? If she doesn't know already?'

'Yes, Phil, I do and you know it.'

'I suppose.' Phil sighed. 'But don't blame me if it all goes tits up.'

'It won't,' Maeve said with pretend bravado. 'The bottom line is that she liked what you wrote. She won't turn down a potential bestseller.' She left the kitchen, keeping her fingers crossed that she would turn out to be right.

Chapter Twenty-Two

Maeve typed the number she had found on the website into her phone, pressed call and waited for someone to pick up. It didn't take long before a nasal female voice answered. Maeve asked for Betsy Malone and was put on hold for several nerve-racking minutes while she listened to piped music. Then a deep voice barked: 'Yes?'

'Ms Malone?' Maeve asked, not sure if this was a man or a woman.

'Yes,' the voice barked again. 'Who the hell is this?'

'Eh, uh, my name is Maeve McKenna and I'm calling from Sandy Cove in Kerry in Ireland. The west coast,' she added, unnecessarily.

'Yeah, I know where it is. One of my authors lives there.'

'Yes, I know. Joe Duffy. I'm his niece. I'm calling about this new book you might want to publish. The one you were sent recently by email.'

The voice softened. 'Oh yes. It's fabulous. But why can't Joe call me himself?'

'Eh, because…' Maeve stopped. 'I explained it to you in the email I sent you a while ago.'

'What email?' the woman asked, sounding irritated. 'You sent me an email? Never got it. Or…' She paused. 'It might have gone into my junk folder. And my secretary cleared all that while I was away.'

'Or you didn't get it at all,' Maeve cut in, cursing herself for using her eircom email service. 'It happens sometimes with that particular emailing service, especially from Kerry. Should have used Gmail.'

'Bad luck. Can you tell me what was in the message?'

Maeve shivered. That email had never been read. So now she had to give Betsy the sad news. How on earth was she going to say it? 'You see,' she started, 'I'm sorry if this comes as a shock but Joe… My uncle Joe…' Maeve swallowed as her eyes filled with tears. 'He… he died a year ago.'

There was a gasp, then silence at the other end. 'Is this some kind of sick joke?'

'No. It's true. Uncle Joe is dead. He had a heart attack and died suddenly about this time last year.'

'Holy shit. I'm so sorry.' There was a long pause and a click as the woman seemed to light a cigarette and inhale, then exhale. 'This is very bad.'

'Yes.'

'Why did nobody tell me until now? Excuse me…' Betsy seemed to be blowing her nose. 'Sorry,' she said in a choked voice. 'This is a horrible tragedy for us. We were all so fond of him and his books were going so well. But then we didn't hear from him for such a long time. I thought he might be unwell, but now I hear it was much worse. I sent him a lot of emails and even tried to call his cell phone but got no reply. So this is why… Oh, God, I can't believe…' Betsy stopped and seemed to take another drag of her cigarette. 'So why did nobody tell me? It's been a whole goddamn year!'

'Well, you see, we didn't know about Fanny and the books until now. We found it all in his laptop only a little over a week ago. My aunt, his widow, didn't have the strength to go through his personal papers and his computer until very recently. And then...'

'You found these amazing new chapters and decided to send them to me? Why? I mean if he's... passed away... there won't be any more. Pity, because they're the best darned writing he ever produced. The others were great, but these are dynamite.'

'They are. I thought so, too. But he didn't write them. It was my aunt. She thought... Oh, it's very complicated. I'll explain later. But we were hoping that...'

'That what?' Betsy snapped.

'We thought we might keep writing this story. My aunt is doing most of it, and I have to say I think she's brilliant. So if she could keep writing and then somehow...' Maeve stopped.

Betsy didn't reply for a long time. Then she laughed raucously. 'Hell yes, I see now. You – I mean, *we* – could keep Fanny l'Amour alive while the author is dead, is that it?'

'Yes, something like that.'

'Hmm...'

'Yes?'

'Hold on. I'm thinking.'

Maeve waited, holding her breath. What was this strange woman going to say? If she said no, they could always try someone else, but she knew publishing was slow and that it could take months, even a year before they even got a reply from anyone in the publishing business. And self-publishing was hard work, even if it could reap good dividends in the end. But here was a ready-made market and a publisher who knew the ropes, and who had all the strings at her fingertips. She was their best – in fact, their only – option if they wanted to make some money quickly.

'Okay,' Betsy finally said.

'Okay – what?'

'Okay, we'll do it.'

'You will? I mean we will?'

'It would be stupid not to. Those chapters that your aunt wrote are too good not to publish. Fanny's new book will be brilliant news for her fans. I mean, Fanny is still alive as far as they're concerned. They have no idea she isn't a real woman. Joe was very good at responding to them as Fanny through online chats on Fanny's Facebook page. They haven't heard from Fanny in a year and there are a lot of messages there. Now your aunt can take over and really *be* Fanny.' Betsy let out a loud laugh. 'Hell yes, this'll be great.'

'And that advance of twenty-five thousand you mentioned to my aunt? Would that still stand?'

'Sure, why not? But we'll have to see the full manuscript first, of course. And I warn you, our deadlines are pretty tight. I'd only be willing to do this if we could publish in double-quick time, and for your aunt to have the first draft finished at the end of October. Do you think she could do that?'

'Absolutely,' Maeve promised, praying that Phil would step up to the plate.

'Great. Hey, could your aunt meet me in person and we'll discuss the deal and the marketing plan? Could she come over to New York? Or…' Betsy paused. 'Maybe London? I'll be there at the end of next week for a conference.'

'London? Oh yes, that'd be fine. I live there myself. I'm only here for a break and to look after my aunt. I'm coming back next week.'

'And you'll bring your aunt?'

'I hadn't planned to, but yeah, why not? We'll both meet you. I wrote a few bits of that novel myself, actually. We're planning to work together. But Auntie Phil will be the main author, so she'll be signing the contract when her agent has gone through it.'

'Agent?' Betsy said, sounding as if the word were something nasty stuck to her shoe. 'Joe didn't have an agent. I told him we'd take care of everything, and he was happy with that. But okay, whatever. We'll sort it all out next week. Let me have your number and I'll get in touch as soon as I get to London.'

'And you'll email us the contract in the meantime?'

'Yeah, sure. If you want. I'll have my assistant draw it up and send over tomorrow. Great to talk to you. See you next week.' Betsy hung up.

Her head spinning, Maeve knew she had to take the bull by the horns and call Stephen. She wasn't quite sure how she felt about him, only that she found him very attractive. He was part of her London life, which now seemed words apart from Kerry – and Paschal. She could email him, but it would be easier to explain everything on the phone. She went upstairs to her room, hoping the card he gave her would still be in her bag. She found it scrunched up at the bottom, and was about to dial the number when Phil flung the door open.

'So? What did she say?'

'Oh.' Maeve plopped down on her bed. 'I'm so sorry. Should have told you.'

'Told me what? That the Malone woman in New York had a hissy fit and turned us down?'

'No, quite the opposite.' Maeve laughed. 'She had this gruff, rough voice with a thick New Yoik accent. Like something from a movie.'

'Yes, yes. Give me the fun details later. What did she say?'

'She was shocked to hear about Joe, of course, and surprised that you had started to write a book in his – I mean Fanny's – name and sent it to her pretending to be him. But…'

'Yes, but?' Phil waved her hands. 'Come *on*, Maeve!'

'Sorry, okay: she eventually agreed the chapters you sent were fabulous and now she wants to keep Fanny's name going and sign us to write under that pen name. She confirmed the twenty-five thousand dollar advance she had mentioned to you.' Maeve drew breath.

Phil's eyes lit up. 'Really? That's fantastic! This will save the house – and me, and you. We can go on and live here together and do up the house and…'

'Slow down.' Maeve got up. 'Don't get too excited. This isn't exactly a lotto win. That money will be paid in many separate chunks I'm sure. I don't think publishers hand out cash just like that. And if we accept the deal, you'll have to hand in the first draft at the end of next month. Do you think you can do that?'

'Yes, of course I can. I've worked so hard, and now I'll work harder,' Phil declared. 'I'll do it.'

'I know that. But I think we need an agent to handle things for you or you might end up working hard for very little. In any case, she wants to meet us in London next week. And before that, I will try to get Stephen Taylor on board – if I can manage it.'

Phil stared at her. 'London? Next week? You mean, you want me to come too?'

'Of course. Betsy wants to meet us both. And you'll be the face of Fanny so to speak, as you've written most of it.'

'London,' Phil said in a dreamy voice. 'How exciting. Where will I stay?'

'In my flat, of course. Not exactly the Ritz, but quite okay. You'll sleep in the bed and I'll take the couch that folds out. It'll be grand.'

Phil's eyes shone with excitement. 'I can't wait. I'll go and have a look at my wardrobe right now and put together a few outfits and accessories.'

'It's a whole week away,' Maeve protested. 'And you'll only have to stay a couple of days. You won't need more than a change of shirts and some clean underwear, a cardigan and a raincoat.'

'Don't be silly.' Phil walked to the door. 'Will you book the flight? I'm not sure I know how to do that online. I'll pay you back, of course.'

'I will. Don't worry about paying me back.'

'We'll take it out of the advance later,' Phil suggested.

'Nah, forget it. This trip is on me.'

'Thank you, darling. I'll see if I can park Esmeralda with the old birds. She'll sulk, but she'll survive.'

'And I'll see if I can get Stephen on the phone to set up a meeting.'

'Good. I'll tidy up the kitchen.'

Maeve followed Phil downstairs and went to the study, where she turned on the laptop and picked up her phone. Her hand shook slightly as she dialled the number on the card. It rang twice before there was an answer.

'Stephen Taylor.'

'Oh, uh, hi, Stephen. This is Maeve McKenna.'

His voice softened. 'Maeve! How nice to hear your voice. You're not calling to cancel our date in December, I hope?'

His deep voice with its posh accent made her smile. 'Not at all. This isn't about anything personal, it's… well… it's business.'

'Business?' he asked, laughing. 'Now I'm intrigued. Is this about some novel you're writing?' he continued, sounding suddenly patronising. 'The story of your life or something?'

'Not me, but my aunt. And it's nobody's life story. She is working on…' Maeve stopped. How was she going to explain this situation? 'It's a bit complicated, but to cut a long story short, my aunt is writing a series in the romance genre under a pen name, and she has just received an offer from a publisher in New York. I'm helping her with a bit of editing and writing and the business side of things. As we have no agent, I thought I'd ask you if—'

'Romance?' Stephen sighed. 'We're up to our eyes in romance at the moment and I'm not sure we can stomach any more. We decided today at a meeting that we would only take on someone with huge money-making potential. So this had better be bloody good.'

'It is.'

'Who's this publisher?'

'Red Hot House.'

'Oh Christ. Not them. Not exactly one of the big five. And the offer?'

'They said an advance of twenty-five thousand dollars for a four-book series.'

'Hmm. Not bad, but not exactly a fortune. But hey, Maeve, old thing, as we had such a fun time and you've agreed to be my arm candy at the premiere, I'll be willing to read the first three chapters. If you agree to go to dinner when you're back.'

'Arm candy?' Maeve asked, frowning. Was he serious?

'Sorry. Bad joke,' he said, sounding contrite. 'But seriously, how about dinner some night when you're back? I'd very much like to see you again soon.'

'Why not? I'll be back at the end of next week.'

'Wonderful. Then we can fix an evening for dinner.'

'Of course. And you'll read the chapters in the meantime?'

'Yes. But I can't promise you that we'll take your aunt on.'

'I think you'll like them. I'll email you the chapters right now. Could you have a quick look and then let me know?'

'Is it sexy?'

'It might make you feel a little hot under the collar.'

He let out a derisory snort. 'I doubt it. But very well. I'll be in touch as soon as I've read the chapters, and then we can meet and discuss it. Don't forget about the dinner. Cheerio for now.' The line went dead before Maeve had a chance to say goodbye.

'Hmm,' Maeve muttered to herself. 'Not quite the Prince Charming when doing business.'

'What?' Phil asked from the door.

'Nothing. I just saw a different side to Stephen.'

'Did he say he'd help us out?'

'No, he moaned about having to read more shite. But he'll have a look all the same because I promised to have dinner with him when I get back. Not impressed with that kind of deal, I have to say. I doubt he'll want to take us on, but that might be a good thing.'

'Send it to him anyway,' Phil urged. 'You never know.'

'It's a shot in the dark, but okay. There might be a better agent out there who'd be more professional.'

'Send it,' Phil ordered, in a voice that didn't allow argument.

'Yes, ma'am.' Maeve made a mock salute and started to laugh. 'He'll probably make us wait a couple of weeks for a reply.'

'Oh well, maybe he isn't the right man for us.'

'You never know.' Maeve logged into her emails and prepared a new message. 'How about this: *Dear Stephen, although you were just a tad more sexist than I like when I spoke to you, as a huge favour I will let you have a quick look at this novel, which promises to set the e-book market on fire…*'

'That's not what you're going to write!'

'No, but I enjoyed it. I'll try to be nice. And I'll send him all we have for now as well, so he'll see the whole picture.' Maeve sat up straighter and started typing. It would have to be business-like and not too personal.

Dear Stephen,

Nice to talk to you today. Please find enclosed the nearly completed first draft of Veronica's Way, which will be book one in the Veronica Fairchild series. As you know, we already have an offer from Red Hot House. I will give you a week's exclusivity, but then it will be sent to other agents.

Looking forward to seeing you when I get back to London.

Best wishes,

Maeve McKenna

She read it out to Phil, who nodded. She attached the manuscript and pressed 'send' before she could change her mind. 'There. Gone.'

'So what do we do now?' Phil asked.

'You keep writing, and if there is nothing from Stephen by this time next week, we'll look up other agents.' Maeve thought for a while. 'Or… We could send it off to other agents right now. Stephen won't know we did it. And then when he comes back with a no, we might have a better offer.' Maeve smiled. 'Isn't this fun?'

'This is not a game.' Phil sat down in the leather armchair by the window. Esmeralda slunk in through the door and jumped up on her lap, glaring at Maeve in her usual way. 'It's all so complicated. But hopefully worth it in the end. Did you read those last two chapters I wrote last night? When the captain sneaks into Veronica's cabin and they…'

Maeve stared at Phil. 'New chapters? No. Why didn't you tell me?'

'I forgot. I couldn't sleep last night, so I decided to do a little work. And then, there in the study, I found a stack of letters from Joe when we were engaged. They were very inspirational, so I thought I'd weave some of that into Veronica's story.'

'Oh, I didn't look at them. So they went off to Stephen before I could check the grammar and stuff.' Maeve sighed and turned to the laptop. 'I'd better take a look.'

'I'll just sit here with Esmeralda while you read.'

'Okay,' Maeve replied, her eyes on the screen. She quickly scrolled through to the new chapters and started reading, her heart racing as she was transported to the ship's cabin in the moonlight, with the sexy captain whispering sweet nothings to Veronica. What followed was a masterpiece in subtle sensuality that was better than anything that she had seen in any of Joe's books. Maeve stopped reading and stared at Phil. 'Ooh,' she whispered, her face on fire.

'This is… I can't describe it. Not explicit, but so subtly sexy I think I need a cold shower. Where on earth did you get this knack for writing such hot stuff?'

Phil's smile was slow and mischievous. 'Joe inspired me. You have no idea what we got up to when we were young and in love.'

'I can imagine.' Maeve cringed slightly. 'No, I don't want to imagine it. But you know what I like about it, apart from the sexy stuff?'

'No, what?'

'It will appeal to women, because Veronica is a woman who's in charge of her own body and her desires. This is not about alpha-male domination of women, it's about a woman having sex when she wants it, or not when she doesn't. It's not spelled out, but it's there. It's not *Fifty Shades*; it's the opposite. That will be the appeal.'

'Joe's books were like that, too. I had a look last night at some more of them. But it's stronger in this one, I think.'

'I love it. And I love Veronica: the way she's so gutsy, and takes the fact that she now has to work for a living on the chin.' Maeve shivered with excitement. 'I'm going to send this to a few more agents, once I have looked up the ones that handle romantic fiction. I'm not sure Stephen is right for us. And I don't know if it would be wise to work with him under the circumstances. I got some strange vibes when we started talking about the book.'

'But isn't he one of the biggest agents in London?'

'I don't care.'

Phil leaned forward in the chair, squeezing a protesting Esmeralda. 'But I do, and it's my book. If he comes back within the week and says he'll take us on, we're going to go with him. Is that clear?'

'But it might affect my personal relationship with him.'

'You'll deal with that, too, if it comes to it.'

'Says who?'

'Fanny l'Amour, that's who,' Phil said, with a determined glint in her eyes.

Chapter Twenty-Three

Maeve walked through the village to Paschal's shop while going through her conversation with Stephen in her head. On a personal level, he had been sweet and charming, but once he'd put on his agent hat he'd seemed like a different person altogether. Would Phil working with him be a good idea? Probably not, if she hoped they would start dating – or even just be friends. She had been so excited when he'd asked her to that premiere, and she was still looking forward to what she was sure would be a glamorous event – one she would never be attending if it wasn't for him. Maybe it would be better if he didn't take Phil on and they could look for a more suitable agent. Then she would be free to see what might happen on a personal level with him.

Energized by the new possibilities, she walked down the street towards the shop, her mind full of what lay ahead. Everything seemed suddenly bright and promising. Only one problem remained to be solved: the wrench of leaving this beautiful part of Kerry.

Paschal was waiting for Maeve in the shop. It was nearly closing time and he was at the till, balancing the cash and the credit card receipts.

The bells on the door tinkled as she walked in. 'Sorry I'm a bit late, but I had to help Phil with something.'

Paschal looked up and smiled. 'No problem. I'm just about to close anyway. Good day today. A busload of Dutch tourists bought up nearly all the T-shirts with the sheep and funny logos. And then I got a car full of French women who wanted to buy maps and postcards. One of them even bought the antique jug that's been sitting here since last year.' He took out a wad of cash and closed the till. 'This goes to the bank in Waterville, along with what's in the safe, but I'll do that early tomorrow on my way to Cork.'

'So what do I do tomorrow?'

'Just keep an eye on things and be nice to the customers. Tomorrow's Friday and market day in Ballinskelligs, so the shop will be closed in the morning. But then you'll open it after lunch and keep things going. I've written down how to work the till and the credit cards.' He handed her a piece of paper. 'Same on Saturday, when I'll be back in the evening. I have a friend who'll come and run things on Sunday while we're in Valentia. I just needed someone here those two days. Then from next week, I'll only keep the shop open at the weekend.'

Maeve looked around the cosy shop. 'I like the mix here. Books and old stuff and touristy things all together. And the shop window arrangement really invites you to come in and browse.'

'It looks like a bit of a mess, but there is a kind of order to it all. And everything has a price tag with a bar code, so it's easy to register. I'll show you how the till works and then I'll close up.'

Maeve looked around. 'It's such an inviting space. You just want to stay and browse and maybe even sit down and read one of the books. Have you ever thought of opening a café in that empty shop next door? You might be able to knock through that wall and make an opening to get through. You could do the café like an old country inn, with wainscoting and framed photos from the old days.'

Paschal laughed. 'Are you looking for a designer job? I'm afraid that would be a very ambitious scheme. And it would cost a lot of money.'

'I suppose you're right. Pity.'

'Fun idea, though. So, if you come around to the counter, I'll go through the drill. And then we could go for a jar at Nuala's and Seán Óg's if you want.'

'That'd be nice.' Maeve stepped behind the counter. 'So how does it work, then?' she asked, as he moved closer, looking at her with a little smile hovering on his mouth. She smiled back, happy to be in his company.

'It's not complicated.' He quickly showed her how the till worked, then stuffed the cash into an envelope and put on a scuffed leather bomber jacket that hung on a peg by the door. The jacket, despite its age and worn state – or maybe because of it – made him look like a hero in one of those old war films, Maeve thought. Sexy, rugged, troubled.

He saw her looking at it and shrugged. 'Yeah, I know. This thing is a bit past its shelf life. I've had it since forever, so now it's part of me.'

She touched the sleeve. 'Lovely and soft. It's got a nice worn texture.'

He grinned. 'That's for sure. Are you ready?'

Maeve nodded, grabbed her bag and followed Paschal out of the door and down the street, towards the pub at the edge of the village. She was admiring his square shoulders in the bomber jacket and his dark curls spilling over the collar, when he stopped suddenly and looked back at her.

'If we bump into someone, we're not together, if you see what I mean.'

She blinked and stared at him. 'No, I don't. Please explain.'

'We're not on a date or anything. I don't want anyone to think that we're...'

'We're not,' Maeve snapped and pushed ahead of him. 'Don't worry. Nobody will know I even like you. Which I don't right now, actually. I think you're a big chicken.'

He grabbed her arm. 'Hang on. Don't get into a snot. It's not what you think.'

She stopped. 'I wish you'd talk to me. Nuala told me what happened to you and I am so sorry. What a horrible accident. I'm sure you'll never, ever get over it. And I understand that...' She paused. 'Oh, God, I don't know what to say. How could I possibly know what you're going through? It's just that I feel there is something happening between us, but you don't know what to do about it. And neither do I.' She looked into his sad eyes and took a deep breath. 'I like you, Paschal, I really do.'

'I like you too,' he mumbled, so quietly she barely heard him. 'You have no idea how much. But Lorna... she was... she *is* standing in your way.'

Maeve's eyes filled with tears. 'I know, I can feel it – her – there: in your eyes, your voice, even in the way you look so confused sometimes. Maybe she doesn't want us to be together?'

'No,' Paschal protested, his voice suddenly loud. 'She wasn't like that. She would want me to be happy.'

'I'm sure she would. She loved you. But if you don't sort it all out in your head and in your heart, you'll never be able to have a relationship again. Maybe you need a lot more time?'

He shrugged, avoiding her eyes. 'I don't know if time is the problem. But do we have to discuss this now? Can't we just have a drink and a bit of craic?'

'I'm not in the mood for craic right now. I think I'll give the pub a miss. I'll catch up with Nuala later.'

'Does this mean you won't come to Valentia on Sunday?'

'I don't think that would be a good idea.' She turned and started walking in the other direction, towards Willow House.

When she had cornered into the lane, she heard footsteps behind her. A hand pulled at her arm. 'Maeve, please stop and listen.'

Her heart thudding, she turned and looked at him. 'Okay. I'm listening.

There was a desperate look in his eyes and he opened his mouth to speak, but no words came out. The cold wind rustled the leaves. 'I don't know where to start,' he said running a hand through his dark curls.

Maeve suddenly felt an urge to lift her hand and smooth his hair back from his face. 'How about the beginning?' she said, softly.

He sighed. 'There is no beginning. Or end. Just…' He shook his head as if to clear it. 'I've been living in a kind of bubble the past four years. The accident… Losing Lorna hit me like a sledgehammer. It took me a long time to get back on my feet. I don't quite know how to explain this, but what helped me the most was my faith. My belief that Lorna isn't gone, that she has just floated into another universe and that she is watching out for me. Sean Óg said the same thing to me. He has been such a great help. Nuala too. They have both helped me accept what happened and to start living again. I want to. I truly do. I'm beginning to feel alive again and to believe I have a future. But…' He stopped.

'But what?' Maeve whispered.

He put his hands on her shoulders. 'But then you arrived and made me feel so confused. Your eyes, your smile, your voice and that sexy laugh were like a beacon of light shining into my darkness. I've started to feel for you something similar to what I felt for Lorna – or the beginning of something that could be as wonderful.'

Maeve leaned her forehead against his chest and breathed in the smell of leather and books, and a hint of turf smoke mingled with soap. 'Me, too.' She looked up at him. 'You're scared, is that it? You think that if we started something, it would happen again? That you'd lose me, too?'

He pulled her close. 'Something like that. You're going back to your glamorous life in London very soon, aren't you?'

She stepped away. 'It's mostly that, isn't it? You think I'm just looking for a little fun? That all we'd have would be a fling, and then I'd leave and never come back?'

'Tell me it wouldn't happen.'

'I…' she sighed. 'Well, yes, I am going back next week as a matter of fact. But I'll come back here for breaks often. I have to earn a living, Paschal, just like you and everyone else.'

'But the bottom line here is that you'll be doing it in London.'

Maeve hesitated, not knowing quite how to put it. 'Yes, but…' She stopped, trying to find the right words. 'I might be able to…'

'Have your cake and eat it?'

'Oh, please. Stop being so judgemental. Yes, I'm going back to work in London like I said. And Phil's coming with me.'

Paschal frowned, his black eyebrows heavy over his eyes. 'She's leaving too?'

'No!' Maeve exclaimed, exasperated. 'She's coming because we have a meeting with someone who might help her make some money.'

'In London?'

'No. She'll be working from here. And I might organise to come here regularly, doing a lot of stuff online.'

Paschal let out a snort. 'Yeah, right. I believe that when I see it. Once you're in London, the big city will swallow you up and you'll forget all about Sandy Cove. And me.'

Maeve stepped further away and pulled her cardigan tighter. 'There's no point standing here in the cold talking to you, when you keep jumping to conclusions and being suspicious about everything I say. Go on and have that jar with your friends. I'll look after the shop for you. And then when you come back…'

'You'll be packing your bags.'

Exasperated, Maeve looked back at him and sighed. 'What's the use trying to convince you when you won't listen? I'm going now. Good night.' She turned on her heel and started to walk away, her heart heavy.

Paschal caught up with her and pulled her by the arm. 'Don't go off in a huff.'

She stopped. 'What else am I supposed to go off in? A taxi?'

He let out a strange sound. 'You're a funny girl. But you're right. I'm a big chicken. I want things to work out in an orderly fashion.

I want for you to stay here and then we could, after a while, work things out.'

'How long would that "while" be? Ten years? I'm nearly forty years old, Paschal. If there is one thing I learned from Phil, it's that there is only now, this moment. Life isn't a rose garden, you know. Nobody owes us a living. Who knows what's going to happen next? We could both be dead tomorrow.' She drew breath, instantly regretting her words. How could she expect anything from this man, who was so sad and so confused? Maybe it was better to break this off, whatever it was, before it was too late and they both got hurt. But then when he took her in his arms, she knew it was already too late.

'Yes,' he mumbled. 'You're right. And now, this moment, all I want to do is this.' He pushed his mouth against hers as if he couldn't stop himself. As Maeve responded, her lips softening, it grew into something so passionate it made her knees buckle. She grasped him by the waist and pressed her body against his, her cardigan opening, his hands straying inside, under her shirt and on her bare skin, which burned at his touch. The cold wind whipped at their hair and clothes but they stayed there, in the lane, holding on to each other as if they were drowning. Maeve forgot all about London, Stephen Taylor and the glitz and glamour waiting for her. All she knew at that moment was that she never wanted the kiss to end, or for Paschal to let go of her.

Finally, she pulled away, breathing hard. 'I need to come up for air.'

He laughed, his teeth gleaming in the gathering dusk. 'Me too.'

They stared at each other. 'What do we do now?' Maeve asked.

'I know what I want to do.'

'Yes, but… It's not…'

'I know. And my house is cold and Phil is waiting for you. And I'm going to Cork tomorrow. But…'

'Yes?' Maeve whispered, her heart singing.

'Valentia. Let's go there on Saturday night. There's a little hotel there…'

'But that's a bit close to here, isn't it? I mean, what if…'

'Someone sees us?' He stepped away, suddenly sober. 'Yes, that's a risk.' He looked at her and ran a hand over his eyes. 'This is so hard for me. I'm sure you think I'm a real coward, but…'

She put her hand on his chest. 'No. You've been struggling with your pain and your sorrow and trying your best to live with it. I suppose you always will.'

He took her hand. 'Yes, that's true. But if you're there, maybe it'll be a little easier.'

'I hope so,' Maeve said, with a feeling he was handing her a very heavy burden. But she was strong enough and more than ready to carry it. 'I'm willing to try. But I'll wait for you. As long as it takes.'

'Thank you.' He gave her hand a squeeze and pressed his lips to it. 'I'll go for that jar, so. See you Saturday night in Valentia. I'll text you the details of the hotel and we'll meet up there, in the bar around six. Just for dinner and then…'

'Let's not rush anything.' Maeve smiled. 'We'll see how we feel. But it's a date. A real date. And a good beginning.'

'Sure is, *mo stór*.' He smiled and walked off, whistling a tune that could barely be heard above the sound of the gale.

She watched him go, the wind tearing at her clothes, thinking about how much she loved him speaking to her in Irish, especially those endearments that sounded like beautiful poetry on his lips. That was a large part of his attraction: his Irish wild spirit and soul. So far away from her life in London. But… She sighed, thinking about his huge emotional scars. Would they ever heal? And what about her own? The heartbreak of being left by a man she thought was the love of her life had left an indelible mark which had crushed her self-confidence and her trust in men. How could she come to terms with that? She looked up at the dark sky and wondered why life was so complicated and why love had to hurt so much. Maybe the trip to Valentia was a bad idea? But she knew she would go, and that whatever happened there would either split them apart or bring them closer together.

Chapter Twenty-Four

Valentia Island, only forty minutes' drive from Sandy Cove, was like another country. As she drove across the bridge in Phil's vintage Jaguar, Maeve looked out at the deep blue sea to the horizon, where she could see the craggy outlines of the Skellig Islands. It was a bright, cool evening with near gale-force winds and clouds scudding across the darkening sky. She hadn't been to this island since she was a teenager, but it hadn't lost its old-world character that gave you the feeling of stepping back in time. Uncle Joe had brought them here on an outing to show them the amazing fossilised tetrapod trackways, footprints preserved in Devonian rocks, on the north coast of the island.

'Look,' Uncle Joe had said, 'about 385 million years ago, a primitive vertebrate passed here and left prints in the damp sand.'

There had been a gleam of excitement in his bright blue eyes. He had loved showing them things that were unique and little-known, trying to instil in them the passion he felt about natural history and the ancient sites of his beloved Kerry. He was the best teacher, never demanding they learn but simply showing them the wonders of nature in a way that made them love it too. It opened their eyes and taught them to look beyond the superficial: something they would never lose.

They had looked at the prints in awe, trying to imagine some kind of huge lizard tramping around right there, millions of years earlier. Then Uncle Joe had bought them lunch in a quaint old pub and they'd forgotten all about the ancient lizard as they'd enjoyed sausages, chips and ice-cream, before taking the little ferry back to the mainland. Remembering this, Maeve suddenly felt a stab of sadness. Those good old days with Uncle Joe were gone and would never come back.

She pulled up at the little harbour outside the hotel and sat there, looking at the sailing boats slowly docking at the marina, the green hills of the mainland and the flags snapping in the wind. It was nearly six o'clock. Would Paschal already be there, waiting for her in the bar? Had he booked a room for them in the name of Mr and Mrs Jones? She laughed and told herself not to be silly. Getting out of the car, she opened the boot to take out her overnight bag, but was interrupted by a voice in her ear.

'You came in the fancy car, eh? Talk about keeping a low profile.' Paschal fished her bag out of the boot.

Maeve laughed. 'How else was I going to get here? It would have been a long walk and there's no bus – or even a donkey – going this way. I handed my sister's car back to my brother-in-law during the week, so this is all I've got. But hey, I thought we were going to keep our date quiet? I'm sure us together in this hotel for a night will be all over the county by tomorrow.'

Paschal laughed. 'I think we might get away with it. I booked the room in the names of Tom Crean and Maureen O'Hara.'

Maeve giggled. 'You're a hoot, Paschal O'Sullivan. I'm sure the receptionist thought this was very funny.'

He shrugged. 'Nah, she's from Dublin and looks about fourteen. She didn't raise an eyebrow. Probably never heard of either of them. How did you manage in the shop?'

'No problem at all. There wasn't much to do, but I sold some books and souvenirs. I put the takings in the safe like you told me and gave the keys to your friend who will take over tomorrow.'

'Great. Thanks for helping out.' Paschal put his arm around her, the physical contact making her heart beat faster. 'Come on. Let's go and settle into our room and…' He stopped and looked at her. 'Maybe you would have preferred two rooms?'

Maeve smiled and touched his cheek. 'No. What would be the point of that?'

He looked relieved. 'Dead right.'

Walking into the hotel, they headed up the beautiful winding staircase to their room. It was large and airy, and dominated by a huge double bed stacked with lacy pillows. The cream wool carpet was soft under their feet and the windows were hung with luxurious flower-patterned curtains held back by red silk ropes, giving the room a sensual, boudoir-like look.

Maeve spotted an ice bucket with a bottle of champagne on the small table by the window. 'What's this? Compliments of the management?'

Paschal put her bag on the floor beside his own. 'No. I ordered it. Thought we'd need a little Dutch courage.' He sat down on the bed and took her hand. 'I have a confession to make.'

Startled, Maeve stared at him. 'What?'

He looked suddenly shy. 'I haven't been with a woman for over four years.'

'Oh.' She sank down beside him. 'You're not the only one.' She played with his hand. 'I haven't had sex for three years. Ever since that pig left me for a girl he had made pregnant behind my back.' She stopped and swallowed. 'It made me numb for a while and then… Well, I never met a man I felt I could trust. Until now.'

He smiled. 'Thank you. I'm glad you feel you can trust me.'

She wrenched off her jacket and pulled the sweater over her head. 'I feel suddenly hot. And in need of a lie down. How about you?'

He took off his jacket and lay down, pulling her down on top of him. 'Let's try this,' he mumbled in her ear. 'Let's learn to love again and make each other happy.'

'Good idea, Tom Crean, hero of the Antarctic.' Saying that name helped Maeve get over her shyness. They were no longer Paschal with the sad past or Maeve who had been dumped, but Tom and Maureen, two lovers who barely knew each other but were dying to learn. As the skies darkened over the harbour, the clouds rolled in and the lights were switched on along the street, they undressed and slipped under the duvet, slowly kissing, exploring each other's bodies, and finally giving in to one other and making love.

Maeve smiled into Paschal's eyes and let out a long sigh. 'Oh, Tom, you were magnificent.'

'You were pretty good yourself, Maureen. Anyone would think you've done this before.'

'It was never as good as this.' And it wasn't. A memory of making love with Lorcan briefly flitted through Maeve's mind. With him, it had been like a performance that hadn't ever felt like love. But with Paschal… She traced his jaw with her finger. 'Not like this, my darling. Not ever like this.' She pulled back and peered at him. 'Do you know that when you kiss me, I feel like I'm fifteen again, being kissed for the very first time.'

'Who was it?'

'I don't know. It happened at a dance in Sandy Cove. This boy pulled me behind the shed and kissed me hard on the mouth, then ran away. I never forgot it.'

He smiled mischievously. 'Did you like it?'

'Yes,' she whispered. 'I did.'

'Good.' He touched her mouth. 'So did I.'

'Oh. So it was *you!*' she said, smiling. 'Oh God, I had no idea. But why did you run away?'

'I was scared. I had been looking at you when you were running around on the beach with your sister. That dark red hair and the long legs… But I didn't dare talk to you. You lived in the big house and were from Dublin, and I lived with my uncle in the little cottage. But then, at that dance, I couldn't help myself. I just grabbed you and kissed you and it was so lovely. But then I felt stupid and ran off. I went to North Kerry to surf with the lads and when I got back, you were gone. I thought I'd never see you again. And then, like a lifetime later, there you were in my shop.'

'How strange.'

'And wonderful.' He kissed her shoulder. 'How about a shower and then some bubbly? And then we'll go down to the dining room and eat something nice.'

'How about room service?'

'Don't think they do that here. This is the only room service you'll get.'

'The best.' She laughed and got out of bed, not caring if he saw her naked body with all its flaws.

'Let's get into the shower, and then we'll open the champagne. Except it isn't. It's Prosecco. Couldn't afford the real stuff, sorry.'

'I love Prosecco,' Maeve declared.

They showered together, crammed into the small cubicle, soaping each other and kissing under the hot stream of water. Then, wrapped in big fluffy towels, they sat by the window and drank chilled Prosecco, looking at the view of the dark water and the stars peeping through the clouds. After a late dinner of Irish stew in the nearly empty dining room, they climbed the stairs again and got into bed, where Paschal, full and content, promptly fell asleep among the pillows and Maeve stayed awake, reliving what had just happened, wondering if it was all a dream. But Paschal snoring softly beside her told her it was real. She could hardly believe her luck.

Her daydreaming was interrupted as her phone rang somewhere in the room, making her jump. She had forgotten to turn it off. Glancing at a still-sleeping Paschal, she crept across the room and found her phone in her bag. She was about to switch it off when she saw it was Roisin.

'Hello?' Maeve whispered.

'Maeve?'

'Yes.'

'Why are you whispering?'

'I'm in bed.'

'At nine-thirty?' Roisin asked incredulously. 'Are you sick?'

'No, I'm in a hotel. With…' She shot a glance at Paschal.

'A man?' Roisin squealed.

'Shh,' Maeve hissed, and tiptoed into the bathroom. 'He's asleep.'

'Who? Don't tell me you've fallen for one of those sexy sheep farmers. I'm sorry, I haven't had time to FaceTime with you like we planned. But the kids have been home and work and everything…'

'Of course. I understand. And no, he's a marine biologist. This just kind of happened recently.'

Roisin giggled. 'Sounds interesting. Is he gorgeous?'

'Yes.'

'Fab! And here I was, calling to cheer you up this cold and windy night. Thought you'd be watching a soap with Phil, drinking cocoa in front of the fire.'

'I hope you're not disappointed.'

'Are you kidding? Tell me all. Where did you meet this hunk? And what about the posh guy in London?'

'Don't ask. I'm not even sure what's happening myself.'

'Let me know when you do. Soon.'

'I promise. Can't go into it all right now.' Maeve shivered. 'I'd better get back into bed. I'm naked and it's freezing.'

'Oooh,' Roisin exclaimed. 'Looking forward to talking to you soon. How's Phil?'

'Why don't you call her and ask? She'd love to hear from you. Got to go. Bye.' Maeve hung up and snuck back into bed, snuggling up to Paschal, who turned and muttered something in his sleep she couldn't hear.

Warm again, Maeve found she couldn't drift off. She mulled over what had unfolded between them, still trying to get her mind around the idea of her and Paschal being together. What about her life in London, her job, and whatever was happening – if anything – with Stephen Taylor? Even if she didn't feel for Stephen what she felt for Paschal, she couldn't give up her career and cut all her ties with London to live in this remote part of Ireland. Paschal couldn't possibly expect that. Or could he?

She had never felt so conflicted in her life. She stared into the black night outside the window, listening to the creaking of boats tied up at the quay and the hooting of an owl, wondering how all this would end.

They woke early the next morning, looking at each other, smiling shyly, before making love again in the light of the early morning sunshine streaming in through the windows. After breakfast in the nearly deserted dining room, they heard the church bells ring for Mass. Paschal looked at Maeve and asked if she'd like to go.

Maeve thought for a moment, finishing the last of her tea. 'I haven't been to Mass in ages. Have you?'

'No. Not since… You know. But now I feel like going. And the church here is beautiful.'

Maeve nodded, got up and took his hand. 'I'd love to.'

Hand in hand, they walked to the little church, which was only a few hundred yards away. They joined the trickle of people hurrying up the path and into the cool dim interior, lit by the sun shining through the stained-glass windows over the marble altar. It was a lovely church with a vaulted ceiling, and beautifully carved wooden pews with embroidered cushions to kneel on. As Maeve sat listening to the service, she felt a strange peace settle over her. She hadn't felt this kind of tranquillity before. She wondered if there really was a God after all, or if it was simply the spiritual feeling of the music and the many voices united in prayer and singing that was lifting her up. She glanced at Paschal beside her, who joined in the hymns sung in Irish, his voice strong and beautiful.

After Mass, they walked all the way to the western point of the island and climbed up to Geokaun Mountain, sitting on a hill that looked over Fogher Cliffs across the sparkling blue ocean. They stayed there for a long time, while Paschal finally told Maeve about Lorna, their brief, happy marriage and the unbearable pain of losing her and their unborn child. Tears welled up in Maeve's eyes as she listened, overcome with a sense of helplessness. There was no cure for such sorrow, no words to make it better; she could only let him speak and hold his hand and hope that her simply being there brought some small comfort.

When he'd finished, she squeezed his hand, not sure what to say or do. But he turned to her and smiled shakily. 'Sorry. Didn't mean to make you sad.'

'I'm sad for you. But glad you talked to me.' Maeve let go of his hand. 'I don't know what to do now.'

He touched her cheek. 'You don't need to do anything at all. You listened and that's enough. I don't want Lorna's shadow to loom over us. I'll never forget her and I'll always have this sad little part in my heart. I'll go off and brood and perhaps shed a tear now and then, but I won't let it wreck the rest of my life. Or yours.'

'It won't.'

'Good.' He took a deep breath, as if he had lightened his burden. Then he gave her a probing look. 'But you have sorrows of your own. That man left you for someone else. That must be hard to cope with.'

Maeve pulled a few strands from the grass. 'It was, of course. Still is a bit from time to time. What hurt the most was that he didn't want to have children with me – but then I realised that I didn't want a family with him either, so maybe it was a good thing in the end. Being here has helped me deal with it all. I'm not into digging into the past and carrying grudges. You only end up hurting yourself.' She tossed the strands of grass in the air and watched the wind blow them away. 'There. All the bad stuff gone with the wind.'

'You're amazing.'

Maeve flicked her hair back and grinned. 'I know.'

'Tell me about Phil and that new project.'

'Oh.' Maeve laughed. 'Such a strange thing. I can't reveal all of it, but in short, she's writing a romantic novel and already has an offer from a publisher. I've helped a little bit, but she can do it on her own now. It's amazing how she just fell into it, as if it had been waiting for her all along.'

'Maybe it did. So that's why she's going with you to London?'

'Yes. To meet this American publisher and to talk about a deal.'

'Fantastic. I'm happy for her. She deserves a break.'

'She certainly does,' Maeve agreed and stood up, rubbing her arms. 'It's getting cold.' She pointed at the horizon. 'Look at those clouds. There could be a downpour soon. We'd better get back to the hotel.'

He jumped up and brushed the grass off his jeans. 'You're right. What was I thinking? I have to go to the museum and pick up some material for my students.' He winked. 'All about the sex life of the jellyfish.'

'Sounds suggestive.'

'Not sure they have that much fun. Not like us.' He threw his arms around her and squeezed her tight, his mouth in her hair, making her shiver with delight. 'Let's get going, then, lovely colleen. Let's get back to life and chores and people and deal with everyday problems. Together.'

Maeve looked up at him and smiled, knowing that this moment would probably change her life forever. Everything was different now. She suddenly knew that there would be no compromise. There couldn't be. She had to either disentangle herself from the life she had thought was perfect and move to Sandy Cove for good, or stay in London and never come back. It made her heart ache to think about it.

The only question was: what was she going to choose?

When they stood at the harbour preparing to leave, Paschal opened the door of Phil's car. 'So we'll say goodbye for a while. I'm going back to Cork tomorrow for staff meetings and other uni stuff, and you're going to London on Thursday, and then…' He paused and took her hand. 'Will you come back?'

She blinked away tears. 'I… I'm not sure. I have to think about it.'

His eyes darkened. 'Yes. You do.' He kissed her cheek. 'It's a dilemma for you – and me. But I don't want you to leave everything you have built up, only to regret it later and blame me for having pressured you. If you do come back, then I want to show everyone we're together. No more hiding and pretending.'

She smiled and touched his cheek. 'That's lovely. I'm glad you want to come out of your shell.'

'But you have to make your choice and then be sure you won't regret it. It's a tough spot to be in. For both of us.'

'Yes.' She stood on tiptoe and kissed him on the mouth. 'But whatever I do, I'll never forget what happened between us. You're a very special person, Paschal.'

'So are you, my sweet colleen.' He hugged her and stepped away. 'Take care. Be happy. Follow your heart and don't do anything until you're sure.'

Unable to reply, her eyes full of tears, Maeve nodded, got into the car and drove off, her heart aching as she looked at the lonely figure in the rear view mirror. How could she leave such a man behind?

Chapter Twenty-Five

'So tell me about him,' Roisin urged when she called that evening. 'The marine biologist you were in bed with. And what about Mr Posh in London? Are you breaking off with him? And when are you going back to the glitz and glamour in London?'

'Oh God, Roisin,' Maeve groaned. 'Please don't ask so many questions. I don't even know the answer to any of that myself.'

'Okay, sorry,' Roisin said, laughing. 'It's just that life is so dreary here and I need a little drama to liven things up.'

'I'd prefer a little less drama.' Maeve sighed and got up from the desk in the study. 'But I can tell you I'm going back to London next Thursday.'

'Oh goody. Then I can come over for a break and do some Christmas shopping at the end of November. And I can help you pick an outfit for that premiere. Can't wait to hear more about it.'

'Oh, that,' Maeve said in a flat voice. 'I nearly forgot about it.'

'What?' Roisin exclaimed. 'Are feeling all right? How could you forget about that? Come on, Maeve, what's going on? Is it that sexy Kerry man? Is it serious?'

'I don't want to talk about it right now.'

'God knows you deserve a little fun after what Lorcan put you through.'

Maeve closed her eyes. 'Let's not go there. Or anywhere. There is so much to sort out and think about.'

'Of course,' Roisin soothed. 'I didn't mean to…'

'No, it's me,' Maeve interrupted. 'I'm feeling a little stressed and confused right now.'

'Oh God, I'm sorry. I didn't mean to put any pressure on you. Call me when you feel like talking. Hug Phil for me.'

Maeve hung up, feeling only slightly guilty about not having told her sister the whole truth, or even about Phil and her new career. But it was all so complicated and she didn't even know herself how she felt or what she was going to do. She only knew that she had to go back to London and reconnect with her life and her job. Only then would she know which was more important: her career or her heart.

London was a shock to the system. After the peace and tranquillity of Kerry, the crowds, noise and traffic were overwhelming. Knowing Phil wouldn't enjoy the long tedious journey from Heathrow on the Tube, Maeve decided to splurge on a taxi. Even that proved to be an ordeal, as the traffic was as thick as treacle.

Phil looked out the window of the cab with a horrified expression. 'What a holy mess. This is not the London I remember. And the flight with that horrid budget airline was an ordeal.' She shuddered. 'All those sweaty people crowding into a small space. As for the air hostesses… Such lack of style and class. Couldn't they at least do something with their hair? And where was the champagne? Things have really gone downhill since the last time I travelled.'

Maeve laughed. 'But then it was first class on Aer Lingus, I bet.'

'Of course. I begin to realise that Joe spending all that royalty money so we could travel in comfort was a very good idea.' Phil shivered and pulled her vintage Burberry mac tighter across her chest. 'It's a little chilly. Do you think we could ask the driver to turn up the heating?'

'I'll ask him.' Maeve leaned forward and knocked on the glass divider. 'Could you turn up the temperature a bit, please?' she asked.

The driver turned to glare at her. 'No.'

'Why not?'

'Because.' The lights changed and the car surged forward, throwing them roughly back against the seat.

'Charming,' Phil said. 'Where are the jolly London cabbies who used to call me "darling"?'

'All dead or gone to Spain, I suspect.'

The taxi finally pulled up outside Maeve's building. Phil looked up at the drab façade through the drizzle. 'This is it? You live here?' she asked, as if it were a campsite for refugees.

'Yes.' Maeve paid the driver without adding a tip, which earned her a nasty look and no help with their luggage, which they had to haul out of the boot themselves before he took off, cascading dirty water from the gutter over their shoes.

'Charming.' Phil took her suitcase from Maeve. 'I take it there is a lift?'

'Yes. If it works.'

It did to a fashion, cranking its way up to the fourth floor. The flat was cold and dark and smelled stale but Maeve turned up the thermostat, switched on the lights and hoped this would make Phil a little less glum. 'Here we are,' she chortled. 'My home sweet home.'

Phil glanced around the living room with the kitchenette in one corner and the IKEA sofa bed in another, and then into the tiny bedroom with its spartan furnishings and framed posters. 'Lovely.'

'No, it isn't,' Maeve sighed. 'But I don't spend much time here. It's only for sleeping and watching the telly. I had plans to look for something better, but now that life seems to be turning in a different direction, I'll just hang on to it for now. The rent is cheap for London, anyway.'

'A different direction?' Phil asked, looking excited. 'You mean you're coming back to Sandy Cove like we discussed on the plane? I thought you were just thinking about it.'

'I'm trying to decide. But if I do, I need to work out how.'

'Of course. I'd love to see you back at Willow House, but you have to make up your own mind.' Phil sat down on the sofa. 'This is comfy. I'll sleep here tonight?'

'It's grand. Roisin's slept here a few times when she's been here on a break. But why don't you take the bed?'

'No, this is perfectly fine,' Phil said. She jumped as her phone rang. 'Oh! Who could that be?'

'You answer and I'll make a cup of tea. Camomile as there is no milk, I'm afraid. No food either, but I'll run down to the corner shop and get a few things. I'll buy some sandwiches for lunch. What would you like?'

But Phil waved her away and answered her phone. 'Hello! How nice to hear from you. Yes, we've arrived and have just settled into Maeve's, eh, *cosy* flat. Lunch?' She checked her watch. 'But it's already twelve thirty.' She smiled as she listened to the person at the other end. 'In a restaurant in Mayfair? Oh, that would be lovely. So kind of you. We're in… I'll give you the address. Just a moment.' She looked at Maeve. 'What's the address?'

'Stockwell. Twenty-four Paradise Road,' Maeve replied, puzzled. Who was calling Phil in London?

'Paradise Road in Stockwell,' Phil said into the phone. 'But it's further from Paradise than I've ever been,' she said with a wink at Maeve, who laughed. Phil nodded. 'Exactly. This isn't too far for you? Oh, excellent. See you in a little while, then.' She hung up and smiled at Maeve. 'It seems I have a luncheon date.'

'Great. With whom? Some old friend?'

'No, a new friend.' Phil got up and got her bag from the front door. 'You know him. The charming man who came to tea.'

Maeve's jaw dropped. 'Who? Oliver Taylor? How did he know you were here? And where did he get your number?'

Phil's face turned a becoming shade of pink. 'Well… We've been chatting a little bit since we met. On that WhatsApp thing. Such fun.'

'But he's engaged to be married,' Maeve said sternly.

'I know that. But why can't we be friends all the same? It's nice for him to talk to someone of his own generation.'

'I suppose. But lunch? And when you've just arrived? We have a meeting with Stephen at four o'clock. You know he said he really likes the book, so I'd say he'll want to represent us.'

'I know. So you said.' Phil took her make-up case out of her bag. 'And we're meeting him at his office near Piccadilly Circus. I'll be there, don't worry. We're having lunch in Mayfair, so that isn't too far away.'

'And after that, we're meeting Betsy at her hotel in Bloomsbury. It's going to be a busy day.'

'I know. And very exciting.' Phil looked around. 'Is there a mirror anywhere?'

Maeve pointed at a door beside the bedroom. 'Bathroom.'

'Thanks. I'll just freshen up a bit.'

'I'll make the beds and then I'll pop down to the shop for a bit of lunch. Then I think I'll call into the office and catch up. Would it be okay if we met at Stephen's office just before four?'

'Perfect.' Phil went into the bathroom and appeared twenty minutes later, freshly made up, her hair arranged in a becoming chignon. She looked radiant and pretty and not a day over fifty. *How wonderful if she and Mr Taylor...* Maeve pushed the thought away. No, that would be too perfect. Belinda would never let him go, in any case. Nice that they were friends, though.

'Is this okay?' Phil asked, gesturing at her black trousers and cream polo neck.

'Lovely.'

Phil touched the gold hoop earrings. 'And these? Not too much?'

'Just right. You look classy and elegant and gorgeous.'

'Thank you.' Phil sighed and picked up her handbag. 'Pity I'm not twenty years younger.'

'Nobody would guess you weren't.'

'You're very kind.' Phil picked up her Burberry trench coat and put it on. 'I hope the rain has stopped.'

Maeve glanced out the window. 'It has. And a navy Mercedes has just pulled up. Must be your date.'

'Not a date, just a friend,' Phil corrected. 'I think he'll take me somewhere posh. I'll see you at Piccadilly. Isn't this exciting?' She kissed Maeve on the cheek and left in a cloud of Chanel No. 5, banging the door shut behind her.

The office was chaotic. As Maeve made her way down the area steps, she could hear shouting getting louder as she came in. Rufus was backing out of Ava's office, holding up his hands.

'Calm down, we'll sort it out.' He spotted Maeve and his face brightened. 'But here she is now. Hello, Maeve, sweetheart. You look fabulous. All bright-eyed and bushy-tailed.' He kissed her on both cheeks. 'Ava will be so happy to see you.'

Ava was nothing of the kind. She appeared in the doorway, her arms folded, glaring at Maeve. 'So here's the prodigal home at last. But don't expect a bloody fatted calf. I'm up to my eyebrows in clients. So there's plenty to get your teeth into.' She shot a sour glance at Rufus. 'You can give her that new client in Notting Hill. Then you can take over the designs of the restaurant in Chelsea. That'll keep you on your toes.'

'I couldn't be more on my toes if I were a prima ballerina,' Rufus shot back. 'But okay, whatever. I wish you would occasionally say no to clients, though. But that doesn't seem to exist in your vocabulary.'

'Damn right it doesn't. "No" is a very expensive word. Welcome back, Maeve. Sorry about the aggro, but you know how it is.' Ava turned and went back into her office, banging the door shut. Then she opened it again. 'Rufus, the new girl took over Maeve's office. Could you share yours with Maeve for now?'

Rufus rolled his eyes. 'I'll take out my magic shoehorn and squeeze her in.'

'Great.' Ava disappeared.

Maeve stared at Rufus. 'What's biting her?'

Rufus shrugged. 'The usual. Plus her mother-in-law is staying with them at the moment, and both the daughters need to have their teeth fixed, which is costing the national budget of Argentina. Her husband got written out of the soap opera he was in and is now on the dole – but hasn't given up his penchant for handmade shirts from Bond Street. Then there's the rest. The usual nitty-gritty of school fees and uniforms and blah, blah, blah. God, I'm happy to see you.' He put his arm around her and gave her a tight squeeze.

'Me too, Rufe.' Maeve extracted herself from his embrace. 'What about the new girl, whatshername – Mona?'

Rufus ushered Maeve into his office and pulled out a chair. 'Monica. She's brilliant. But Ava keeps taking on new jobs, so we're really stretched. If we could only get a really big job, like a hotel or some billionaire's new London pad, we could slow down. But no such luck. Maybe after the feature in *Tatler* next month. But this new client of yours seems nice. I bet you're dying to get stuck into that one.'

'Well, it sounds great, but I haven't seen it in detail yet. I'll have a look and draw up a plan. And we have the trade fair the week after next.' Maeve sighed and sat down. How on earth was she going to leave the firm? She looked around Rufus' office. It wasn't the tight cubbyhole he had pretended, but a bright, airy room with fawn grass cloth wallpaper and white sheer curtains pulled across the windows, hiding the view of the rubbish bins and the dreary little courtyard. His desk was an old table painted a distressed white, and the chairs were white with light-blue upholstery. A rug in hues of blue and green lay on the floor, and the walls were hung with posters from various art galleries. The whole effect gave a feeling of tranquillity and peace. Maeve breathed in the lavender scent from a candle on the desk and relaxed for the first time since she had arrived. 'This room is heavenly. Can I stay here and work with you?'

Rufus looked surprised. 'Of course. But I thought you liked your own space.'

'That was a long time ago. Or seems like a long time. I'm a different person now.'

He peered at her. 'Yes, you are. You look… serene.' He sat down on the other side of the desk and continued scrutinising her face. 'You've put on a little weight, which suits you. And your cheeks are rosy, you have freckles on your nose and your eyes are shining.' He leaned forward. 'You're in love.'

Maeve felt her cheeks flush. 'Yes. I think so. But not only with a man. I think I'm in love with a place, and a whole new way of seeing the world. It's been such a strange experience to be there in Sandy Cove, walking on the beach, collecting seashells, reconnecting with the locals. It has opened my eyes to the small things in life.'

'"To see a world in a grain of sand and heaven in a wild flower,"' Rufus quoted.

'Oh, that's beautiful. Who wrote that?'

'William Blake. Nineteenth century poet. It goes on: "Hold infinity in the palm of your hand and eternity in an hour."' Rufus waved his hand. 'And on and on. It's a lovely poem.'

'Yes. And those lines really sum up my feelings. When I'm there. In Sandy Cove. But then…'

'Then you come here and you get an adrenaline rush from the big city and the challenge of work and the fun of creating homes for people, even if they're rich bitches.' Rufus grinned. 'I do, anyway.'

'I can see that.'

Rufus turned on his laptop. 'But now we have to get down to the nitty-gritty.' He handed a piece of paper to Maeve. 'These are the jobs I've covered for you while you were away. Most of them are nearly finished, except for the house in Holland Street. I had to spend a whole day humouring that barracuda Belinda to make her go back the original plans. But now it's all painted and furnished downstairs, the carpets have been laid and the beds should have been delivered this morning. Maybe you could pop over there and make sure it's all done? The wedding is in three weeks and they want to move in straight away before they go on their honeymoon in the Seychelles.' Rufus drew breath. 'Could you also have a word with Monica to tell her you're back, and see if she's available for some of the new clients?'

Maeve nodded, her mind getting back on track with work. Rufus was right; there was an addictive buzz in London and in this line of work that would be hard to give up.

'Okay,' she said, when she had checked the list. 'That looks grand. I'll go and take a look at Holland Street and then get back here and we'll go through the new assignments. Then I have an appointment at four, so have to leave early. What else is happening? Anything exciting?'

'Yes. Lots of things. But I'll tell you later, when you get back.' He made a shooing gesture. 'Go on, get out of here. I need a little peace to work on the trade fair stand and what theme we're going to go for.'

Maeve laughed and got up. 'Okay. I'll leave you alone. But when I get back, we'll have to get stuck in.' She glanced at the list Rufus had given her and thought of all the jobs she had done during the past year, all the homes she had created, the difficult clients she had tamed, the workmen and shop assistants who had become her friends, and the buzz of deadlines and the race to finish on time. That was what had landed her in hospital with panic attacks, sending her to Sandy Cove and Phil. *And to Paschal.* His beautiful brown eyes swam before her, his lovely smile, his hands caressing her… Could she give that up for the excitement of her career in London? She blinked and focused her eyes on Rufus, who had forgotten all about her as he worked on the designs on his computer. She got up and tied the belt of her trench coat. 'I'm off now. See you later.'

Rufus nodded. 'Good luck with the coddiwomple.'

'What?'

He laughed. 'Don't look so suspicious. It's old English slang meaning to travel purposely toward a vague destination. Isn't that what you're doing?'

Maeve sighed. 'Yeah, I suppose so. But once I get there, it won't be vague any more.'

'Fingers crossed.'

'And everything else,' Maeve said, with a strange foreboding that soon things would come to a head. Was she ready to face it?

Chapter Twenty-Six

In the meantime, Phil was having a wonderful time. Oliver had not taken her for lunch at an expensive restaurant in Mayfair but had changed his mind. They had ended up in Nostalgia Café in Soho, where they served sausages and chips and baked beans, and an old-fashioned jukebox played sixties music.

They sat on spindly chairs at a Formica table and sipped Coca-Cola, listened to the Rolling Stones' greatest hits and talked. *So much to talk about,* Phil thought, as she told him about her life, the cities she had lived in and the movies, music, fashion and books she had loved. Oliver, in turn, talked about his own youth and how he had been a rebel at university: grown his hair long, smoked pot and lived in a commune, much to the horror of his bourgeois parents, who had hoped he'd become an accountant like his father. Oliver had dropped out of university and travelled to India in a Volkswagen van with a group of friends. He had returned after a year and taken a business course, met Marjorie – who was to become his wife – and started a business in electronics that had grown and grown and made him very wealthy.

'Seems I have knack for making money,' Oliver said, with an apologetic smile. 'I tried to pretend I was from a working-class family but my accent gave me away. My wife used to laugh at that. She was from a titled but poor family and grew up in a dilapidated manor house in Norfolk. Her father thought a good horse was more important than a new roof. I loved them. And her. You would have too. Everyone did. She was…' He stopped and coughed. 'Sorry. Can't really talk about that.'

'How long ago did she pass away?'

'Two years. Still hard.'

Phil put her hand on his arm. 'I know. It's only a year for me. It's as if it happened yesterday. I cope well most of the time, but then sometimes it hits me like a sledgehammer.'

He nodded. 'Yes. Exactly. And then there's the loneliness.'

'I know. Even when there are people around, you still feel lonely. I think…' She paused. 'The most important thing is to learn to be alone without being lonely. That's my greatest challenge. And I'll get there. One day.' She focused on Oliver. 'But you're getting married again, I hear?'

He looked at his plate. 'Yes.'

'But that must make you happy.'

'Yes of course. Very happy. But…'

'But?' Phil said, alarmed. 'There's a "but"? Is it because you're worried she's only doing it for your money?' Phil leaned forward. 'Much younger wives can be dangerous, you know. In so many ways.'

Oliver laughed. 'No, she can't get her hands on my money. There'll be a pre-nup, and she knows Stephen will inherit most of my estate.' He smiled. 'So she won't try to kill me, in any case. The "but" is just about our difference in age. Oh, she's fun and beautiful and sexy and all that. But after the lights are out and we've had – *you know* – I want to talk. About life and the meaning of it and such. She just yawns and picks up a magazine, or rolls over and goes to sleep.'

'But she's great in bed?' Phil asked, despite herself.

He blushed. 'Wonderful. But sometimes I just want a cuddle. And—' he eyed his empty plate '—to eat sausages and chips and HP sauce.' Looking at her with his twinkly blue eyes, he laughed. 'I'm a dinosaur from the sixties, so shoot me.'

'Then they'll have to shoot me too.' Phil smiled as the music changed from the Rolling Stones to Elvis. 'Oh, listen to this song. "Are You Lonesome Tonight". I used to play that whenever I had broken up with a boy, and cry my heart out.'

'And I used to listen to Tom Jones and "I'll Never Fall in Love Again".'

'Such happy times,' Phil murmured. 'Even when they were sad.'

His eyes were tender as he looked at her. 'We didn't know real sadness then, did we?' He took her hand. 'You know what? I think we can dance to this tune. Plenty of room by the jukebox.'

Phil nodded and got up. Oliver put his arm around her waist and together they floated across the floor in a perfect, slow foxtrot. Forgetting all the people in the restaurant, Phil closed her eyes as she felt his arm around her and pretended just for a moment that she was dancing with Joe, the way they used to. She opened them and saw that Oliver's eyes were also closed, and it touched her more than if he had shed tears. She felt a stab of guilt, as if she was being unfaithful to Joe – or his memory. It was too soon. She couldn't feel anything but sympathy for this nice, elegant man she was dancing with. Joe was still here, all around her and in her heart. She looked at Oliver and knew he could guess her thoughts and that he understood. He had been there too, and maybe still was.

Then the music changed to Chubby Checker and 'Let's Twist Again' and they laughed and pulled apart and did the twist as if they were teenagers. Eventually, Phil had to stop to catch her breath, while there was a round of applause from the other customers.

Oliver smiled and bowed. 'Pity we had to stop. I think they like us.'

'But my old knees are complaining,' Phil said and laughed.

'Mine too,' Oliver confessed. He took her hand and led her back to the table, and ordered a knickerbocker glory for them both. They dug into the concoction of ice cream, whipped cream and chocolate sauce, laughing again at their antics, and Phil suddenly felt that it was possible to feel young and carefree, whatever your age.

When it was time to leave, Phil kissed him on the cheek. 'Thank you, Oliver. This was the best lunch I've had in a long time.'

He held her hand for a moment. 'I can't tell you how much I've enjoyed it. I hope we can do this again sometime.'

'I'll let you know if I come back to London. In the meantime, let's keep chatting on our app.'

'Do you want me to drive you to wherever you're going?'

'No, thank you. I'll try the Tube. Must learn to manage on my own, you know.'

'Without being lonely.'

'Exactly.'

She walked away from the restaurant feeling, for the first time in over a year, a flash of pure joy. Would they meet again? She sent a brief prayer to one of her favourite saints and continued to the Tube station with more pep in her step than ever before.

*

After checking on the Holland Street house, where everything was in order, Maeve went back to the office and sorted out her files and client lists. Rufus was out on a job, but Monica, the now not-so-new girl, was a huge help with the invoices, and they worked together at Rufus' desk until it was time for Maeve to leave for the appointment with Stephen at his office.

As she walked the short distance from the Tube station, she breathed in that special smell of London: petrol fumes laced with spicy food from the many ethnic restaurants, freshly made coffee and the odd whiff of perfume from the open door of a beauty salon. All around her, people were hurrying to appointments and meetings, or just heading home after a long day. The noise of the traffic was deafening and the mix of languages from animated conversations added to the buzz of the city that always made her heart beat a little faster. *Do I really want to leave all this?* she wondered, as she ran across the street just before the lights changed. The pulse of this vibrant city was intoxicating and addictive. The stress had made her ill, but what would the bucolic life of a small village do to her?

She shook her head to rid her mind of the problem. One step at a time. Right now it was all about Phil and her writing. The rest could wait.

Phil was sitting in the gleaming chrome and glass entrance hall of the literary agency. She looked relaxed and happy, with a new sparkle in her eyes. 'Hi, there. I got here a bit early. I came on the Tube, which wasn't too bad actually.'

'The Tube! I'm impressed. Did you have a nice lunch with Oliver?'

'It was fun. We ended up in this amazing café place where they played our kind of music on a jukebox. Great craic.'

'Sounds fabulous. Are you ready for the meeting?'

Phil nodded. 'Yes. If Stephen is even half as charming as his father, it'd be a great partnership.'

'I'm afraid you might be disappointed,' Maeve said glumly, and pressed the button for the lift.

But Stephen had switched on the charm big-time, greeting them with a huge smile and kisses on the cheeks, followed by tea and muffins in his plush office. Phil beamed and sat down, tucking into the muffins as if she hadn't seen food for a week. 'How lovely,' she said, between bites. 'I knew you'd give us a wonderful welcome. Didn't I say that, Maeve?'

'Yes you did,' Maeve replied, trying to avoid Stephen's flirtatious eyes. Sitting beside her, he pressed his knee lightly against hers, which made her stiffen. This was a business meeting. Why couldn't he be more professional? Their eyes met briefly and all she could see was a glint of mischief. He even had the nerve to wink at her. She subtly shuffled away from him.

'I had lunch with your father,' Phil continued. 'Such fun.'

'I'm sure he was happy to have lunch with you,' Stephen remarked. 'He loves attractive women. Just like me.'

Maeve squirmed and nibbled on a muffin. She cleared her throat. 'Let's get down to business. You liked the book?'

Stephen straightened up. 'Yes, very much. Despite not wanting to handle more romance, we all felt that this one is different. It'll sell very well, we feel. That's why I want to suggest we go with another publisher, as Red Hot House isn't big enough for us.'

'Excuse me,' Maeve cut in. 'Aren't we getting ahead of ourselves here? I think we need to discuss your terms, and the kind of agreement Phil might be signing with you.'

Stephen's smile was stiff. 'Of course. Sorry. I rushed ahead there. But only because I'm so anxious to go ahead and get you the very best deal.' He moved his leg closer to Maeve's again, but she didn't know how to deal with it. It was important to appear friendly, or Phil would lose out.

'And what is the agreement?' Phil asked.

He cleared his throat. 'My terms are the same as most agents. I take fifteen per cent of whatever you earn in the UK, and then twenty per cent for any foreign rights and sales. That's because I have to employ a sub-agent for those. Those are the basic terms.'

'What if you and Phil fall out and she wants to leave?' Maeve enquired, finally easing away from his leg.

'She'll just give me thirty days' notice and the right to represent her for any work that I might have submitted to publishers. And of course, the fifteen per cent of any book deals before that.'

Phil nodded. 'But ultimately, I decide which publisher to sign with?'

Stephen smiled. 'Of course. The author decides where they want to go.'

'Thank you.' Phil glanced at Maeve then back at Stephen. 'That's fine. I'll accept your offer to represent me.'

'But…' Maeve started, but was silenced by Phil's stern look. 'Fine.' She shrugged. 'It's just business anyway,' she muttered to herself.

'Exactly,' Stephen filled in. 'It's not as if we're going to have a love affair or anything, is it?'

Maeve was about to say something cutting, but stopped herself. What was the point? Plus, she didn't want to spoil this for Phil.

Phil finished her tea. 'Excellent. So if we could sign the agreement, we'll be off. We have another appointment this afternoon, and then I will need to put my feet up after this very hectic day.'

Stephen took a bunch of papers and handed them to Phil. 'You might like to read through this before you sign.'

Phil laughed. 'Nonsense. I don't like to read a lot of bumph. Give me a pen and I'll sign.'

Maeve snatched the contract from Phil. 'We'll go through this and call you tomorrow.'

'But…' Phil protested.

Maeve stuffed the contract into her bag. 'We have to think about this very carefully, Phil. There's no rush.'

'I suppose,' Phil agreed, looking deflated.

'I'll call you tomorrow morning, Stephen.' Maeve got up, wanting to get out of there. 'We have another appointment in half an hour, so I'm afraid we have to leave.'

'I need to use the ladies' before we go,' Phil said, gathering up her coat and bag.

Stephen stood and opened the door. 'Down the corridor. First door on the left.'

When Phil had gone, Maeve was left standing by the exit, poised to leave. 'Nice office,' she remarked.

'Yes.' Stephen touched her arm. 'I was hoping you might be free for dinner tonight.'

Maeve looked coolly at him, less attracted with every minute. 'I'm afraid not.'

He looked suddenly annoyed. 'I thought that was part of the deal?'

Maeve frowned. 'What deal? You mean you'll only represent my aunt if I… go on a date with you tonight?'

'Not quite. I just thought it'd be nice to catch up, now that you're back.'

'But we have that date in December. The premiere, remember?'

He smiled broadly. 'Oh, yes, that. It'll be an exciting evening. But I thought that tonight, we'd be more… casual, if you see what I mean.' There was a leery look in his eyes Maeve didn't like. Did he think she was easy? He stepped closer. 'We could have dinner somewhere nice, and then maybe…'

'Maybe what?' She stepped away.

'Oh, we could go on somewhere. Like my flat.'

Maeve stiffened. 'I think you're moving a bit too fast, Stephen. That's not what…' She stopped, trying to find a way to put him off as politely as she could. 'I'm not…'

'That kind of girl?' he filled in, grinning. 'Isn't that a little old-fashioned? I've heard that Irish women are…'

He suddenly didn't look so handsome any more; nor did his posh accent impress her like it had in the beginning. Maeve pulled herself up and gave him a steely look. 'I have no idea what you've heard, but I'm afraid I'm going to have to decline. And you can forget about me coming to the premiere, too.'

'What?' He stared at her. 'You're not coming? Does this mean what I think it means?'

'Yes. I don't want to go on any kind of date with you,' Maeve replied stiffly. 'I don't think we hit it off, actually.'

'I see.' His eyes narrowed. 'Fine. I get the point.'

'Good.' She smiled stiffly at him and left to join Phil, who had just emerged from the ladies'. 'Bye, Stephen. We'll talk tomorrow. Come on, Phil.'

'She's in a hurry. Bye for now,' Phil said, waving goodbye. 'Thanks for tea and all the—'

'Goodbye,' Stephen snapped, slamming the door.

'What was that all about?' Phil asked in the lift. 'Is he cross with you? But I thought he was flirting with you during the meeting.'

Maeve shrugged. 'Yeah, he was coming on to me all right. And then he got annoyed when I said no to his invitation to dinner and entertainment afterwards, if you see what I mean.'

'How unprofessional. But never mind. The main thing is that I have an agent who's interested in representing me. Isn't that terrific?'

'Fabulous,' Maeve muttered, wondering if their meeting with Betsy Malone would turn out to be some other kind of disaster. It was that kind of day.

Chapter Twenty-Seven

Betsy Malone was waiting for them in the hotel lobby. Dressed in wide black trousers and a matching velvet top, she was tall and rangy with short grey hair and a pair of bright red spectacles on her straight nose. She looked at them with a critical eye before she held out her hand and gave Maeve a bone-crushing handshake. As she shook Phil's hand in a similar fashion, Phil winced and said, 'Hello,' in a small voice.

Betsy nodded and hitched her large tote bag higher on her shoulder. 'Let's go into the fancy space they call the guest living room. There's nobody there.'

'She's very, eh, powerful,' Phil whispered as they followed Betsy into the living room, which would have been inviting if it were not for the loud wallpaper.

'I know what you mean. She's a little intimidating,' Maeve whispered back.

Phil nodded, smiling at Betsy when they all settled on the couch in front of the fireplace. 'Wow, this is really plush,' she remarked.

Betsy extracted some papers and a mobile phone from her bag. 'Yeah, it's great, except for the wallpaper.'

Maeve laughed. 'Yes it's a bit overwhelming. I think they thought William Morris but got some kind of Alice in Wonderland nightmare instead.'

'She's an interior designer,' Phil said to Betsy.

'Okay,' Betsy replied. 'But let's go straight to why we're here. Sorry, I'm from New York. We don't do small talk.'

'Of course.' Maeve cleared her throat. 'So, straight to business, then. We've just seen an agent who has agreed to represent us.'

Betsy frowned. 'Who's the agent?'

'Stephen Taylor,' Maeve replied.

'Stephen Taylor?' Betsy raised one of her black eyebrows. 'Seriously?'

'Yes,' Phil said. 'But we haven't—'

'He seems to think Red Hot House is too small for this book,' Maeve cut in with a warning glance at Phil. 'He said something about submitting to bigger publishers.'

Betsy's eyes narrowed. 'Yeah, right. Good luck with that. So… Stephen Taylor, eh? The big literary agency?'

Maeve bristled. 'That's the one. You don't believe us?'

'Sure I do. Why would you make something like that up?' Betsy paused. 'Joe didn't have an agent. Being a lawyer, he could go through the contract himself. And we worked very closely together on everything, including foreign rights, which we didn't succeed in getting for him – but I think we can for you. Your writing is slightly different and it will have even more appeal than Joe's. We have an incredible editor who has just started and she's dying to work on the book. We would also organise a book tour across America for you, Philomena, as I think you should be Fanny's face, so to speak. You look very like the photo on her website, give or take a decade or two.'

Phil's eyes sparkled. 'Oh, that sounds very exciting.'

'I think you'd be fabulous on TV, actually,' Betsy continued. 'Inspirational for older women out there.'

Phil blushed. 'That's very sweet of you.'

'I'm not sweet, I'm telling the truth. So,' Betsy continued, shooting a steely look at Maeve. 'I'm upping my advance to double of what I said before, which was…' She frowned. 'What was it again?'

'Thirty thousand dollars.' Maeve looked at Betsy with an innocent air. 'That's what you said to me, in any case.'

'Did I? Okay, then. If that's what I said, the new deal is sixty thousand, plus travel expenses for the book tour, of course. But then we want full rights.'

Phil nodded, looking determined. 'I accept.'

'What?!' Maeve exclaimed. 'Are you mad, Phil? You have to speak to your agent first, before you—'

'I don't have an agent,' Phil snapped. She turned to Betsy. 'We didn't lie when we said Stephen wants to represent me, but I haven't signed a contract with him yet. I wanted to sign there and then, but Maeve said no because she thought I should read the contract through first. And she was right. But I have been thinking about it… I feel I just want to go with Betsy, and not have an agent at all.'

Betsy and Maeve looked at each other in silence.

Maeve touched Phil's arm. 'Is that really what you want?'

Phil looked close to tears. 'Yes,' she whispered. 'I want to work with Betsy like Joe did.' She looked at Betsy, her eyes glistening. 'I got carried away in Stephen Taylor's office and I've changed my mind. I love the idea of continuing Joe's work, taking up his mantle and keeping in touch with his readers. I feel that this was the huge gift he left me, even if it took a long time to find it. It will keep me connected to him. I want to do him proud – he would want me to work with Betsy, not sell my soul and chase the money. I don't want to be rich, I just want to be… solvent. To have enough to do the repairs to my lovely house, so I can keep living there. That's what Joe would have wanted me to do. That's all.'

Maeve suddenly felt her own eyes sting. How right Phil was. She was living in the most beautiful place, surrounded by kind friends and caring neighbours. All she needed was something to keep her busy and a little extra cash to repair the house she loved. She cleared her throat. 'Okay,' she said, turning to Betsy, who was dabbing at her eyes with a tissue. 'We accept your very generous offer and we'll tell Stephen Taylor to go to… I mean, that we don't need him.'

'And we can ask a lawyer to go through your contract,' Phil cut in.

'Great.' Betsy blew her nose. 'I sent the contract already, but read it through before you sign. Then we can get started on the editing.' She patted Phil on the arm. 'Thank you. You're wonderful.'

'So are you.' Phil leaned over and kissed Betsy on the cheek. 'I'm not surprised Joe liked you so much.'

Betsy smiled and patted Phil's cheek. 'We were a team.' She got up. 'Okay, gang. We have it all sorted. I have to go. Talk to you later. Bye, Maeve. Nice to meet you, too.'

When she had left, Phil and Maeve grinned at each other. 'We did it,' Maeve chuckled. 'And got more money.'

Phil beamed. 'And we don't have to share it with that agent. I mean, Stephen. I liked him at first, but then after he snapped at you… I can't believe he's Oliver's son. I hope you're not disappointed.'

Maeve shook her head. 'Not at all. You're so right. Life's too short to be greedy. And I think you'll love working with Betsy and her crew. A very happy ending, I feel.'

'For me, yes. But what about you? What are you going to do?'

Maeve shrugged. 'Stay here, for now. I have to give Ava at least a month's notice if I decide to leave.'

'If?' Phil frowned. 'You mean you haven't decided?'

Maeve sighed. 'No. I'm afraid to let go of all I have here, but at the same time worried that I'll lose something more important if I stay.'

Phil nodded. 'Either way, you have to give something up. You're at a very important crossroads.' She put her hand on Maeve's cheek. 'Try not to think too much. Things will fall into place and work out for the best. I'm sure of it.'

Maeve sighed. 'I wish I could believe that.'

When they got back to the flat, Maeve ordered Chinese takeaway for dinner and sat down at the table in the kitchen to check her messages. Before she could look them up, the phone pinged with a text from Paschal, who wanted to FaceTime. Maeve sighed, knowing she didn't look her best, but turned on the video anyway. She smiled as Paschal's face appeared. 'Hi, handsome.'

'Hello from the bog of beyond,' he replied, and smiled that sweet smile that always made her weak at the knees. 'How are things in the big smoke?'

'Not too bad. But I miss you like crazy. We've had a meeting with a literary agent who was dying to have Phil, but we said no. Then we met scary Betsy the publisher, who despite being very intimidating and probably smoking forty a day, turned out to be a real charmer. But who could resist Phil's sweet face?'

He laughed. 'Nobody could.' He paused. 'So… How's everything else?'

'I'm not sure.' Maeve sighed, knowing what he wanted to hear. 'I don't know what to say to you right now, Paschal. I'm so confused and scared. But I will let you know when I come to a decision.'

'I hope you'll manage that very soon.'

'I'm thinking about it.' Maeve smiled reassuringly. 'How are you? The shop behaving itself?'

'It's been a bit mad to be honest,' he replied. 'Loads of tourists one day, none the next. But I've sold all the Aran jumpers, and the woolly hats with the pompoms are flying off the shelves. I have only two left. Not to mention the shillelaghs. The Yanks go mad for those, even when I tell them they're just walking sticks and nothing special.' He suddenly laughed. 'And you know what? I had to pose in one of the jumpers and a hat in front of Mad Brendan's donkey, who had happened to stroll by. "So ethnic!" they squealed, snapping away and then pressing dollar bills in my hand before they took off in their bus. Jesus, girl, I think I'll give up university and just become a local attraction instead.'

Maeve giggled. 'You'd make a fortune.'

'Yes, and just imagine what the two of us could do. We could live in the cottage and wear peasant clothes. You'd look great with a shawl on your head. And we'd go "top of the mornin' to you, kind sir, to be sure, to be sure". Then we could charge for all the photos and serve tea and brack. What do you say?'

'Are you proposing to me, Paschal O'Sullivan?'

'Could be, girl.' He paused and winked, and Maeve could hear the faint roar of the ocean in the distance and the crackling of the fire in his cosy living room. She was instantly transported to Sandy Cove and the cottage. 'Oh, Paschal,' she whispered, and touched the screen, as if she could feel and smell him. 'I want to be with you, but I'm scared to take that final leap.'

'You need to get out of there.'

'I know.'

'So do it.'

'I would, if…' She stopped. 'There is only one little problem. What am I going to live on if I quit my job?'

'There are plenty of jobs over here. You could look for something in Cork city and commute like me. We could get a bigger flat and…'

'You make it sound so easy.' How could she explain to him how hard it would be to give up everything she had worked for? And London, the city she had come to love. 'I'll think about it,' she said, trying to sound confident.

'Good. I'll say good night now, as you seem very tired. Let me know if and when you're coming back. I won't call you again,' he added. 'You have to figure this out on your own. And…' He paused. 'If you're not going to come back, I think we need to end whatever we have started.'

Maeve felt a jolt of fear and sadness. He didn't sound angry, just resigned and ready to face the heartbreak of losing her. 'I know,' she whispered. 'There will be no compromise. I'll call you when I know. Bye for now, Paschal. I'm sorry if…'

But he had hung up, leaving her racked with guilt about the pain she was causing him. And herself. She hung up, tears stinging her eyes, and slowly got up and joined Phil, who was setting up the Chinese takeaway that had just arrived on the coffee table.

She looked up. 'I thought we could watch the news while we eat.'

'Great.' Maeve sank down onto the couch.

Phil shot her a look of concern. 'Are you all right?'

Maeve sighed. 'Yes. It's just… Paschal and everything.'

'It must be hard for you. Such a dilemma. You have to do whatever is right for you, or you'll regret it.'

'I know.' Maeve tried to pull herself together. 'But right now, back to business. I have to call Stephen to tell him what we've decided. '

'I tried his number just now. I thought I'd save you the trouble.' Phil joined her on the couch. 'But he wasn't available and I just got his voicemail. So instead of asking him to call me back, I thought we could send him a text.'

'Okay. Good idea.'

'But what should we say?'

Maeve smiled mischievously. She took the phone from Phil and started typing.

'What are you writing?' Phil asked, craning her neck to see.

'I'll read it to you. "Dear Stephen, thank you for reading our book and for the offer to represent us. But I'm afraid you are not the right agent for us, so we have decided to pass. We wish you the best of luck with your agency. Best wishes, Maeve and Philomena."' She looked at Phil. 'Was that okay?'

Phil giggled. 'Perfect.'

'I bet he has never been turned down like that before. Especially by text. That'll teach him not to hit on women during business meetings.'

After a moment, the phone pinged and Phil looked at the screen. 'He replied.'

'Oh? What did he say?'

Phil held out the phone. 'Here. Read it.'

Maeve peered at the phone, where it said: *Thank you for letting me know. You've just made the worst decision of your very short writing career. You'll regret it when that second-rate publisher fails to sell your books. Sincerely, S T.*

'He's in a major snot.'

Phil shook her head. 'How on earth can he possibly be Oliver's son?'

'Maybe he went to a posh boarding school where he learnt to behave like a superior little shit? I believe that's quite common among such men.'

'So sad for Oliver. I'll get some forks and glasses.' Phil walked to the kitchenette and rummaged around in the drawers. 'I'll bring a jug of water too,' she said.

'Brilliant. Thanks, Phil.' Too tired to move, Maeve was grateful for Phil's energy and enthusiasm. Her company was like a comforting blanket, just like when, years ago, she had soothed any upsets with her wise words and a cup of steaming cocoa. But she was going home tomorrow, while Maeve stayed behind to sort out her own life.

Even if she decided to leave, she might have to stay on for a couple of months before Ava found a replacement designer. But what about that new client with the office in Covent Garden? It had seemed like the kind of project she'd love. It might lead to other exciting jobs, too. Was this really the right time to leave? The dilemma seemed impossible to solve. Giving up her job seemed such a huge upheaval – but the thought of breaking up with Paschal was even harder. Could she burn all her bridges for him? How was she going to feel if she gave up everything for a life in a very remote part of Ireland? Would being in love be enough to make it right? So many questions that needed answers. But she knew one thing. Paschal would always stand by her. She trusted him completely.

There was only one problem. She didn't trust herself.

Chapter Twenty-Eight

In the end, it was easy. When Maeve arrived at the office the next day, Ava was on the warpath, standing like an angry statue, her arms folded, in the doorway of Rufus' office. She checked her watch with a raised eyebrow. 'Nine fifteen? Don't tell me, the Tube broke down.'

Maeve shrugged off her wet raincoat. 'No, I overslept. Sorry.'

'Have you gone through the stuff about the trade fair?' Ava asked. 'I emailed it to you last night. And also the news that Oliver Taylor's selling the house, so now we have to do a house doctor job on it.'

Maeve's jaw dropped. 'Are you serious? Why?'

Ava shrugged. 'No idea. Maybe Belinda or whatever her name is has changed her mind and wants a different house. She might have discovered that Holland Street isn't as trendy as she thought. What Lola wants Lola gets, as the song goes.'

'Maybe,' Maeve mumbled. 'Sounds very typical of her.'

'But whatever,' Ava breezed on. 'He's a decent old chap and has said he'll pay the last of bills, and he's given us the house doctoring job, so maybe you could get on that straight away? And perhaps explain to me why you don't check your emails? Now that you're back, I need you to be on the ball. So many new clients, the trade fair and all those outstanding projects...'

Emboldened by a sudden surge of anger, Maeve glared at Ava. 'I checked my emails around seven last night. Then I spent the rest of the evening with my aunt and we watched a movie on TV. A lovely romantic comedy that made us feel good after a long day. If you want me to work overtime, you'll have to pay me accordingly.'

Ava looked shocked. 'What do you mean? It was only nine o'clock when I sent those things. You usually…'

'Yeah, I used to work late at night, that's true. But that was before I had a life. Now I do, and I'm going back to it as soon as I can.'

'Back?' Ava exclaimed, her voice in falsetto. 'Back to the sticks in… Ireland?'

Maeve nodded. 'Yes,' she said, with more determination than she felt. A cold ripple of fear ran up her spine. *What am I doing?* she thought. *What am I going to do for work if I leave my job for good?*

'Why?'

Ava's tone made Maeve even more determined. *Feck this*, she thought. *I can't stay here and be dictated to like this.* She fixed Ava's eyes with a cold stare. 'Because, dearest Ava, I'm fed up.'

'Of what? You love this job… And you're bloody good at it,' she ended, as if it pained her to admit it.

Maeve dropped her wet raincoat on the floor. 'I know I am. And I did love it. But then I had so many jobs going I didn't have time to think, let alone use any of the creativity that I used to thrive on.' She sighed. 'I have nothing against you personally, Ava, but I'm tired of marching to the beat of your drum. I know you're pretty squeezed financially because of your family life but I don't see why I, or anyone else here, should have to work themselves into the ground to pay for your daughters' braces and school fees. Or keep your husband in expensive shirts.'

Ava didn't reply. She stood there, her hair and clothes a picture of glossy perfection, as if nothing could pierce her armour.

'Why can't they go to a state school and put up with their crooked teeth?' Maeve said defiantly. 'And maybe your husband could come in here and help out? I mean, if he has nothing better to do than lie on the couch watching soaps all day long.' She picked up her coat, afraid to meet Ava's eyes. She knew she had gone too far.

Ava moved aside to let Maeve pass. 'You know what, Maeve?'

Maeve froze. 'Yes?'

'I'm going to let you go.'

'Go where?'

'Out of here. You're fired, to put it bluntly.'

'Oh, I…' Maeve struggled to find the words. 'Thank you. I mean… God, I'm sorry, Ava, I didn't mean to…'

Ava sighed, looking suddenly deflated. 'I know. It's been hell here for the past couple of months. I've been a real bitch to work for, I know that too. As you said, I'm squeezed, both financially and emotionally. But I shouldn't have tried to make others pay for that. So I apologise, too.' She put her hand on Maeve's shoulder. 'I have to confess, I'm jealous. You came back from Ireland glowing with happiness. I knew then I'd lost you, and that you'd probably fallen for some rough and handsome fisherman in the west. And now you'll go back there and live a simple but happy life with someone you love. Is that it?'

Maeve laughed. 'Not quite. Ireland isn't some backward country inhabited by peasants. That was two hundred years ago. But whatever. Yeah, it's the simple life I didn't know I wanted until I lived it for a short while. And yes, I'm in love,' she added, not being able to hold it in any more. 'And he's a university lecturer in marine biology, not a fisherman, but that's not important.'

'Oh.' Ava looked blankly at Maeve.

'I'll stay another week to tidy things up and do the house doctor job. And then Monica can take over from me, as she is already in my office.'

'Thank you.' Ava smiled. 'I'm sorry it had to end like this. But let's not part on a bad note. Why don't we go out for a drink tonight after work?'

'I'd love that.'

'Fabulous.' Ava looked suddenly a lot brighter. 'You know what? You've given me a great idea. I'm going to haul in that sorry excuse for a man and get him to work.'

'Who? Rufus?'

'No. My husband. Never thought about it before, but he could be a huge asset to the firm. Not great at designs, but he's handsome and nice and could be a great filter when those women get stroppy. And at the trade fair, too. Why didn't I think of that before? See you later, darling.'

Dizzy with relief, Maeve went into Rufus' office and sat down at the desk, her knees like jelly. What had just happened? Had she really given up a job she had loved for a new life in a small village back in Ireland? She nodded, smiling, her shoulders relaxing and a warm feeling of happiness spreading from her toes all the way up to her face. It was true. It was happening. And… A thought suddenly hit her. She could start her own firm in Ireland! It might even be a better choice. There would be less competition, and she could start small and build it up slowly. She stretched her back and rolled her shoulders, then turned on her laptop, her head full of ideas. Her life was finally changing for the better.

Chapter Twenty-Nine

When Phil heard the news later that evening, she threw her arms around Maeve. 'Oh, darling, I'm so pleased. I know losing your job must be hard, but now everything will be much better, you'll see. How do you feel?'

Maeve laughed and pulled out of the embrace. 'I feel scared. This is a huge change for me. And I'm broke and have nothing to live on, except a few thousand in the bank I managed to put away so I could buy a flat in London – which would have taken, like, twenty years considering how pricey everything is around here.'

'If your problems are only financial, you have nothing to worry about, Joe used to say.'

'Yeah, that's grand when you're not a pauper like me. But I'm planning something that might work.' Maeve looked at Phil's bag in the hall. 'You have to catch that flight. I'll go with you on the Tube.'

'No, I'll manage on my own,' Phil protested. 'I have actually ordered a taxi. A bit extravagant, but with all this money coming in…' She paused. 'You know what? I'm going to offer you a job. I need an assistant now that I have a writing career. I can't handle all that Internet stuff on my own. What do you say?'

Maeve laughed. 'I'll think about it. I am also going to think about Paschal's suggestion of working in Cork while I get myself organised to start up on my own. There might be interior design firms there who need staff. Ava will give me a good reference despite everything that has happened. All is not lost because I'm leaving London, even if it's sad and I'll miss the buzz.'

'You can always buzz back over here for a visit,' Phil said putting a hand on Maeve's cheek. 'I have to go. .'

'I'll help you with your bag,' Maeve said. They headed to the taxi waiting outside. Putting Phil's suitcase in the boot, she called out, 'Have a nice trip back.'

'Thank you.' Phil settled into the back seat of the cab. 'I'll be waiting for you in Willow House. There will always be a room for you there, whatever happens. But take your time and do what you need to do before you leave. And don't rush into anything. It'll be all right, I'm very sure of that.'

'I hope you're right.' Maeve waved as the taxi drove off and went back upstairs, where she spent the rest of the evening doubting that she was doing the right thing. But whatever happened, she knew there were two people who would always be there for her. Phil – and Paschal.

A week later, Maeve landed at Cork airport, just ahead of Storm Anita, which was forecast to hit the west of Ireland later that evening. Paschal was waiting for her at arrivals and threw his arms around her as she emerged with her suitcase.

Melting into his embrace, Maeve closed her eyes, breathing in his special smell of soap and a hint of turf smoke, resting her cheek against the rough wool of his sweater. The slight sadness she had felt at quitting her job and leaving the buzz of the big city disappeared like the memory of a distant dream. 'Home at last,' she whispered, and held on to him as tight as she could.

'So you are, girl.' Paschal bent his head and kissed her long and hard. They stood there in the arrivals hall for a long time, hugging, kissing and laughing, until Paschal pulled away. 'We've got to get out of here before the storm hits.'

'I know. I just wanted to show you how happy I am to see you.'

'You can show me that when we get to my flat. Okay for you to spend the night there? It's a bit cramped but I have evening lectures later, so can't drive to Sandy Cove until tomorrow.'

'That sounds like heaven.'

'Hardly heaven,' he said with a laugh. 'It's just a studio flat with a sofa bed that we'll have to share. But it's quite big, so I think it'll be okay. We have to get a move on as it's already five o'clock but then we'll have to stay in and risk my cooking and batten down the hatches. Storm Anita is said to be pretty vicious.'

The flat was tiny, just one room and a small kitchenette, but it was bright and airy. Although it was sparsely furnished with just a sofa bed, a small table and two chairs by the window, and a flat-screen TV balanced on a bookcase, it felt like paradise to Maeve because she was there with Paschal. She walked around, admiring the framed posters of marine life, touching the clothes that hung from pegs near the door. She peered out the window at the park, where the leaves were already beginning to turn yellow, and at the blue ribbon of the river Lee that snaked its way through the city. A gust of wind rattled the windows, and the trees and shrubs were suddenly bent by the force of it. 'Here she comes,' Maeve said.

'And we're warm and snug.' Paschal wrapped his arms around her from behind. 'Are you going to stand there all day?'

She turned around in his arms. 'No. I feel cold. The wind is scary.'

'We're safe here. I have to go to college for two more lectures and then I'll be back and we can celebrate. We'll stay here and grill some sausages, if that's okay? It won't be safe to drive anywhere. The rain is going to be heavy and the river might burst its banks, too.'

'That's fine.' Maeve touched his face. 'Is it safe for you to go out?'

'The campus is just a minute or two away by foot. No trees there, so it'll be fine, and then there's a covered walkway. I know some of the students might not be able to get there, but I have to give the lecture to those who turn up. I'll be back in a couple of hours. You can watch TV or take a nap while I'm gone.'

'I have my Kindle so I can read, too. Don't worry, I'll be fine.'

He kissed the top of her head. 'Great. See you in a little while.'

'Be careful out there.'

'I will.' He pulled her into his arms. Maeve closed her eyes and felt his soft mouth on hers in a spine-tingling kiss that seemed to last forever.

He pulled away and laughed. 'You're making it impossible to leave. But I have to go. See you later, sweetheart.'

Putting on his jacket, he headed out into the storm. Maeve watched him from the window as the wind howled outside and made everything rattle and shake, blowing twigs and leaves around. Just after he rounded the corner, it started to rain and the skies darkened even more. Maeve prayed he would be safe, and then chided herself for worrying. Paschal was used to these kinds of conditions and knew how to take care of himself. She wondered if Phil was safe at home, and picked up her phone to call her.

Phil replied after several rings. 'Hello, this is Philomena Duffy, also known as Fanny l'Amour. How can I help you?'

'Phil!' Maeve exclaimed. 'It's me, Maeve.'

'Oh,' Phil said, sounding embarrassed. 'Sorry. I was so taken up with it all that I didn't think of anything else.'

'What all?' Maeve sat down on the couch.

'The author stuff. Betsy made me admin on Fanny's author page on Facebook and I've been busy chatting to my readers. Such fun.'

Maeve let out a giggle. 'Oh gosh. Take it easy. You don't have to answer everyone at once.'

'I know, but it's so lovely to have all these new friends on Facebook. I can see why Joe was so taken with it.' Phil paused. 'But where are you? I thought you'd be here by now.'

'I'm in Paschal's flat in Cork. He didn't want to drive all the way to Sandy Cove in this storm, so we're staying the night.'

'Ooh,' Phil cooed. 'How romantic. So happy for you both. But I've known you'd end up together ever since you met. Never seen a man so smitten so fast.'

'Really?' Maeve smiled. 'I didn't notice. I was too busy being smitten myself.'

'I knew that, too.'

'Is the storm very bad over there?'

Phil laughed. 'Yes. It's pretty wild already and I think we've lost a few tiles off the roof. But I have buckets out upstairs and the Aga is going full blast, so we're fine. Not the first time this old house has ridden out a storm.'

'That's true. So you're okay then? Not too lonely?'

'I have Esmeralda. She sulked for two days after I got back, but now she has forgiven me. It took a lot of salmon and several saucers of cream. She's a real diva.'

Maeve laughed. 'She sure is. I'm going to have a look in the cupboards here and see if I can rustle up something for dinner. Take care, darling Phil. I'll see you tomorrow.'

'Lovely,' Phil chortled. 'But before you hang up, I thought I should tell you something…'

'What?'

'It's about my friend Oliver. He had some news.'

'Oh?' Maeve said, preparing herself for an update on the house.

'Good news, actually,' Phil breezed on. 'He's broken up with his fiancée.'

'Really?! Any idea why?'

'He didn't spell it out, but it was something to do with her changing her mind about that house they were going to move into. She wanted them to buy a trendy loft in Camden instead and he refused. Then she sulked, and I think he finally got fed up with her. So that was that.' Phil sighed and let out a giggle. 'Sorry, but…'

Maeve smiled. 'I know. That seems like good news to me too. Such a nice man. He was blinded by her, ahem, sex appeal, and now he's found out she wasn't worthy of his love. And maybe…' Maeve stopped. 'No, forget it.'

'Maybe he will now turn to someone his own age?' Phil asked.

'Yeah. I was hoping that perhaps…'

'Me too,' Phil murmured. 'But give him time – and me, too. We're already becoming firm friends and speak every day. We're helping each other out and that's very nice. He says he wants to come over and see me, and I said maybe for Christmas. So we'll see. Building a relationship takes time. But at our age, time is a precious commodity. So maybe we'll hurry slowly, if you see what I mean?'

'Yes, of course,' Maeve said softly. 'I'll leave you to work it out.'

'Thank you. But now back to work. I've finished the first draft, would you believe? And I've sent the contract on to a lawyer friend of Joe's who has a bit of experience with authors. He said he'd come back to me after the weekend and then I can sign and get cracking on the next book. Unless you want to help me write it?'

'No, *you* can,' Maeve cut in. 'I'm going to leave the writing to you from now on. You're so good at it. I'd only ruin the freshness of your writing. You'll be flying solo from now on.'

'Oh, that's a lovely compliment. Thank you. I'll still ask the old birds to beta read all the same.'

'Good idea.'

'As a matter of fact, I have decided to tell them everything,' Phil continued. 'They've invited us to tea tomorrow. We should make an announcement then. I don't want to hide what I'm doing any longer.'

'Terrific. Could be great for publicity, too. I mean it won't take more than ten minutes for it to be all over the village.'

Phil laughed. 'Yes, that's my plan!'

'I'm so happy you've settled in to your new career.' Maeve sighed. 'I only wish I could get into something that would work for me now that I've got myself fired. But as I told you, I'll look for work in Cork until I can set up my own firm.'

'Maybe you should fly solo straight away?' Phil suggested. 'Why don't you start your own business and be your own boss? You have the experience, and all those clients whose homes you've designed. Set up a website and post photos of those interiors. Go out there and show yourself, and what you can do. Haven't you taught me how powerful the Internet is?'

'Oh.' Maeve laughed. 'That's what I'm planning to do eventually. But it will take a little time and work to set it up.'

'Of course it will. But now you have plenty of time to think and plan. And you already have your first client.'

'Who?'

'Me, you silly girl! You will do up Willow House when we get the repairs done. I have already contacted a builder who will come and give me a quote and then we can get started on the interior.'

'Ooh…' Maeve sighed. 'I've been redecorating the house in my dreams since I arrived. I know *exactly* how we're going to do it. I think a very pale primrose for the walls in the living room, and then a floral design for the curtains, and a new sofa and…'

Phil laughed. 'Slow down, girl. We have to get a new roof first. And the rewiring, and the plumbing, and I'm sure there has to be rising damp and rotten timbers in a few places. That'll take time to fix. And I haven't even been paid any of the advance yet.'

'I know. But it's fun to plan. Can't wait to get stuck in.'

'I'm just looking forward to putting all those buckets away. I'm getting tired of hearing dripping everywhere.'

'I know. First things first, as you say.'

'We'll talk about it when the builder's been here. But I'd better get back to my writing before there's a power cut. I have to earn that money before we can spend it.'

'Of course you do. Good luck with the writing. I'm sure it'll be fabulous.'

'I'll do my best. Bye for now, love. Take care.'

Maeve hung up with a smile. Good old Phil. What trooper she was. And Oliver would come around and the two of them would be – if not romantically involved – dear friends who helped each other. Belinda had gone too far and Oliver had escaped a marriage that would have been a scam. Thank God he had finally seen the light. Win-win for Phil. And bless her for asking Maeve to do up Willow House. And for being so sure Maeve would be successful in her new venture. Maeve felt a dart of excitement. It'd be hard work, but what did she have to lose? Only her pride, if it bombed. But why would it?

She decided to bite the bullet and get started right away. Ava wouldn't mind if she used the photos of her completed projects, and they'd look great on a website. She could contact some of her nicer clients and ask them for testimonials, too. She'd have to hire a web designer and start an Instagram account for her new business. Maeve felt a thrill as she considered her options. This would be great fun. She could finally be her own boss, finally pursue her passion. Her stomach fizzed as she spent a long time looking at websites of other interior design firms and their social media pages. They were good, but she knew she could do better.

Maeve nearly forgot time and place as she drew up plans, but when her stomach rumbled, she checked her watch and discovered two hours had passed since Paschal had left. He would be back soon. She got up to see what she could put together for dinner. The fridge contained eggs, sausages, butter, milk and two tomatoes. She could fry sausages and eggs and grill the tomatoes. More like breakfast than dinner, but it'd have to do. She hummed to herself as she turned on the hotplate, dreaming of her new plans, and placed the sausages in a frying pan. But just as the sausages started to sizzle, there was a roar outside from the wind and the lights went out. Feck. A power cut, just when she was about to start cooking.

Maeve stood in the dim light for a moment to get her bearings, and then went to the window to see if Paschal was on his way back. He should have finished his lectures by now. But even if he were out there, she couldn't see a thing. All was dark, the wind howled and the rain drummed against the window. She could see a faint glimmer of the river and the outlines of trees bent double by the storm-force winds. It was scary out there. But where was Paschal? She listened to the roar of the storm and imagined him out there, struggling to get back. She wrung her hands, thinking of a possible explanation, trying not to imagine the worst. He had said he'd be straight back, so why wasn't he here? Had he been delayed by the power cut and was lost in the dark somewhere? Then a terrible thought struck her. People got killed in storms like this. What if she never saw him again? Tears welled up in her eyes as she imagined the worst, wondering how she would cope if…

Just as she was close to a panic attack, the door banged open. 'I'm back,' Paschal panted, entering the flat. 'Where are you?'

Relief flooded through Maeve like a wave of warm water. 'You're back,' she croaked. 'Thank God you're all right.'

'Of course I am,' came the cheery reply. 'But it was a struggle to walk with this wind. I nearly blew into the river. Where the hell are you?'

'Here.' Maeve groped along the wall to join him. 'It's so dark. I thought something had happened to you. There's nothing to eat. I tried to cook something but then the power went out and—'

'Fear not, my woman. I hunted down some prey and brought it home.'

'Prey?' she asked, confused. 'You killed something and brought it home to eat?'

'Yes,' he said proudly. 'I killed a pizza and flung it over my shoulder and brought it back. The very last pizza in the Italian takeaway. They were supposed to send it out, but then found they couldn't so they gave it to me. For free. Howzat, eh?'

'Brilliant.' Maeve reached him and took the box he was holding. 'Turn on your phone so we can see where to put it.'

Paschal directed the light from his phone across the room. 'There's a torch somewhere. And two candles in the cupboard over the cooker. Scented candles I bought at the market from some charity or other. Vanilla, I think.'

'That'll be fine. As long as we can see.' Maeve shivered. 'Just listen to that wind.'

'Incredible. Let's eat and go to bed. I can't wait to be tucked up with you.'

'Good idea.'

'Not the romantic evening I had planned, I'm afraid,' Paschal said with a touch of regret. 'Cold pizza, smelly candles and no heating. But we're here together, and that's all that matters.'

'"A loaf of bread, a jug of wine and thou",' Maeve quoted from the old poem by Omar Khayyám as she laid the table.

'No wine, I'm afraid. But Mary's excellent blackcurrant cordial, also from the market. No idea who this Mary is, but she makes a mean juice. Good vintage, too. Last year, which was an excellent year for blackcurrants.' He sighed. 'Oh shit, this is terrible. I can't even ply you with booze to get you into bed.'

Maeve laughed and sat down. 'No need to ply me with anything. Sit down, ya fool, and have your dinner.'

'Yes, missus.'

They quickly gobbled down a few wedges of cold pizza, washed down with the blackcurrant cordial, kissing and laughing between bites. 'Pineapple?' Maeve said as she chewed. 'Didn't know they grew that in Italy.'

'It adds a bit of class, though, you must admit.'

'Definitely,' Maeve said, reaching across the table to push his wild dark curls out of his eyes. 'There. Much tidier.'

'Thank you.' He grabbed her hand and kissed it, his brown eyes so full of desire it made her shiver. Then he leaned over the table and touched his lips to hers. His breath was laced with a delicious mixture of herbs, pineapple and blackcurrant.

'I think I've had enough to eat,' she whispered as she returned his kiss.

He groaned and pulled back. 'I'm getting a crick in my neck.'

Maeve moved around the table and slid onto his lap. 'Better?'

'Much better.' He wound his arms around her waist, letting his mouth wander from her face to her neck, and down the opening of her shirt to her cleavage. 'Your skin is softer than silk,' he whispered.

His warm lips made her skin tingle and she touched his face, full of longing. 'Let's go to bed.'

'Good idea.' Getting up, Paschal led her to the sofa bed and they undressed in the dark, lit only by the candles, and slid under the covers, hugging each other to get warm again. As the wind continued to howl outside and the rain lashed the windows, Paschal showed Maeve how much he had missed her. Afterwards, they looked at each other in the soft glow of the candles, smiling and caressing each other until Maeve couldn't keep her eyes open any longer. She slowly drifted off, feeling safe, loved and protected. *This is it*, she thought. *This is how it feels to come home.*

Chapter Thirty

The wind dropped during the night and the skies cleared. They woke up to a bright, sunny morning with the broken branches, twigs and leaves strewn across the park the only signs that the storm had raged all night. With the power back, they enjoyed a breakfast of eggs and sausages before they drove to Sandy Cove in the golden light of the autumn sunshine. They reached Willow House in the early afternoon, where they found Phil in the study, hard at work on the laptop. Dressed in tracksuit bottoms and one of Joe's old cardigans, two pencils stuck in her hair, she looked at them as if she didn't quite know who they were.

'Phil?' Maeve said. 'Is everything all right?'

Phil blinked. 'Absolutely perfect.' She laughed and shook her head. 'Sorry, pet. I was somewhere else there for a while.'

'And where was this?' Maeve asked.

'In Peru. Veronica has just landed there to climb Machu Picchu. She's going to fall in love with the guide along the trail. I think. Or she might fall for one of the men in the group. A handsome doctor who saves her from altitude sickness. What do you think?'

Paschal laughed. 'How about her running away to Kerry and falling for a poor local lad who is mesmerised by her beautiful green eyes and dark red hair?'

Phil's eyes focused on the two of them standing there, hand in hand. 'Oh that's so lovely.' She got up from the desk and hugged them both. 'This is so perfect. I knew it would happen ever since that first day in the bookshop. I even prayed at Mass it would. And it did. And now Maeve is back for good. This makes me so happy. Let's go and celebrate somewhere.'

'What about Veronica?' Maeve asked.

'She can wait.' Phil touched her hair and pulled out the pencils. 'I look a fright. I need to pull myself together. And I think we're expected to tea at the old birds' house later anyway. So why don't we celebrate there? Go and take a look in the basement and see if Joe left a nice bottle of something. He was planning to put together a wine cellar, but I think he drank most of it instead. There might be one or two left, though.'

While Phil went to 'pull herself together', Maeve and Paschal decided on some port from the basement, Paschal having suggested that the old ladies would love it. Phil, having changed into her good trousers and a grey cashmere sweater, appeared shortly afterwards and they all walked through the village, Paschal and Maeve holding hands, laughing at shouts of 'When's the wedding?' and 'Let's see the ring' and other remarks from everyone who spotted them. Nuala whizzed past them on her bike but came to a screeching halt and doubled back.

'Mother of God, what do I see? The two of ye smooching in public. Behave yerselves, there are children watching.'

Maeve burst out laughing. 'You're a scream, Nuala.'

Nuala beamed. 'So it's true, then? You're staying, and will be moving in with your man here?'

Paschal rolled his eyes and laughed. 'I suppose it was all over the village before we even got here. Jesus, someone must be psychic in this village.'

Nuala shrugged. 'I heard you drove down the lane to Willow House with Maeve about an hour ago. That was enough to start the rumour.'

'But there's another bit of gossip that's about to start,' Phil cut in. 'It will push these two lovebirds off the front page, I promise you.'

Nuala stared at Phil. 'Yeah? What would that be?'

'How about this,' Phil continued, her eyes dancing. 'Someone in this village has been writing romantic novels under the pen name Fanny l'Amour. And this person has just signed a very lucrative contract with a publisher in New York.'

Nuala's jaw dropped. 'What? Who? How come I never heard this before?'

'Because this *someone* has been keeping their cards very close to their chest,' Maeve said with a wink. 'And they know how to keep a secret.'

'Oooh.' Nuala's eyes widened. 'So… When will we know who it is?'

'Soon,' Phil said darkly. 'Next time there's a full moon. The author might even do a book signing when the first book is published. That could be the big reveal. But we have to ask the author first, of course. He or she might want to stay incognito.'

'He or she?' Nuala looked confused. 'You mean it could be a man?' Her eyes homed in on Paschal. 'Nah. Couldn't be.'

Paschal grinned. 'But it could be someone very close to you.'

Nuala's eyes widened. 'What? You mean…' She got back on her bike. 'The sneaky little shite! Just wait till I get my hands on him. See you later, lads.' Nuala pedalled away down the street and disappeared around the corner at breakneck speed.

Maeve pushed at Paschal. 'You cruel man. Now she thinks it's Seán Óg and will give him hell until he confesses.'

Paschal laughed. 'I'll give her a call later. And Seán Óg took the boys to hurling so he won't be home until teatime. This'll teach her to believe in gossip.'

'And he was telling the truth,' Phil chimed in. 'I was standing very close to her when he said it.'

Maeve laughed and put her arm through Phil's. 'You're a hoot. Come on, let's go and have tea with the ladies. They're waiting to hear the latest news, which will have reached them before we even get there. And then, after tea, I'll…' She stopped and turned to Paschal. 'Oh God, I haven't told you about my plans. It's something I've dreamed of doing for a long time.'

He smiled at her with a quizzical look. 'What plans? You're not leaving again?'

'No, no!' She laughed and grabbed him by his jacket. 'Just listen. Call me mad but I'm going to start my own interior design business straight away instead of looking for work. I'll set up a website and do some PR through social media, and then work around Kerry and Cork when I get some clients.' She drew breath and stared up at him. 'What do you think?'

He smiled and nodded. 'I like it. I'm sure it'll be a success.'

Maeve sighed. 'It might fail too, but I won't know until I try.'

'Absolutely.' Paschal looked suddenly contrite. 'You've solved the problem beautifully.'

'And I will be her first client,' Phil said, grinning. 'I can afford the best now that I've got all this money. Willow House will rise from the ashes and be the most beautiful house in Sandy Cove.'

'That's a promise,' Maeve declared.

'All problems solved, then.' Paschal held out the bottle of port. 'Here. You go on to the tea party and I'll get going to the shop and see what the lads have been up to during the week. I'll see you later.' He kissed her cheek and half-ran down the street to the shop.

Maeve watched him go and turned to Phil. 'Isn't it all so fabulous? Me and Paschal and my new firm and your writing and everything?'

Phil smiled and touched Maeve's cheek. 'I couldn't be happier. It's all perfect. I think you arrived here like a whirlwind and shook us all up. I am so happy you did. I was hoping you'd stay but didn't know how it would be possible to offer you something that could compete with your exciting life in London. But then Paschal happened. And Fanny happened. And Oliver, too. And now your business. I suddenly feel alive again, and know that I have to go on living. I really owe you a huge thanks for all of that.'

Maeve's eyes welled up. 'No,' she whispered. 'I should thank you.' She shook herself and looked up at the dark clouds. 'But come on, it's going to rain. Let's go and break the news to the old birds. They'll be so excited. It won't be long before everyone knows, after that. We will have to draw up a plan for the launch and maybe do a press release. You're going to be famous, Phil.'

'Oh.' Phil stopped walking. 'I never thought of that. I just wanted to earn some money for the house and write stories. I wish Joe could be here and experience this with me.'

'But he is,' Maeve said softly. 'I can feel it. Can't you?'

Phil smiled. 'Yes I can.' She suddenly laughed. 'What a legacy he left. Who would have thought he'd stay alive through a woman called Fanny l'Amour? It's so strange, don't you think?'

'Stranger than fiction,' Maeve declared.

Epilogue

Phil's book launch, held in Paschal's shop just before Christmas, turned out to be the best party in Sandy Cove since old Mrs Madigan's wake. Everyone in the village turned up dressed in their best party clothes. The shop had been beautifully decorated for Christmas by Maeve, with strings of lights around the doors and windows. Inside, there were silver garlands with hearts and angels, and a cardboard reindeer beside the small but perfect Christmas tree, which was decorated with red bows and silver bells. It was the first job of her new business and the photos had already been put up on her website – earning her a few assignments for shops in nearby Killarney. It was a fantastic way to kickstart her business and make a name for herself locally. The Willow House project wouldn't be possible until the roof had been sorted, and all the other repairs had been carried out by the builder Phil had hired. But Maeve had already done a mock-up on her computer, and had picked out fabrics and new pieces of furniture. It would be beautiful. She couldn't wait to get started and do the old house justice.

'Holy mother, I didn't expect so many people,' Phil whispered as they stood by the counter, where Maeve had arranged Fanny l'Amour's books in decorative piles.

'Any excuse for a party,' Maeve whispered back. 'And then with the shindig Sean Óg and Nuala are throwing at the pub, this'll go on all night.'

'I know.' Phil patted her hair in place. 'Do I look all right?'

Maeve studied Phil for a moment. In a red vintage Dior dress, her hair in a French twist and her gold hoop earrings, she looked her very best. 'Apart from the frightened look in your eyes, you look splendid.'

'Oh.' Phil blinked and squared her shoulders. 'I'll try not to be scared.'

'But why would you be? They're all people you meet every day.' Maeve looked at the group at the door. 'Oh! Here are your beta readers, all dressed up to the nines.'

'Louise is wearing sequins,' Phil said with a giggle.

'They have all made a huge effort. Mary's even put on lipstick, look – and Oonagh's had her hair permed.'

'They look terrific.' Phil beamed at them as they approached. 'Hello, beautiful ladies. Thank you for coming. You all look lovely.'

'We had to dress up for Fanny – I mean, *you*,' Louise said. 'You're fierce elegant, Phil. Like a film star. And Maureen looks beautiful, too.'

'Thank you.' Maeve ran her hand over the front of the green wool dress Paschal had bought in the Woollen Mills shop in Kenmare, guessing her size correctly. Was there no end to the perfection of this man?

A tall bearded man in a tweed jacket pushed through the crowd towards them. 'Hello,' he called. 'I'm John O'Callaghan from the *Examiner*. Could I have a word with the author before the launch?'

'The *Examiner*?!' Phil exclaimed, looking as if she was about to faint.

'How did you hear about this?' Maeve asked.

'The publishers in New York were in touch and told me all about Phil Duffy and her work. Amazing, that she has been writing under this pen name for years in secret.'

'I decided to come out this year,' Phil said. 'I felt I needed to show my face at last.'

Maeve smiled, relieved that Betsy had kept quiet about Uncle Joe. It would make life much easier for Phil.

'Would you mind if I took a picture?' O'Callaghan asked. 'With you and the books, and…' He glanced at Maeve.

'And my niece, who assists with marketing and all kinds of stuff. And these four lovely ladies, who are my beta readers, of course.'

'Grand. We'll do a couple of shots,' O'Callaghan agreed.

They managed three different poses with Phil on her own, one with Phil and Maeve, and a group shot with the excited old ladies, who couldn't stop laughing. Then Paschal called the party to order.

'Hello everyone,' he shouted, 'and welcome to my shop for the launch of Fanny's latest romance. Fanny, as you all know by now, is none other than our own Philomena Duffy, who has been fooling us all into thinking she was busy gardening and baking, when all this time she was writing sizzling love stories. And now she is finally coming out into the limelight and showing her talent to us all. We are so proud of you, Phil. Aren't we?'

'Yes!' the crowd replied in unison.

Phil burst into tears. 'Oh, you're all so very kind. I can't think of a better place to launch this new series.' She picked up a book and pointed at the woman on the cover. 'This is Veronica, my new heroine. I hope you'll love her and enjoy reading about her adventures. The story is a little… ahem… racy, in parts, so don't give it to anyone under eighteen.'

There was a burst of laughter. 'Phil, you brazen hussy,' someone shouted. 'And here we were, thinking you were all straight-laced and well behaved.'

'Ah, sure life's too short for that,' Phil quipped, dabbing at her eyes with a tissue.

'So let's start the signing then,' Paschal cut in. 'If you're not too into your wine and nibbles. But there'll be more food and craic at the pub later. Sit down behind the counter, Phil, and you lot all form an orderly queue. Maeve will take your money and nobody gets out of here without buying a book.'

There was laughing and shuffling while the crowd lined up. Phil took out the fancy Montblanc fountain pen Betsy had sent her as a gift on publication day, and started to sign as if she had done it all her life. The old cash register pinged repeatedly as Maeve took the money and handed out change. When all the books were gone, there was a wad of cash for Paschal to put into the safe before he shooed the last customer out and locked the door.

They merrily followed the laughing, chatting crowd down the street towards the Harbour pub. It was a frosty night, with the stars sparkling above in the black sky. Maeve tucked her hand under Paschal's arm. She was still getting used to her new life, and from time to time she missed the excitement of London, the hustle and bustle, the buzz she used to get from just walking down the street. But then whenever she walked out into the little garden of Paschal's cottage on a crisp, sunny morning, and watched the sun rise over the mountains in the east, looking out over the expanse of blue sea and the seagulls swooping down to catch fish, she felt a warm cloak of calm settle on her shoulders. The infinity of the ocean, the silence and the peace was like a balm to the soul. She knew this was where she wanted to be for the rest of her life. This place was home.

And then there was Paschal. She knew they were together for good, and that he would never let her down. They grew more in love with every day that passed. Not that their relationship was without glitches, as their recent little tiff while furniture shopping had confirmed. They had borrowed Sean Óg's van and driven to Cork to get the bits and pieces they needed for Maeve's 'update' of the cottage, as she had diplomatically called the total refurbishment necessary to make it habitable. The interior designer in her hadn't been able to put up with the drab curtains, the narrow uncomfortable bed, the two saggy armchairs and the wobbly table. 'My uncle will turn in his grave,' Paschal had said as they'd loaded the items into the van. 'You're turning his fisherman's cottage into a doll's house. But, okay. Looking forward to soaping your back in the new bathroom with some of that cute soap you insisted on buying.'

Maeve stepped closer. 'And cuddling under the new duvet with those soft sheets I chose,' she murmured in his ear.

'That too.' He put his arm around her. 'I'm sorry, but I can't stand shopping. Especially on this scale. I'm glad it's over.'

Maeve smiled, thinking that putting together the furniture would be another battle. She was no good at it, and knew Paschal would have to do the bulk of it, which would mean a lot of swearing and dirty looks in her direction. But it would be worth it in the end.

And it was, despite more grumbling and swearing, and another tiff that ended in laughter and love-making under the sheets on top of the new mattress on the floor – as putting the bed together demanded engineering skills of major proportions. But days later, when it was all finally done – the couch by the window, the colourful carpet on the floor, the lamps lit, the new kitchen table and chairs in the kitchen, the bed and the cushions that added that extra touch – they stood back and sighed with fatigue and happiness. They finally had a lovely little home, big enough for the two of them and… maybe a third 'very small person', Paschal had whispered in Maeve's ear as she drifted off to sleep.

'What?' she asked drowsily. 'A third… what? You mean…?' Her eyes flew open. She turned and put her arms around him. 'Oh, sweetheart, of course I would want a third little person – a baby, I mean. Our baby.'

He let out a long sigh. 'I didn't dare ask you – I mean, you said you never wanted a family with that guy who left you.'

'Not with him,' Maeve said hotly. 'Nor with any man I've ever met, except you. Isn't that strange? Must be hormones or those ferro… thingies, whatever they're called. '

'Pheromones,' he corrected. 'It's to do with smell or scent.'

'Ah.' Maeve rolled onto her back, smiling into the darkness. 'Must be that soap you use.'

'Yeah. I'm sure Palmolive is responsible for half the population of Europe.'

Maeve giggled. 'You nutcase. But,' she continued, feeling a dart of fear, 'I might be past my sell-by-date when it comes to baby-making.'

Paschal took her hand and kissed it. 'We'll just have to keep trying and hope for the best. It'll happen if it's meant to be. I believe in fate and the universe and… love.'

'Me too,' Maeve had mumbled, drifting off to sleep, knowing somehow that third little person would arrive one day.

And then the last little piece of the jigsaw had fallen into place in the oddest way. Phil had been in the greenhouse, clearing out old flowerpots and throwing away what was left of Joe's seeds and dried-up plants, something she hadn't got around to until now. She'd lifted the biggest pot and had discovered an envelope encrusted with earth and mud. She'd opened it, and found a card with a heart and a tightly written message inside that read:

My darling Phil,

Please forgive me for not sharing my secret with you until now. I tried to tell you, but lost my nerve when you dismissed the very thing I have been doing for a while: writing romance. I know it will seem strange to you, but I found solace in this kind of fantasy when I retired from the work that I'd loved. I fell into it by accident when I was fooling around with the idea of writing a novel. I started to write anything that came into my head – expecting literary Nobel-prize material to come out. But instead, out came my romantic streak, laced with a feminine touch. This made me laugh at first, and then I found I couldn't stop. Fanny l'Amour was born, and she just kept growing. I thought the book might be marketable and sent it out to a publisher called Red Hot House, where an excellent editor called Betsy Malone helped me and urged me to keep writing. The first book sold very well, and then they asked for more, so I kept writing – and the books kept selling, to my surprise. It made me some extra cash that we could use for our trips and other things we couldn't otherwise afford. I feel bad about not having told you, and will slip this card under your teacup tomorrow morning so you can read it in peace, and then we can have a good laugh and make plans for our next trip. I was thinking about that little hotel on the Left Bank in Paris, where we spent our honeymoon. What do you say?

Waiting eagerly for your reply.

Joe

Maeve had found Phil in the greenhouse in floods of tears, pressing the card to her chest. 'I can't believe it,' she sobbed, handing Maeve the card. 'He kept this secret all this time and was afraid to tell me. Why was I so stupid and snobby?'

'It wasn't your fault,' Maeve soothed, when she had read the message. 'He should have had the courage to tell you. But he was afraid – like all men who think they have to be so strong and silent all the time.'

'But why didn't he do what it says? Slip it under my teacup?'

'Maybe he lost his nerve. Deep down he was quite a shy man, as you know.'

'Yes, but I wish I had found this message when he was still alive.'

Maeve gave the card back to Phil. 'But you didn't. At least you know now he wanted to tell you. Isn't that a comfort?'

Phil nodded, drying her tears. 'Yes. I'm sad that he didn't dare to in the end – all my fault. But I'm so glad I've continued his work.'

'He'd love that,' Maeve declared.

'I know. And now I'm not angry any more.' Phil had smiled through her tears. 'The naughty rascal. He loved playing jokes. And this was the best one.'

Maeve looked up at the stars now as they walked to the after-party, and wondered if Uncle Joe was up there somewhere, smiling, happy that Phil had found his secret and made it into her own, that Maeve had come back and found love, and that Willow House would be saved. A soft breeze suddenly touched her face and blew in her hair. It felt like the whisper of a kiss, a message from someone far away. She smiled into the darkness and rested her head on Paschal's shoulder. Minutes later, they arrived at the pub and the door opened to let them into the bright, warm interior where everyone was already gathered. The musicians struck up a jig as they came into the pub. The floor was cleared for dancing, and a few couples were already limbering up. Paschal took Maeve's coat and put it on a chair. He held out his hand. 'How about a dance, now that we know each other better?'

Maeve shrank back for a moment, but then she took his hand and laughed. 'Okay. If you can cope with my two left feet and don't care if I make a fool out of you.'

'You already did, my darlin'. Come on, just look into my eyes, listen to the beat and forget everything else.'

Maeve nodded, their eyes locked, and suddenly, she felt the beat in her head, her heart and her soul – that Irish music that was nearly hypnotic. She started to dance in perfect time with Paschal, their feet tapping the floor, their shoulders touching, smiling at each other, twirling and jumping, dancing faster and faster until, suddenly, the music stopped and they stood rooted to the spot, breathing hard. There was a stunned silence and then the applause rang out with shouts of 'Bravo!' and 'Encore!'

Maeve shook her head and said, 'Maybe later.'

Sean Óg handed her a glass of Guinness, giving a full pint to Paschal. 'Here. A bit of the black stuff to give you strength.'

'How about a toast?' Nuala shouted from behind the bar.

Paschal lifted his glass. *'Sláinte mhaith,'* he said. 'To us and the future.'

'And to Willow House,' Maeve filled in. 'And Sandy Cove and all its people.'

'And Fanny l'Amour!' someone shouted. 'May she keep writing and selling by the million.'

'I'll drink to that,' Maeve said and took a sip from her glass. It tasted both sweet and bitter, with a slight fizz. *Just like life*, she thought, and smiled at Paschal. 'I'm beginning to take to this drink,' she confessed.

'Be careful,' he warned. 'It can be addictive.'

She laughed and looked into his velvet eyes. 'Too late. I'm already hooked. Forever.'

A Letter from Susanne

Thank you for reading my book. If you want to keep up to date with my new releases, please click on the link below to sign up for my newsletter. I will only contact you with news of a new book and never share your email address with anyone else.

www.bookouture.com/susanne-oleary

I hope you enjoyed the visit to Kerry as much as I did writing it. This series is the result of my love affair with Kerry that started when we bought a holiday cottage there seven years ago. I will keep going back to this beautiful part of Ireland in the next books in the series.

I would love to hear your reactions to the book in a short review. Getting feedback from readers is hugely helpful to authors, as it might help new readers want to pick up one of my books. I will continue writing and hope you will keep reading my stories!

While you're waiting for my next book, you might like to try one of my earlier releases, which you will find on my website.

Many thanks,
Susanne

www.susanne-oleary.com

authoroleary

@susl

Acknowledgements

Once again, I want to thank my amazing editor Christina for all the hard work she put into making this book as good as it can possibly be. Also, Kim and Noelle and all the wonderful people at Bookouture. I also want to say a huge thank you to all the lovely Kerry people I've met ever since we started spending our summer holidays there. And last but not least, everyone in the lounge, always there to help and laugh and mop up the odd tear.